ON THE EDGE

A RURAL TALE OF JEALOUSY & OBSESSION ON THE SOUTH WEST COAST PATH

CLARE S. MUDD

Edited by David Holwill
Cover design by Ellie J
Layout by Oliver Tooley

ISBN: 978-1-83778-048-8

For my husband's legs.
They made this book possible.

Prologue

How I Lost My Husband to the South West Coast Path.

Obsession: A persistent disturbing preoccupation with an often unreasonable idea or feeling (Merriam-Webster).

Fixation: An obsessive drive that may or may not be acted on involving an object, concept or person (Sigmund Freud).

Obsessive behaviour: An overwhelming desire to achieve an ambition, desire or outcome.

Types:
- Fast: An idea or concept that requires immediate action
- Medium: A thought that starts as a bud then blossoms into a blooming necessity
- Slow: A gradual perception that simmers slowly to boiling point

(Lara Sedgefield).

I have been truthful in my account apart from a couple of exaggerations. I cannot speak for Sebastian. This is not intended for general readership, but if perchance you stumble across it, you must make up your own mind.

Lara Sedgefield

Chapter One

Bruised Apples

Lara

My husband is off out again for the day. Pleasure not business. A hike around the South West Coastal Path, something he has always wanted to do, apparently. Although I only knew about it two months ago and he has never mentioned it before even though we have both lived in North Devon all our lives. And he's fifty-five. I thought that sort of pursuit was for retired people with time to kill, a good way to keep fit and active after years of work. Is he going on his own? With a group of friends? No. He's going with MY friend, my best friend.

"Bye, see you later. I'll text you if I can but there may be no signal." He kisses me quickly and darts out of the front door, backpack and walking boots in hand.

I resign myself to another day alone. There's a lot to do on a farm with cattle, sheep and chickens, and the house itself is rambling, inconvenient and high maintenance. At least Sebastian went up to the attic this morning to place a bucket under a hole where two slates had come off the roof in the night. Unfortunately, when he opened the loft hatch, several dozen dopey flies flew out, so my first job is to grab the hoover and vacuum them up. After that there's paperwork and phone calls to make, picking in apples from the orchard and spreading them out on newspaper, checking on cows and calves and bringing in logs. Son Bobby works all day on the general farm work, except a couple of mornings a week when he works for an elderly farming couple next door. So between us we can manage, which is just as well, as Sebastian is now out hiking every Monday on top of his regular three days a week working on various gardens. He gets asked all the time to take on more gardens but declines as he's needed on the farm. Besides, he "doesn't have time" as he's so fond of saying.

I fill my day with chores, sorting out some old clothes for charity as we intend to redecorate our bedroom soon and need to reorganise. I even manage to squeeze in half an hour in the gym (an outside shed with some bits picked up from the council tip) jigging to an old '80s CD. Don't want Seb and Rosa being too much fitter than me with their eight-hour marathons. I know I'm wasting my time as there's no way I'll ever look as fit as Rosa.

She and I bumped into each other (literally) at the local garden centre, buying plants. We both dropped our plants, apologised, laughed and ended up having a coffee together and discussing our gardens; we've been friends ever since. She is tall, slim, blonde and beautiful. I am short, sturdy, and have uncontrollable frizzy, brown hair. She has a lovely nature and is artistic with many hobbies: she can dance, sing and belongs to an Am Dram group. I am critical, snappy and have no hobbies apart from collecting recipes and cooking, which is the only thing I can do quite well, apart from eating. Rosa cannot cook, and on the rare occasion I go to her house, she buys brownies or ham rolls from the bakery. When she comes to visit I make lots of delicious goodies. Rosa, even though she has a willowy figure, tucks in with appreciation so we have a love of food in common. I do not think she spends time googling recipes, though, or looking at restaurant reviews. She has persuaded us to join a "Simply Dance" class so Seb and I can now execute a quickstep after a fashion; not well, as neither of us is a natural dancer. Rosa can waltz, foxtrot, tango and quickstep with ease.

She has a perfect two-bedroomed cottage, tastefully furnished with pale grey sofas, soft grey and white throws artfully draped, small side tables with lamps, a flame effect fire and some good watercolours adorning the walls. Her bedroom is pink and white with a tiny spotless ensuite shower room. The second bedroom is yellow and white with daisy-printed curtains and a separate gleaming bathroom. She has an attic for her art studio where she produces paintings good enough for a commercial market, but she works part time for a firm of solicitors: family connected so she can be flexible with hours. Her outside area consists of a patio with a large collection of tubs, pots and hanging baskets cascading with green foliage and a mix of yellow, white and blue plants.

In contrast, Seb and I live in a draughty old farmhouse with ancient, sagging chairs covered in brown blankets and dog hairs. Dust from two wood burners is impossible to control so I don't bother much. The kitchen has an old Aga, a large scrubbed top table and an uncomfortable wooden settle piled with old newspapers and *Farmers Weekly* magazines. The cupboard under the stairs is jammed with kids' toys. Rosa came round soon after we first met and didn't mind dog hairs or cobwebs. It wasn't until I went to her immaculate place that I realised our old place must have been a bit of a shock, but she has never commented about the mess and even puts up with our labrador's slobber. She and Seb got on from the off and talked about plants and gardens.

The three of us went to the RHS Rosemoor Gardens near Torrington and took a couple of walks around Appledore and

Westward Ho! In fact, it was the afternoon at Westward Ho! that gave Seb the idea for the stupid walks. I had a backache from carrying some heavy logs and decided I would sit on a bench near the sea front with a Hockings ice cream while he and Rosa walked along the cliff edge a short way. On their return, Seb's eyes were shining. "Fabulous views, Lara. We could see for miles. I'd like to do some coastal walking."

"That sounds fun, Seb," Rosa agreed. "If you want company any time, count me in."

Sebastian finally returns at 6pm as I'm stirring a parsley sauce to pour over a home-cured gammon. "Sorry I've been so long," he apologises. "I went into Rosa's to mark the route we've done today on her map: Westward Ho! To Appledore."

"Did it rain?" I query. "We've had quite a lot here this afternoon. Bobby fed hay to the cows in Square Meadow, so it's a good thing the two ponies weren't in the next field as he had to drive through there. There's no goodness in the grass this time of the year."

Sebastian ignores me and continues burbling on about his day while I'm chopping apples for sauce. "We bumped into John someone or other, who used to live in the village, remember? I didn't recognise him at first but we soon got chatting. He's married again and into photography. That took up about half an hour, then we reached Appledore; Rosa insisted on buying me lunch in the Market Arms. She wouldn't take no for an answer. It was lovely. We had brie and cranberry toasties, salad and a huge pot of tea."

"Bobby and I had yesterday's leftovers with a fried egg," I manage to squeeze in.

"That took an hour," Sebastian continues, oblivious. "Then the rain really came down so we waited a bit before abandoning the idea of walking around the Appledore coast, although I half regret that," he muses, scratching his head. "We'll have to do that short stretch another time now. Anyway, we caught a bus back and by the time we had walked to Rosa's and marked the map, well… that smells good."

I'm now beginning to get really irritated. Where's "hello, how's your day been"? I pick out two bruised apples from the bowl and eye them speculatively. Funny how one bruised apple can rapidly affect another, and it seems to me that Seb and Rosa have become like the apples. Rosa's enthusiasm for the walks has become as compulsive as Seb's and it's all either of them can talk about.

His phone beeps and I wave him away while I finish the apple sauce, make the gravy for dinner and mix a Martini and ice to calm myself down. We go to bed early. He's exhausted and we want to catch up on a *Death in Paradise* episode we've not seen. After fifteen minutes he's snoring.

Seb.

I was awake from 2am to 4am going over the walk Rosa and I did yesterday. I really love it, it's so much fun exploring bits of countryside and coast you can only see from the path. It's so exhilarating. I wish Lara would come with us but she says it's too much for her, clambering over rocks. She would slow us down too; Rosa's like a mountain goat. I reached over to put my arm round my lovely wife as I sensed she was half awake, but she was flapping the duvet off in seconds and flailing her legs in the air. I guessed she was having another hot flush.

Unfortunately, there were two slates off the roof yesterday, so my first job was to get out the ladders and roof hook to survey the feasibility of replacing them but it was no use, they were out of reach at a difficult angle on the roof. Nothing for it but to go to town to buy another ladder hook. Before I left I checked on the two ponies grazing on a small strip of land near the log shed; they're being there is annoying because, as the area is very close to the house, it's my daily job to scoop their poops onto the muck heap. If they were in the paddock this wouldn't be necessary. I said as much to Lara. "How long are the cattle going to be in the Square Meadow and the Small Paddock? I haven't got time for the ponies by the log shed. I need to put them back in the paddock."

She slammed the door. What had I said?

Lara

I can't believe that man. Did he really say he hasn't got time for the ponies as the cows are in the Square Meadow and adjoining paddock? He needs to remember the cattle are our livelihood. The ponies are pets.

"Sebastian," I say when he comes in to change clothes, ready to drive into town. "The reason you haven't got time is nothing to do with the cows, which incidentally have been in that field for TWO days, but because you spent the whole day out yesterday. No doubt you'll be out again in the next few weeks, and you're planning to go to Somerset at some point. So no way is it the cows' fault that you don't have time!"

He has the grace to look sheepish and we have a quick peck on the lips before he heads out the front door.

The weekend away in Somerset, which has been in the planning stage for a couple of weeks, looms, and I'm not sure if I'm looking forward to it or not. Sebastian and Rosa will be discussing their stupid walk (oh, did I mention I call the South West Coastal Path the stupid walk?) nonstop; I will have to drive them to various vantage points, which basically means I will spend most of the day alone. On the other hand I get a short holiday, time to myself for reading, watching tv, having a leisurely wine/coffee and pootling about Somerset. I have given Sebastian the cash for my third-share of a night's B and B. We'll see what happens when we come to paying for any extras. I have two conditions before we go: one, We have a nice evening meal and possibly some entertainment; two, They must not be too late returning from the stupid walk, so we have time for getting ready at leisure. Meanwhile, I face the prospect of Seb and Rosa constantly phoning each other to go over arrangements and planning their walk.

Chapter Two

Combe Martin to Ilfracombe

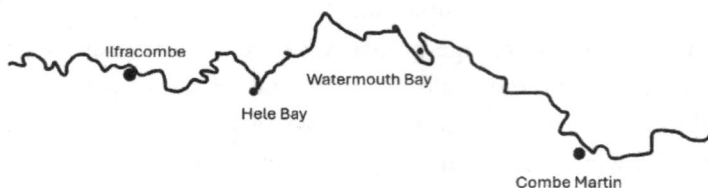

Lara

We are decorating our bedroom, a job that has been in the pipeline for over three years and having seen Rosa's lovely home I realise I really must try to keep the old place a bit more respectable, so Sebastian and I spend hours online looking at wallpaper sites. Amend that, I spend hours. He glances over and dismisses everything. We have different tastes: he likes botanical designs, I prefer subtle Laura Ashley-style designs with small prints to cover our bumpy old walls. I'm googling special offers when I wonder if Brewers has a sale on. "Let's look in Brewers together on Monday," I suggest.

Sebastian looks shifty. "Err, I can't do Monday. I'm probably walking Ilfracombe to Combe Martin."

Hmm! I spend the whole weekend weaning cattle with Bobby, cooking, cleaning, preparing a large roast lunch for family, children, stepchildren and offspring, so on Monday when I'm balancing on top of a step ladder painting the bedroom window whilst Seb is strolling through Combe Martin in the sunshine, I'm feeling piqued to say the least.

When he returns at 6pm he burbles something about parking in Ilfracombe, catching a bus to Combe Martin and walking back, but frankly I can't be bothered to listen.

"Sebastian, we have to get the bedroom finished by Christmas. The two spare rooms are chock-a-block with our furniture and clothes. I have a houseful of people staying over. I need those two rooms and we're running out of time. We seriously need to choose some wallpaper and crack on!" I wave my hands, noticing that I have white blobs of undercoat on my palms.

"Oh, don't worry, we'll get it done." He takes his mobile from his pocket. "Look, we took some great photos."

Seb obviously had an exciting day, but after perusing five hundred shots of Watermouth Bay and *Famous Five* locations, and to add insult to injury learning they tucked into lobster salad and prosecco, I tune out. Really! He can have beans on toast for supper.

Seb

Combe Martin to Ilfracombe. Another Monday, another great day. Rosa and I parked at Ilfracombe near the harbour and caught the 301 single decker to Combe Martin, a picturesque village nestled in a deep valley with one of the longest high streets in England. We ignored the tempting-looking bakery as today we had decided to have lunch in Ilfracombe. Having made use of the handy public toilets in the car park, we started our walk, heading eastwards and climbing straight away along the scenic rocky coastline, with great properties overlooking the sea. Looking back we could see the Hangman Hills. Passing the impressive-looking Sandy Cove Hotel, we then turned inland along a very short stretch of the main road before resuming the path to Watermouth Harbour, where there were many boats moored. Watermouth Bay was where some of Enid Blyton's *Famous Five* tv adaptations were filmed. We negotiated some steep ascents and descents. We paused briefly at the pretty small cove of Hele Bay (again handy public toilets) before reaching Ilfracombe, pale sunlight breaking through the clouds and shining on Hirst's statue of Verity standing proudly on the quay.

Having spent quite a time admiring scenery, examining film sites and undergoing some arduous climbs, we needed a rest, so treated ourselves to a lobster salad lunch and prosecco in S and P's harbour café, discussing our next expedition. After an excellent meal, we strolled along the harbour, over and around Capstan Hill, took some photos of the Landmark Theatre with its pointed domes, colloquially known as Madonna's Bra, then Rosa bought a scarf and some candles in a couple of the High Street shops whilst I admired the tall Victorian buildings.

Chapter Three

Heddon's Mouth to Lynton

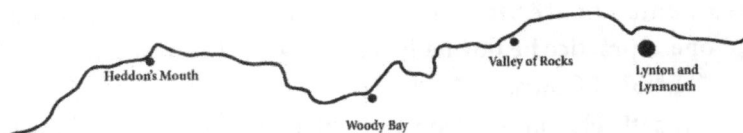

Lara

We've had a busy Christmas week: the usual huge turkey dinner with all the trimmings, a further family day with children and grandchildren, having a whale of a time shrieking with laughter, toys strewn across the living room floor, chocolates and satsumas consumed at will. Seb and I have four children between us from previous marriages. Luckily the stepbrothers and sisters get on really well and we have some great family gatherings. Bobby lives with us; my daughter, hubby and their two children live just down the road; Seb's son, partner and two children live nearby and his daughter lives in Exeter, about an hour away. Parents-in-law and Seb's brother are frequent visitors, usually staying overnight, so parties are hectic but fun, with Ben the labrador getting spoilt with extra treats. He endures the tinsel around his neck to snaffle an extra chunk of turkey. I have cooked, cleaned, scrubbed, polished, picked up toys and crumbs, and unblocked the vacuum cleaner. I am therefore pleased when Seb suggests a Wetherspoons breakfast for the two of us as he needs to buy some wood from Wickes and to spend his Next vouchers. I also need to stock up on party food for New Year's Eve as we have planned a leisurely supper by the fire, playing board games and seeing in the New Year with the tv.

Having enjoyed our traditional breakfast, I sip my coffee and relax until I notice Seb seems to be permanently dabbing on his phone, a practice he normally disapproves of at mealtimes.

"Hello?" I frown.

"What!" He jumps. "Do you want another coffee? I'll do you a refill."

"Thanks." I'm grateful. He's good at the Wetherspoons refills, and I rarely get my own.

"Who are you texting?"

He immediately turns his phone over. "Rosa's talking about a short walk tomorrow. There's a small stretch along this part of the coastline we haven't done yet."

The car park ticket is about to expire so we head off to Wickes and Tesco. It had better be a small walk, I think to myself; it's New Year's Eve and I have plans.

We're having a cup of tea later at home when Seb muses aloud, "Do you think taxi firms operate on New Year's Eve?"

I shrug, not knowing. I haven't used a taxi for years.

"Hang on." He disappears to the back door where there's a better signal. "Good." He smiles. "They do. I've booked one for 9 o'clock tomorrow."

"Where are we going? I thought we were staying in and having our own private party here."

"Umm, we are. I've booked for 9 o'clock in the morning. Rosa and I have decided to walk from Heddon's Mouth to Lynton, so I've booked a taxi from Lynton."

What happened to the short walk? I think ferociously. "Well, you'll be shattered. Remember, we have a long evening planned. I'm not retiring at 8pm with reruns of *Only Fools and Horses*. You better stay awake!" I reach for my tablet and google cattle prods. I'm surprised to discover they're legal and readily available. If there was a next day delivery, I'd be sorely tempted to buy one. For use on Seb, obviously, definitely not on the cattle, who are sweet and docile.

Seb

Heddon's Mouth to Lynton. I set the alarm for 6.30am to meet up with Rosa early, prior to driving to Lynton for the 9am taxi to Hunters Inn. All went well, and we arrived at Hunters Inn in anticipation of a good day, morning sunlight peeping through the clouds. Having no time to linger, we soon set off, as the walking app quoted about eight miles to Lynton.

Crossing a small stone bridge over the River Heddon, we soon reached Highveer Point after a steep climb. We took some time to enjoy the glorious views before descending to a waterfall, which looked lovely, but there was no avoiding wet feet. Nearing Woody Bay we had to take a detour as the path was closed due to fallen trees. There was a faded A4 laminated notice in explanation, but as neither of us had brought reading glasses, we soon gave up squinting and took the alternative route. The path then took us to Lee Bay and Lee Abbey (a Christian retreat), both beautiful, before reaching the famous Valley of the Rocks where we spotted some goats, much to Rosa's delight. We went off path to explore and climb over the rocks for a while, sat to take in the views and scenery, before descending to Lynmouth. We had a late lunch at the Ancient

Mariner, fabulous. I had mussels, Rosa had a brie, bacon and cranberry sandwich with salad.

Lara

I am so annoyed I cannot speak. I certainly cannot listen to Seb's ramblings and open a bottle of wine before settling down to play Uno.

The evening is muted to say the least. Seb is so tired he throws a teaspoon in the bin, puts a hot chocolate sachet in the washing up bowl and puts his mug in the fridge.

He then subsides on the settee and goes to sleep. I see the New Year in on my own. Even the chimes of Big Ben striking twelve loudly on the tv do not wake him. I leave him alone and consider once again purchasing a cattle prod.

Chapter Four

Minehead to Porlock Weir

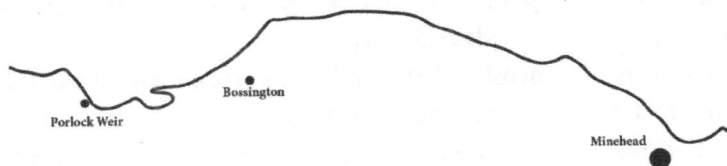

Lara

Minehead. I can't believe I suggested it myself. I saw an incredible offer on a holiday site for the Northfield Hotel; the reviews were good so, having checked with Rosa, Sebastian booked two rooms with the hotel and upgraded to deluxe.

The three of us set off early on a Sunday morning. Rosa spent the night with us as we all went to a mutual friend's birthday party last evening.

A thick mist is rolling over Exmoor and we wonder what view there will be on their walk, but after Simonsbath and Exford the weather clears considerably, and we arrive at Bossington to a reasonably clear sky. What a gem is Bossington. Ultra quaint and pretty, set down a long and narrow winding country road. I feel nervous about facing the prospect of driving it alone to reach the hotel.

Sebastian and Rosa have a long discussion on whether to take brollies, macs or both, chocolate, nuts or both. I'm just impatient to get going before I chicken out of the drive. In the event, it's easy; the satnav takes me directly to the hotel through some small and winding streets but there's very little traffic and I reach my destination, albeit pink with concentration, in about fifteen minutes.

"You look as if you could do with a coffee, dear," says the sympathetic receptionist when I announce we have two rooms booked and I'm the advance party.

"Oh yes, I remember." She nods. "I spoke to your husband. You must be the driver, you poor thing."

She makes me a welcome cup of coffee in the Residents Lounge, where another lone lady soon arrives, ordering a large brandy, then the three of us regale each other with various driving adventures.

"Oh, you are a good sort," exclaims brandy lady. "You're stuck on your own whilst your husband and friend go off for the day."

"I don't mind," I lie. "I get to have coffee, read a book, explore the town. It beats getting blisters, aching calves and wet hair."

I walk the whole length of Minehead sea front and back, from the lookout on Culver Cliff to the golf course the other side of Butlins, and explore the shops, before buying myself a ham and cheese sandwich and a large bar of chocolate to take back to the room.

"You must have walked three miles at least," praises the receptionist.

Room 24 is fabulous, huge with a large tv and sofa, king-size bed, massive bathroom with a claw-footed bath and a separate walk-in shower. On the dressing table there's Miles tea, coffee and chocolate, bottled water, sweets and two small bottles of red wine. Heaven. I open a bottle of water and settle down with my lunch and book. It's not long before my phone rings. It's Sebastian to say they're in the car park. They have been quick; I haven't had time for a glass of wine yet.

Seb

Bossington to Minehead. It seems ages since we first started planning this trip but at last we're here. We set off from Bossington, not rushing as this was only a short walk. Also, being mainly moorland and not too many steep climbs, it was an easy one for us. We saw some Hereford cattle that seem to be roaming over a large tract of land and wondered where their water supply was.

The information I looked up said there are two options for the walk, one being more difficult around Selworthy. We opted for the easier one, as we were worried about Lara being on her own. When we reached a sign saying "Steps to Quay" we weren't sure, but as I guessed the hotel was on a hill, we decided not to go down if it meant climbing up again, and opted for the top cliff path, arriving at the hotel easily with no complications.

Lara was waiting for us at the car, so we took off our walking gear to leave in the boot overnight. "We made good time," I answered to her query as to why we had not been long. "We didn't actually see the sea at all, as the walk was all inland."

"Ha," replied Lara, "I've spent over two hours walking along the sea front. I reckon I've covered almost as much as you two."

Lara

Having enjoyed coffee, wine and chocs, and relaxed in our rooms for a while, the three of us spend an hour and a half using the pool, jacuzzi and steam room before getting dressed for dinner, booked for 8pm. The meal is delicious. I'm thinking the stupid walks aren't so bad after all if I get to stay in hotels like this.

After breakfast, another splendid repast, we stroll down to the town to take photos posing against the giant-hands-holding-a-map monument that depicts the start of the South West Coastal Path, 630 miles.

Then it's back to Bossington for the stupid walk in the other direction. I spend an hour in Porlock, but most of the shops are closed on Mondays, so I buy a newspaper to read in the car before setting off to Porlock Weir to pick them up. They make good time but we're too late for lunch at the welcome-looking pub with its roaring fire, so return to Porlock where we have soup and scones at a great café serving homemade food.

Rosa falls asleep on the way home. Seb warbles on about having seen Kirrin Cottage on the path.

As we near home, I can see Seb shifting about in his seat, so I brace myself for a revelation and sure enough: "Lara..." Seb concentrates on the road but gives a quick sidelong glance. "Rosa and I have really enjoyed these walks and seeing that sign in Minehead has made me realise I want to do the whole 630 miles from start to finish." He risks another glance at my stony face. "We were thinking that, now we've walked Minehead to Porlock Weir, we'll start from now and do the walk in the correct order around the coast."

"Hang on," I interrupt. "You've already done a few stretches. Surely you're not going to do them again."

"Erm, well yes." Seb shifts nervously. "We'll have to if we want to do the whole route properly. But I expect we'll be much quicker now we're getting so fit."

I glance down at my short legs and wine-baby stomach, which doesn't seem to shrink however many bales of hay I throw around. "Sounds like you and Rosa have thought it all through."

"Just think of the holidays in Cornwall we can have." Seb brightens up. "It'll take a while to walk the North Devon coast, then we can spend some weekends in Cornwall. It will be great."

Seb

Bossington to Porlock Weir. Lara dropped us off at Bossington. Rosa was in raptures over the picturesque village so we wandered around for a while before setting off on the easy walk across mostly flat, marshy ground, close to the coast most of the way. We passed the house they used as Kirrin Cottage in the *Famous Five* series, now used for tourist accommodation, took some photos and then continued along the scenic route towards the pebbly beach approaching Porlock Weir.

Having visited Minehead and seen the monument, Rosa and I have decided to walk the whole coastal path to Poole, if possible, in the correct order geographically, if not always in the correct direction. Of course, this will not always be feasible due to weather, tide times, wind direction and whether we want to walk into the sun or not. There are also bus routes to consider; it is better to get the bus at the start of the walk rather than relying on catching one at the end when you are governed by time as well as the possibility that the bus does not turn up at all. When we reach the Cornish Coast, we shall have to stay overnight, so those walks will have to be over the winter months, for several reasons: price of the stay, busyness of the tourist season, the farm work in the spring and summer months, and the weather probably being too warm for steep walks.

We have realised the importance of having stout, waterproof walking shoes or boots, lightweight waterproof coats, walking poles, water bottles and studying the walking app before setting off; the whole prospect is thrilling, and I cannot wait for next week.

Chapter Five

Porlock Weir to County Gate

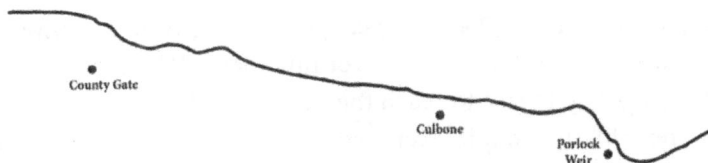

Seb

Having picked up Rosa early this morning, we had a pleasant drive to Porlock Weir, where I had already arranged for a taxi to take us to County Gate, for the five-and-a-half-mile trek back.

County Gate is a large car park at the point where Devon and West Somerset meet and has sweeping panoramic views. (Also, very handy toilets.) The taxi driver advised, "Take the lower path, otherwise you'll end up on the wrong route." The path meandered mostly through woodland where there were lots of trees down, one right across the path. We caught occasional glimpses of the sea through the trees.

At Culbone Church, there was an elderly couple, both leaning on walking sticks fashioned from branches picked up on their way, leaves sprouting from the top. "Where have you come from?" enquired the lady. "Have you come far? I've just about had enough and can't go any further." She leant heavily against the wall.

"Well, it's about four miles to County Gate, all up and down and fairly strenuous." I glanced at her walking stick.

"Oh no." Her face dropped even further. "What shall we do, Herb?" She turned to her husband, who looked equally as shattered.

Leaving them to their deliberations, Rosa and I explored the tiny church, reputed to be the smallest in England and used as a location for *Lorna Doone*. Rosa spent a long time exclaiming over the pews and font until I got impatient. "Come on, Rosa, let's get going. I want to reach the pub before it closes."

The elderly couple were still slumped across the wall discussing their options, so we waved them goodbye and set off along the track towards Porlock Weir. The track was in good condition, although I guess it could be slippery in wet weather. Luckily, it was a beautiful day, the sun sparkling over the canopy of the majestic oak and ash trees and the sea shining through the gaps.

We had a lovely lunch in the pub and were entertained by a couple of musicians having a jam session in the car park.

Lara

Seb arrives home about 5.30pm and plonks himself down at the kitchen table, rubbing his calves. "It was good." He sips a coffee, nodding at me. He proceeds to tell me about the taxi, the walk, fallen trees etc. until I interrupt, "What about lunch?"

He looks away.

"Er, a sandwich at the pub, look." He gets his mobile from his pocket. "There were lots of trees down." He scrolls through various shots of trees and paths until one grabs my attention.

"What's that?" I try to snatch his phone.

"Ermm, we just had a small prosecco."

Mm, I'm pretty sure I glimpsed two large glasses clinking over two humungous plates of food.

"What was your sandwich?"

Seb looks away and mumbles, "Crab."

When he goes out to check on the ponies, I google the pub in Porlock Weir and the menu looks fabulous with rave reviews. The "sandwich" turns out to be a crab baguette with all the trimmings. I head to the freezer. If he's lucky, he can have a fish finger sandwich for supper, minus the bread.

Chapter Six

Spa Weekend

Lara

Rosa has suggested a spa weekend for the two of us. Is she nuts? My idea of hell. Green smoothies, carrot sticks, cucumber slices, grapes (but not trodden) and water. No bread, potatoes or chocolate. Exercise regime. Masseurs pummelling your fleshy bits.

"I don't think so, thank you, Rosa. It's not my idea of fun."

"Oh go on, Lara. You may enjoy it. I've been before and you don't have to do any of the activities if you don't want to. You could just relax by the pool."

"I'll think about it, but I don't have time, anyway."

"You do. I ran it past Seb and he thinks it will do you good and is happy to help Bobby on the farm while you're away. It's only a couple of days. So, you see, you have no excuse."

I'm going to kill Seb. Why did he not warn me? Why did he say he'd help Bobby? Why did he say it would be good for me? And why oh why are he and Rosa discussing me as if I am a specimen? Seethe.

"Please, Lara. I'm sure you'll love it when you get there."

I weaken. What a sucker. "Probably. I'll let you know tomorrow."

"Thanks, Lara." Rosa hugs me. "I'll speak to you tomorrow. Fingers crossed."

Oh hell. She seems so pleased. How can I let her down?

***

"Seb, I'm furious with you." He backs away. "Why did you not warn me about this ghastly weekend?"

"I didn't think it was important. Rosa mentioned it and I said 'fine by me' but said she should ask you. Why? Are you going?"

"She's insisting. But I don't want to."

"Why not? It will be nice for you to have a bit of me time together."

"Me time? No, Seb, it will be me and Rosa time, not me. If only! I would love some real me time, which would be seclusion in a four-star hotel with room service, four books, a box of chocolates and no phone."

Serendipity Spa in reality is not too bad. I'm slightly worried our bags may be checked for contraband as I have stowed two large bags of Maltesers and a bottle of red wine, but it's fine. Rosa scans the activities and signs up for everything. I have a leisurely swim and participate half-heartedly in one yoga class. Having showered and dressed for dinner, making full use of the Elemis body lotions, I relax in the room with a book and a glass of wine. I wave the bottle of Rioja and the chocs towards Rosa. She is appalled but accepts three Maltesers.

"Oh, Lara, you are naughty. You don't mind breaking the rules."

"What rules?" I look around nervously. "Have they got cameras on us?"

"Of course not. That's what I love about you. Your fearless spirit."

"What me?" I gulp my wine. "Please have a glass, Rosa. I feel silly drinking on my own."

"Okay, just a small one." She gets a toothbrush tumbler from the bathroom.

"Cheers," I say. "You were right, after all. I am enjoying myself."

Rosa relaxes with her wine and twiddles the glass. "You're lucky, Lara. You have a great husband and family."

"I wouldn't say that, but they're okay, I suppose."

"I'd love to be you."

"Really? Wallowing in mud? Overdraft? Constant worry about weather?"

"I wouldn't like the mud, but I would love your life on the farm with a wonderful husband and family."

"You have your sister, a good job and a lovely home."

"Not the same. Tell me, how did you and Seb meet?"

"I've told you already. Twice in fact," I admonish.

"Tell me again. I love it."

"It was a coach holiday to the Isle of Wight."

"So romantic," Rosa acknowledges with a grin.

"Tell me about it! I was taking my mother; Seb was with his grandmother and somehow we were given adjoining tables at dinner on the first night in the hotel. The oldies started chatting, which left Seb and I in painful silence staring into space. In retrospect, they weren't that old, I suppose. The food arrived, mediocre, but better than expected. Mother and Grandma tucked in with gusto. Seb and I looked at each other across the tables and burst into laughter. That broke the ice. After that, the four of us got on like a house on fire. We spent three days on excursions: Cowes, Ventnor, Osborne House, ate all our meals together. Seb was so solicitous towards his grandmother I think I fell in love with him then."

"He's a caring person," Rosa intervenes. "Go on."

"The rest is history. I've told you everything. Wait, do you mean the quiz night? Mother and Grandma were nodding off, having giggled their way through the comedian's terrible jokes. Seb and I ended up with a quiz questionnaire, most of which had us completely baffled. We felt so ignorant not having a clue and just made up some daft answers, until we got to the '70s and '80s music questions, which we knew. We surreptitiously passed our answers to an elderly couple sitting next to us and they won a box of fruit jellies, which they gave to us."

Rosa sighs and looks dreamy. "How lovely."

"Shall I top you up? Just a small one."

"Yes please. How naughty." Sighing. "You and Seb and the family; they all love you, you know?"

"Well, yes, I suppose they do in a funny sort of way. It's probably because I feed them."

"No, it's more than that. There's a magic."

"Rosa, you've had too much Indian head massage, or whatever. Basically, we bumble along from one crisis to another: TB, fly strike, still births, failed crops, no rain, too much rain, bank demands, kids squabbling. Seb has to go out to work or the farm would crumble. Most of the time we're too exhausted or irritable to even switch on the tv, let alone watch anything."

"Seb seems fine on Mondays."

"He looks forward to it. It's his one day off, I suppose. But I can assure you we have plenty of ups and downs. We've fallen into quite a rut recently. It's probably why he loves the walks so much. They get him away from the constant workload, which never seems to lessen."

"Yes," replies Rosa. "I can see that. He says he loves striding along on the edge of the world, looking over the vast expanse of ocean and scaling the cliffs. He can forget all else and enjoy the freedom and the sheer beauty of nature."

I gaze at her in disbelief. "Did he? How eloquent. Come on, let's go for dinner. I'm starving. I hope there are chips."

Chapter Seven

County Gate to Lynton

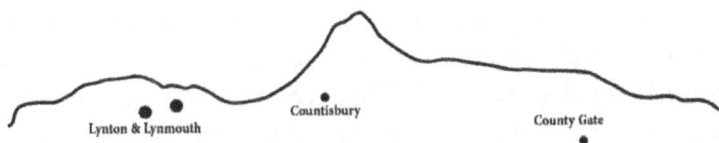

Lynton & Lynmouth   Countisbury   County Gate

Lara

Seb and Rosa are walking County Gate to Lynmouth and Lynton today. I am painting the kitchen walls so must move brasses, pictures and clock to the table, along with the toaster, bread bin, storage jars and a stack of *Farmers Weekly* gathering dust in the corner.

I am envious to say the least, and as I take the lid off the paint pot, reflect on the last time Seb and I had a lovely day out in Lynmouth, a couple of years ago. I remember the weather was sunny, cold and crisp, rather like today. We drove down the precipitous hill into the picture-perfect village, surely among the prettiest in Devon, and parked in the car park. We ambled along Lynmouth Street, which before the flood of 1952 was the riverbed, enjoying the fabulous shops selling all sorts of arts, crafts, kitchenware, interiors and much more. I bought a teacloth, which I still have. After wandering over the bridge across the river and admiring the stunning coastline and towering cliffs, we retraced our steps and had a delicious lunch in the Ancient Mariner, one of the many great places to eat in the village.

Along the harbour, the Memorial Hall has photos, information and a pre-flood scale model of the village as it was before mid-August 1952, when the huge torrent of water which had built up on Exmoor on already waterlogged ground, combined with weather factors and the bursting of a dam formed by fallen trees and debris, coursed through the valley and completely overwhelmed the culvert that had been built, flooding the whole area. Thirty-four people died, hundreds were made homeless, over a hundred buildings were destroyed or damaged along with bridges and cars washed out to sea. The village was rebuilt with the river being diverted around the village.

No trip to Lynmouth is complete unless you travel to Lynton on the iconic Cliff Railway, an incredible feat of engineering, built in 1888 and the world's highest and steepest water-powered railway. A unique and inspiring experience, which we took great delight in.

At Lynton we had an ice cream and strolled around the shops before descending to Lynmouth again on the railway.

I suddenly realise I have not started painting yet. I've been so lost in my memory of a wonderful day out together, and I recall Seb and I agreed that we were so lucky to live in this lovely part of the world. I pick up my paintbrush, sighing. Seb and I rarely go out together these days and certainly not for a full day, mooching about. He's too busy on his stupid walks.

Seb

We parked at Lynton and got a taxi to County Gate car parking area. We hadn't realised there is a bus stop there; we must have walked past it the last time we were here, so we took note of the times for future reference. It seems to be a stop for the Exmoor coaster, Minehead to Lynmouth. At the car park there are great views across *Lorna Doone* country so we spent a while there before crossing the road to start on the path. The path was easy walking at first, across fields with views towards the Bristol Channel and Wales. After crossing a farm track, we soon reached the church at Countisbury. We had a quick look around, decided not to stop for a break in the Blue Ball Inn, tempting though it looked, but pressed on to Lynmouth, the path at first being alongside the main road then descending very steeply down to Lynmouth through woods, and along the cliff edge with dramatic and wonderful views. We crossed the bridge over the East Lyn River and spent a short while looking around the village as Rosa wanted to look in some of the shops, then decided to have a late lunch before rejoining the path to walk up to Lynton.

Chapter Eight

Heddon's Mouth to Combe Martin

Seb

I picked up Rosa and we drove to Combe Martin car park, used the toilets and set off in misty conditions. We bumped into an acquaintance of mine and Lara's, who looked at Rosa with interest. "Who's this then?" he asked, raising his eyebrows. He always was blunt. I introduced Rosa briefly but we didn't stay to chat as we were anxious to set off on our walk.

We walked at first alongside some houses, then a short section of shrubby growth before emerging onto open land, climbing all the time. We paused briefly to rest on a bench then continued upwards to reach a summit, heaving a sigh of relief and congratulating ourselves on our fitness. The mist cleared and we looked ahead and realised we had only climbed Little Hangman and the huge cliff ahead must be Great Hangman, reputedly the highest cliff in England at 1043 feet. We looked at each other in dismay, then laughed. "We can do it." It was strenuous to say the least, a steady but arduous climb to reach the summit with stupendous views. We both stood on a pile of stones and took photos to record our success. Then began the gradual descent through some moorland, before a very difficult steep drop down to almost sea level. We were glad we had decided to do the walk from Combe Martin to Heddon's Mouth rather than vice versa because of the steep steps. After a wooded valley, another climb took us up again to moorland; we guessed we were at roughly the highest point before descending again so I called a taxi for an hour and a half's time to take us back to Combe Martin. We reached Hunters Inn in half an hour and had a light lunch.

Lara

It sounds like Seb and Rosa had a great day out. They had a fabulous lunch at the Hunters Inn. I can probably count on one hand the number of lunches Seb and I have had on a day out, unless you count a picnic, or a quick pit stop at McDonalds. As for a taxi, this is unheard of. Days out, lunches, taxis. How can he afford it? Is he charging double to his gardening customers? The money does not come out of the farm account, which is solely for essentials, not fripperies.

"Taxis, lunches." I frown at Seb. "Quite the gentleman of leisure these days, aren't you?"

"It's only because there was no public transport there," Seb defends himself. "And it was a bit of a trek to take two cars. We went halves on the fare. And the lunch wasn't expensive. I'll go upstairs and change."

I'm assuming he went into Rosa's for tea as well. I contemplate the chicken breast I've laid out on the work surface and give it a thwack with the rolling pin. Why am I bothering with herby chicken escalopes with shallots and sauté potatoes when Seb has partaken of a delicious Exmoor pub lunch? I give the chicken another thwack. Seb can have half a thin end. Bobby can have extra. He and I had beans on toast for lunch.

Chapter Nine

Ilfracombe to Braunton

Seb

Ilfracombe to Woolacombe. Approx eight miles. We parked at Woolacombe, caught the 31 bus to Ilfracombe and started on the path near Torrs Park. The walk at first was winding and double backed on itself and we wondered if we were on the right track. Lee Bay, about halfway, is my kind of place, caves and smuggler paths galore. I spent a good half hour exploring whilst Rosa chatted to another hiker. We ate our snack of chocolate bars, which Rosa had brought, sitting on a rock, gulls screeching overhead. Reluctantly leaving, we ascended the steep path, which is also part of the Tarka Trail to Bull Point Lighthouse, then south to Rockham Bay, before going around to Morte Point with its fabulous views towards Woolacombe. The path was then fairly easy walking to Mortehoe along the road to Barricane Beach, famous for its shells that get washed up regularly.

Woolacombe has a wonderful, huge sandy beach, very popular and busy in the summer months, and has numerous hotels, guest houses and B and B establishments. We were thankful to relax in the Red Barn for a lunch of toasties and a cold cider.

Seb

Woolacombe to Croyde. Five miles. We parked at Croyde and caught the bus to Woolacombe, looking anxiously at the gathering grey clouds.

Unfortunately, it pelted with rain, so it was heads down, unable to appreciate the miles of North Devon sands at Woolacombe and Putsborough. The official coast path goes through the dunes but we walked mostly along the beach then took the steps up to the cliff top to go around the headland to Baggy Point. We were disappointed not to fully appreciate the views because of the bad weather. My jeans were soaked through when we returned to the car but Rosa had spare leggings and, although extremely tight on me, they were better than dripping all over the car seat. We debated a pub lunch, an appealing idea, but the thought of being seen in the leggings put me off.

Lara

Sebastian came home wearing Rosa's leggings! He warbled some excuse about getting wet. "It was teeming with rain."

"We had a couple of showers here." I stare at his legs. "Bobby and I brought a couple trailers of logs round to the log shed. Umm, what was Rosa wearing while you borrowed her leggings?"

"She had spare ones." He has the grace to look abashed.

"Didn't she want them herself? Surely she must have been wet through as well or did the downpour only home in on your pins?"

Seb mumbles something about waterproof trousers but frankly my mind is fixated on a mental image of Rosa, who having stripped off her leggings and handed them over to Seb, also stripped down to his underpants, then reclines back on her car seat in a red thong, whilst watching Seb raise his bottom off the car seat to wriggle into her leggings.

"We didn't have any lunch." Sebastian's eyes drift towards the mashed potato I'm pounding furiously. "Rosa wanted to go the pub but I was wearing her leggings."

My eyes are now as big as those of the mackerel, whose head I've just chopped off. "Fish pie for supper." I turn my back. "Very fishy."

Seb and Rosa are dancing a tango on Croyde Beach in the rain. She is wearing a clinging dark red sheath dress with a slit up to the waist revealing toned bronzed legs. Seb is clad in tight black leggings and a red bow tie. They dip and glide. Rosa expertly slides her leg between Seb's thighs, pointing a golden high-heeled dance shoe and arching her head back with perfect poise. Seb holds her close and leads her into a series of sensual intricate flicks and manoeuvres.

The judges, sitting on a nearby rock, Craig Revel Hake, Motsi Mackerel, Shirley Sole and Anton du Lobster all have eyes on stalks and are gaping open mouthed at the intensity and passion of the most dramatic and perfect tango they have ever seen. Anton du Lobster waves his claws in ecstasy and even Craig Revel Hake is flapping his fins.

The dancers conclude with a controlled but perfect clinch and the judges clap their fins and claws and wave their tails enthusiastically before awarding four perfect tens.

Seb

Croyde to Braunton. This was a fairly easy one with wonderful scenery. We parked at Braunton and caught the 9.04am 21C bus to Croyde. Croyde is a charming village by a huge, sandy, family-friendly beach with rock pools and dunes and is known as the surfing capital of North Devon.

Starting from the car park, the path went past the dunes then ascended narrowly to Saunton Down, which has wonderful views over Saunton and Braunton Burrows.

We used the toilets in the car park at Saunton, then walked along the fabulous sandy beach leaving the fine-looking Saunton Sands Hotel behind us getting smaller whilst Westward Ho! got bigger as it came into view, the famous pebble ridge becoming distinct. We could discern Bucks Mills, Clovelly and Hartland Point in the distance, and we discussed how much we were looking forward to our future walks.

On reaching Crow Point, part of the Braunton Burrows Nature Reserve, we walked along the toll road by the estuary. The rivers Taw and Torridge meet at this estuary, which creates unpredictable tides.

Chapter Ten

Braunton to Westward Ho!

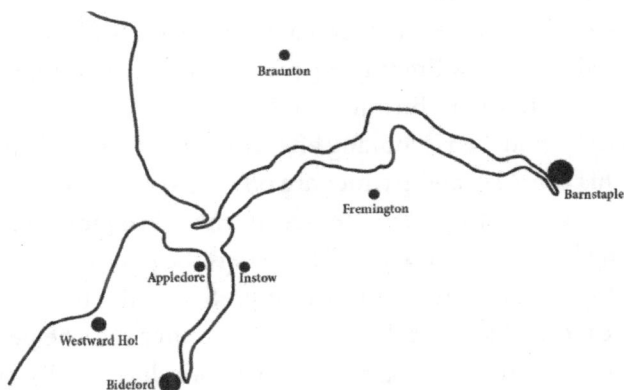

Lara

A month off from stupid walks. Yea! We had a week's holiday in Lanzarote, enjoying the all-inclusive facilities, and Seb forgot about his middle-age spread. A week of bliss, then back to catching up with farm and family. Seb had planned a possible short break to Cornwall (seemingly bypassing the proposed methodical order) with Rosa, but she had an unexpected last-minute wedding invitation, so the plan was thwarted.

So, first Saturday at home with no family commitments, back in our occasional Saturday night routine, work permitting, i.e. my making a fakeaway in advance, for nuking later, an early glass of wine at 6pm ready for relaxation with a bag of Kettle crisps. So far so good. I run a bath and Seb even brings me a glass of wine to savour while I'm wallowing in the bubbles. Returning to the bedroom, warm, scented and mellow, I frown as Seb is banging his phone in frustration. "One bar! This is the pits. I need to call Rosa to see if she wants me to bring the bedding for Monday and Tuesday."

Bedding? What bedding?

"What do you mean? Why would you want bedding?"

"Well, you know I'm staying over at Alex and Corinne's next week while they're in Birmingham?"

"Yes." I nod. Seb is looking after his two little grandchildren while his son Alex and partner are off on a short break.

"I'm just texting Rosa to see if she's bringing her own bedding but there's no signal." He bangs the phone again.

"Why would she want bedding? She only lives twenty minutes from Alex. She'll surely go home after she's helped you with the bath time." Rosa absolutely adores kids. Unlike me, I only tolerate them. Give me a dog or a cow any day. She's volunteered to help Seb look after them for the days he is staying, only a few miles from her home.

"Oh, she may stay the night." Seb waves his hand dismissively. "Then she can be there when they wake up."

What! This is the first I've heard of it. I stomp downstairs to steam some beans to go with the Thai green curry I've prepped from scratch and wonder if I can find some laxatives to add to Seb's.

Seb

I packed my bag and took the clean bedding off the spare room bed, a couple of diet cokes, a hip flask of rum and three Snickers bars. Lara said she would make a cottage pie and an apple crumble for me but I don't want her to go to any trouble and I can easily buy some ready meals from Tesco so Rosa and I can microwave them at our leisure after the children have settled. I'm apprehensive about looking after them for three days but Rosa is on hand and she'll be great with them.

I'm disappointed we didn't go to Cornwall so I have spent an hour or so looking up cottages for future reference.

Awful weather, such a nuisance. Alex and Corinne got off okay at 8am, Rosa turned up soon after and together we took the two little ones to Nursery for 9am. We picked them up at 2pm. We had arranged a short walk from Barnstaple to Braunton while they were there but decided against it because of the lashing rain.

Lara

Cows, mud, rain. Phoned Highways South West complaining about potholes, subsidence, dreadful condition of roads but got cut off! No internet because of weather. No word from Seb. Bed early with a book, a hot chocolate and four shortbread biscuits.

After I've helped Bobby with feeding the cattle and brought in two wheelbarrows of logs, Seb turns up exhausted at 10.30am with the kids, as there was no Nursery today, eyes slits and asking for paracetamol, almost incoherent when I asked him how the evening and morning had gone. So when he leaves again at 3.30pm, I have no idea of his plans for the rest of the day, (i.e. Rosa).

I have a busy afternoon, then my phone pings "Alfie sick. Rosa has forsaken her amateur dramatics night and is helping me."

"That's good of her" I text back before frowning and reaching into the fridge for a bottle of Sauvignon blanc. "What's happening?" I text back later having downed two large glasses.

"All okay, Alfie seems fine. We've put a bucket by his bed. R and I having supper. Chinese takeaway from Tesco. Night x."

Grr. I know Seb won't indulge while he's in charge of the kids but I bet he's popped a hip flask in his jacket pocket. I retire to bed with the bottle and six shortbread biscuits, and catch up on the last two episodes of *Cold Feet*. I toss and turn most of the night, dreaming of prawn toasts, Chinese wontons and red silk kimonos embroidered with yellow dragons. The rain lashes against the window and I worry about the sheep.

Two beautiful people wearing embroidered silk hooded jackets are sitting cross-legged and bare-footed on a red and gold mat with a bowl of Chinese tisane in front of them. They bow to each other and sip, then rise in one fluid movement to join hands and stroll along a wide, vibrant avenue, festooned with bobbing red lanterns under a clear, starry sky. They stop to allow a huge iridescent dragon pass, golden scales gleaming in the moonlight. The dragon stumbles into a giant pothole and lets out a roar. The two beautiful people rush to the rescue and help him regain his balance. The dragon swishes his glowing tail, breathes out a small curl of fire and showers them with golden fortune cookies.

Seb

Rosa and I had a nice evening, ready meal on laps, chatting and watching a bit of tv. Both children were fine today so we were able to leave them at Nursery. We just had time to walk the Braunton to Barnstaple stretch as the weather was much improved. I parked at the Leisure Centre long stay car park in Barnstaple, and we caught the 21C bus to Braunton from Barnstaple Bus Station, getting off at the main car park in Braunton.

The path follows the old railway line, starting off at Wrafton Wildlife Pond where we saw some swans swimming about serenely. We passed Chivenor Air Base, where there is a lot of new housing being built, then Heanton Court, following the estuary to Barnstaple, under the new bridge, then along the old Long Bridge back to the Leisure Centre.

Barnstaple is the main town in North Devon, situated alongside the River Taw, and is one of the country's oldest boroughs. It has a thriving pannier market with stalls ranging from homemade jams and chutneys to bric-a-brac, books and plants. There are many interesting and historic areas: the iconic nineteenth-century Butchers Row with its great range of produce shops, the Grade 1 listed Queen Anne's Walk and the ancient Long Bridge among others. The High Street, Boutport Street and side streets have an array of different shops and eating places.

It was a flat, easy walk so we got back in plenty of time to collect the little ones.

Barnstaple to Bideford. This was another easy one as the path is flat along the Tarka Trail, which was the old railway line connecting Barnstaple to Torrington, via Bideford. There were several cyclists as well as walkers on the trail.

We had a pit stop at the Fremington Quay Café, a renovated railway station, for coffee and cake and made a note to go back sometime for the delicious-looking lunch.

Walking towards Instow we passed Yelland, where we could look across the estuary, then along the sandy beach at Instow, which has a boatyard with yachts moored. Instow also has a preserved level crossing and listed signal box.

Leaving Instow, we continued along the Tarka Trail to Bideford and across the old bridge, which connects the old part of the town with East the Water. The mediaeval bridge is one of the longest in England and has twenty-four arches.

Lara

Seb has been reticent about his stay with the children, just mumbling something about going to Barnstaple, and that Alex and Corinne had a good time away, but not at all forthcoming. I have tried to call Rosa a couple of times but there has been no reply and she hasn't got back to me.

My mind is working overtime wondering if there was a problem. Did they fall out? Seb can be quite annoying sometimes. Perhaps he made her clear up Alfie's vomit and she realised she is not so keen on kids after all. Perhaps he fell asleep leaving her to clear up the dishes. After all, she lives alone and is not used to other people's mess. I doubt it was easy looking after two under-fives and Seb may have taken her for granted. This seems unlikely. Rosa is very patient, but she's not a doormat and would stand her ground.

What's the alternative? Maybe they got on too well; maybe they enjoyed each other's company and cosy evenings together so much that they nearly...

"Do not go there, Lara." I pinch myself. "You're being ridiculous and fanciful. This is your husband and best friend. And we live quiet lives in the country. We're not in a soap or a Hollywood film."

Seb

Bideford to Westward Ho! Approx three and a quarter miles. Rosa and I walked along Bideford Quay and through Victoria Park, past some houses overlooking the estuary, under the new Torridge Bridge opened in 1987, and along the embankment, where there were a couple of houseboats moored. We discussed living on a houseboat and discovered we both quite like the idea. We walked along the rear of Appledore Shipyard, then along the road of Appledore sea front with views across the estuary to Instow. Appledore itself is a quaint and charming fishing village with a maze of narrow streets and small terraced cottages, formerly fishermen's homes. There are some great pubs and eating places but we carried on over the salt marshes and dunes to Northam Burrows and the beach, the golf course just inland on our left. The Pebble Ridge at Westward Ho! is always impressive and we strolled along the huge sandy Blue Flag award beach, as fortunately the tide was out, until we reached the town. We had a snack of a hot sausage roll and a Hockings ice cream before catching the 21 bus opposite the car park back to Bideford.

Lara

Seb has gone to Bideford today and, as it happens, I have papers to drop in to the accountants so I decide to have a morning out myself. Parking near Victoria Park, I stop to admire the quay with its famous arched bridge and see there are a couple of cargo ships unloading. I personally think Bideford is one of the prettiest towns in North Devon with its picturesque riverside, small winding streets, pannier market and interesting shops. Victoria Park is great for children and adults alike and boasts lots of kids' amusements and lovely landscaped gardens, as well as the Burton Art Gallery.

There are many great places to eat in Bideford, but today I decide to have a coffee and cake in the Burton's Café du Parc, all the while wondering where Seb and Rosa are. It's a very short stretch to Westward Ho! so in theory Seb could be home before me.

Chapter Eleven

Westward Ho! to Morwenstow

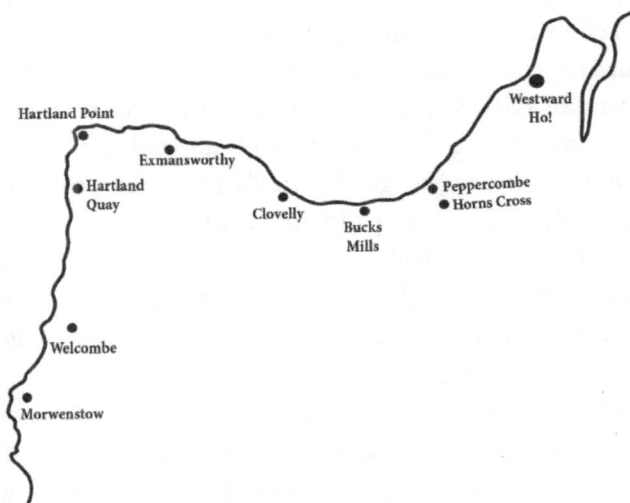

Lara

The stupid walks are back on a regular basis. There was our holiday, Rosa's wedding weekend and another short break somewhere, the Alfie and Lily babysitting, so all in all the walks have been disjointed and occasional rather than the regular Mondays. Seb spent most of yesterday evening using up the 4G data allowance on his mobile to look up cottages in Cornwall, for later in the year. The Wi-Fi is off again. Living out in the sticks this is a regular occurrence. He found a couple of options he'll discuss with Rosa later.

They've gone to Hartland today. Or is it Horns Cross? Maybe Westward Ho!? Seems to be a lot of walks around there; I've almost lost count how many times I've heard Hartland this, Hartland that, Westward Ho! and Appledore.

I've brought in some logs but my main job for the day is scrubbing the kitchen floor, prior to resealing it tomorrow. Sackcloth and ashes spring to mind I know, but this a yearly chore (in reality every two years as I keep putting it off), which I hate, but a necessity as the floor gets filthy. We all tiptoe in and out in our wellies occasionally, with an apologetic "forgot my phone" or "I need to get Bluebell's cattle passport" and then there's Ben, the love, padding in and out, skidding on his slobber, so occasionally I must scrub the old flagstones and reseal. They look good for about a week while we all remember to remove boots but then revert to the usual pattern of tiptoeing, "only for a few seconds".

The weather has been so wet lately that Bobby and I are falling behind with fencing and field work. The cattle are housed, so he is scraping dung from the sheds and putting down clean bedding. I think about Seb sitting on a rock somewhere gazing at the ocean or maybe sheltering in a secluded cave sharing a bar of chocolate and having cosy chats with Rosa.

He sends me a picture of himself by a coastal signpost, blue sky overhead. I growl over my scrubbing brush.

Seb

Peppercombe to Westward Ho! Great day again. Started off a bit drizzly but the sun came out and it was glorious. We ended up driving to Horns Cross instead of travelling by bus as there was a mix up with the app timetable. Rosa and I both got it wrong somehow. Also, Rosa had left her walking boots in her car at Westward Ho! where we had arranged to meet, only discovering this as we approached the bus stop in Bideford, so we had to return for them. She kept apologising, then realised she had also left her phone, so we had to go back again but it was no problem. It only took a few minutes to change her boots, pick up the phone, double check she had locked the car and put her keys in my glove compartment for safe keeping.

We waited a while for a bus but then decided to drive, parking in a layby at Horns Cross. We had to walk along the A39 for a bit, then turned right by the pub (parking for patrons only) to reach a signpost with both left and right arms pointing to Peppercombe. We took the right though a National Trust gate, down a winding path through Peppercombe Woods to the pebbly beach. We then retraced our steps a short way back to take the footpath to Greencliff. There is a coach house there with a sign: "Feel free to rest a while."

The views and the scenery from Peppercombe to Westward Ho! are fantastic. Quite a strenuous climb in places but exhilarating. We walked along the cliff tops until at one of the dips we decided to do a stretch along the pebbles as the tide was low. Not easy walking. Someone had made a hut from driftwood under the cliffs and appeared to be living there. We continued along the beach for a while before climbing up the path again where the cliff dropped to near sea level. We paused on a bench to munch a couple of chocolate bars, anticipating having a late lunch in the Pier House restaurant on our return to Westward Ho! Continuing on the path past Abbotsham, we chatted idly about what we would choose on the menu. "I'm starving," declared Rosa. "I'll quickly change my walking boots when we get to my car, and we'll go straight back to Horns Cross to get yours. I'll just put the car keys in my jacket pocket in readiness."

She rummaged in her bag, frowned, then met my eyes in shock as we realised simultaneously that her keys were safely stowed in my glove compartment back at Horns Cross.

Dilemma! We had walked over three and a half miles, and it would take us a long time to walk back to my car. Consulting the walking app, we realised that Abbotsham village was only a mile and a half inland and that there was a bus going from there to Horns Cross in three quarters of an hour, so we decided to hotfoot it and while away a pleasant half hour in the pub, before catching the bus. By the time we got back to Westward Ho! we were still just in time for a late lunch.

Lara

Honestly! I don't think those two are safe to be let out. Seb finally arrives back clutching a bottle of rum, two packs of paracetamol and a bunch of flowers, looking sheepish. He stopped at Asda. He witters on for a while about views and sunshine and chocolate but I can tell he's twitchy and not telling me the whole story. I wait patiently, knowing he'll divulge eventually. It transpires that Rosa left her boots and her phone in her car at Westward Ho! which involved driving back from Bideford twice, they waited at a bus stop for a bus that never came, they had looked at an out-of-date app (or probably a different area of North Devon, who knows?). So they drove to Horns Cross, parked in a layby, walked to Peppercombe Beach, scenery, views, seagulls, blah, blah, blah. Then, when they had passed Abbotsham, discovered Rosa had left her keys in Seb's glove compartment at Horns Cross! What? As if! I find this hard to believe. They had a drink in the Thatch pub, caught a bus back to Horns Cross, returned to the Pier House, needing a substantial late lunch of mussels and beef nachos, washed down with a gin and tonic, to recover from their ordeal! Seb says it was only a small g and t, but I don't believe him. I'm not sure I believe any of it. It's too ludicrous. Perhaps they just lazed about on Westward Ho! beach, had a leisurely lunch at the Pier House and bought me the flowers as a distraction...or a guilty conscience.

Seb

Bucks Mills to Peppercombe. This was a short circular walk today, about five miles all told and covering two miles of the coast path. Rosa has extra work at the moment, and I have a list of things to do on the farm but we could not resist squeezing in a quick one. We parked in the free car park on the edge of the village, then walked through the picturesque street towards the harbour, which is rocky and had some odd fishing nets and crates dotted about along with the remains of some old lime kilns. We retraced our way back through the village to join the coastal path to Peppercombe and, after negotiating some steep steps, climbed up to the woodland path, which was charming and offered glimpses of the sea.

We descended to Peppercombe Beach, a secluded cove backed by red sandstone cliffs, and had our lunch sitting on a large piece of driftwood. We had the beach entirely to ourselves and I wished we had more time. It was beautiful, but we reluctantly found our way back to the path, only for Rosa to exclaim that she had left her umbrella behind. I quickly ran back to retrieve it, while she ambled slowly on, and then we returned to Bucks Mills car park via the inland route.

Bucks Mills to Clovelly. Approx four and a half miles. This was an easy walk. We parked at Bucks Mills and walked up the hill to the A39 to catch the bus to Clovelly, going to Hartland Village first as the bus only stops at Clovelly on the return journey. Not a hardship in this lovely area and a good way to appreciate the scenery.

We walked through the Clovelly visitor centre where we were allowed to go through free of charge as we were not descending to the village but sticking to the coast path. At the SW Coast Path signpost we turned right to Bucks Mills to walk along the Hobby Drive, built in Victorian times for coach and horses. It is a wide, flat path, tree lined either side and highly elevated. An easy walk with a few infrequent glimpses towards the sea as we were fairly inland. After the Hobby Drive, we walked along the normal coast path down to Bucks Mills before heading up the road back to the car park.

Lara

Seb and I are going away for two days visiting distant relatives, so there's lots to do, checking the animals, going around the farm and the garden, covering semi tender plants, cleaning the house, washing the bedding etc., but as it's Monday and we are not going until tomorrow, Seb has managed to squeeze in a short walk somewhere between Hartland and Clovelly. "I know we went to Clovelly last week but there are great walks around there and this small stretch will take us nicely towards Hartland where the walks will be longer and harder. I'll be back by one or thereabouts." He pecks me on the cheek at 7.15am.

"The roads are icy with a hard overnight frost, so I'll take the truck."

"Wait," I yell as he disappears through the door. "Have you remembered Rosa's birthday present and card? We'll be away on the day."

"Don't worry." He pats his rucksack. "I have it here."

I glare at his back sourly. Our wedding anniversary was last week, and he didn't even get me a card. I didn't give him one either but that's beside the point.

At 12.45 my phone pings. "Won't be back for lunch."

After our lunch of soup and toast, Bobby goes out to check the sheep whilst I wash up and put the kettle on for another cup of tea. I'm having to get used to solitude. Seb and I used to have the odd day out: visiting a garden centre, buying plants, a stroll around Rosemoor Gardens or Saunton Sands, even the occasional picnic on Exmoor. Just a couple of hours away from the farm and a change of scenery. Now it's only Seb going out. Truth be told I'm envious. Not about the stupid walks – no way! I'm envious of his enjoying a leisure pursuit with an agreeable companion.

A couple are strolling along the cliffs above Hartland, carrying a picnic hamper, a golden labrador scampering at their heels. The labrador stops every now and then to sniff the air, nose twitching, then darts off to investigate some interesting tufts of grass. The couple smile indulgently at their pet, turn to each other, nod and unroll a red plaid picnic blanket in a sheltered grassy hollow. They unpack the picnic hamper of a whole roast chicken, cheese, salad and a French stick, uncork two small bottles of white wine and munch contentedly. Satisfyingly full, all three lie back for a snooze, the warm sunshine making them euphoric. The dog whimpers in his sleep chasing a rabbit, then tries to snatch a fly hovering overhead.

A smell of burning rouses me from my reverie. Hell's bells! The kettle has boiled dry and Ben is nuzzling my leg to be let out.

Seb

Clovelly to Exmansworthy. We parked at Hartland Village approximately two miles inland from the coast path, to catch a bus to Clovelly, popping into the shop for pasties and chocolate. Reaching Clovelly, we walked through the visitor centre, which they kindly allowed us to do, as before, on the promise that we were not going to walk down the cobbled hill through the village to the harbour. Instead, we turned left onto the coastal path, noting an acorn signpost, "Minehead 99, Poole 531". We were so busy talking about the possibility of going all the way to Poole that we missed the South West Coastal Path sign and found ourselves at the bottom of the steep hill, by the sea. We asked a fisherman and he pointed us back up the hill, where we soon located the sign, it being obvious.

Rain came down heavily as soon as we set off through the Clovelly Estate. We passed a cabin then took shelter in a folly, Angels Wings, which was built in 1826 as a lookout. The rain eased slightly so we resumed our way along the towering cliffs of Gallantry Bower, a steep climb, before descending to Mouth Mill, a fascinating secluded small beach with amazing rock formations. I made a note to return in better weather. After several more ascents/descents we came across a grassy cliff top where a Wellington bomber had crashed in 1942 with the loss of all crew. We ate our soggy pasties before rejoining the path to walk the two miles to Hartland, along the edge of a boggy field. Even the road, which we thought would be drier, was flooded as the river had burst its banks and our feet got soaked. As soon as reached the truck, the rain stopped, and the sun came out. Typical.

Seb

Exmansworthy to Hartland Quay. Nearly five miles. There are no buses near this part of the coast, so Rosa and I met up in Bideford and drove in convoy to Exmansworthy National Trust car park (free). We left her car there and I drove on to Hartland Quay. We decided to walk west to east as there was quite a westerly blowing today, and Rosa did not want to walk with the wind in our faces.

We set off up the hill to the coast path and over the cliffs, where we could see a large stone arch sitting on the cliff top. We came to Blackpool Mill, location of the television dramas *Sense and Sensibility* and *The Shell Seekers*. Hartland Abbey is inland from there and is also the location for many films and tv programmes.

A steep climb, involving steps, was quite a challenge but we did not hang about as a snake slithered across the path by Rosa's feet, making her scream. The cliff top gave us magnificent views over the jagged rocks and swirling water, and we spotted a waterfall. More steps, ascents and descents, then we caught a glimpse of Hartland Lighthouse before the radar mushroom came into view and we paused to read the monument to "those who perished in the Glenart Castle Hospital ship, torpedoed 26th February 1918, (20 miles out to sea)."

We could now see the lighthouse clearly. At this point there is the Hartland Point Refreshment Kiosk, selling drinks and cakes, but Rosa had brought sandwiches, so we went a little further before pausing to rest and gaze in awe at the views.

After a NT sign, "East Titchberry", the path became flatter and easy going, and passing the fingerpost "Exmansworthy ½m" we soon reached the car park where Rosa had parked.

We had a drink at the Hartland Quay Hotel and looked around the museum. All in all a great walk. We both agreed that this coastline is truly breathtaking and has to be among the best in the country.

Morwenstow to Hartland Quay. This was a fantastic walk, getting on for nine miles and strenuous in places.

We took two cars again. Rosa left her car at Hartland Quay and I drove on to Morwenstow and parked by the church, near the Rectory Farm Tea Rooms, which Rosa said is highly recommended by a friend of hers.

The coast path pointed two ways and we took the right, firstly through a field, then along the cliff top before four very long zigzag ascents and descents to sea level and up again. We could see Lundy Island across the sea in the distance. The path was very steep, stony and narrow in places. Rosa slipped a couple of times and I had to grab her before she fell.

A flight of extremely steep steps, new looking, which seemed to go on forever and positioned perilously near the cliff edge, had us puffing, and we agreed this challenging walk with its incredibly steep valleys is not for the faint-hearted.

A signpost informed us "Tamara C2C, Plymouth 87m, Plymouth 300m coast."

A bridge over Marsland Water had Cornwall on one side and Devon on the other, so we spent some time taking photos. Marsland Cliff is the home of Ronald Duncan's writing hut. The hut started out as an Admiralty lookout during WW2. It was dismantled after falling into disrepair; consequently the poet built himself a hut on the same site, with its wonderful open views affording him peace and inspiration for his work. It was rebuilt again after his death in the 1980s.

We descended to the picturesque, quiet Welcombe Beach, which has a small car park, and crossed over stepping stones near waterfalls to access the coast path on the other side. A gentle slope, then the path became steep again to reach the flat cliff top around Knap Head and Embury Beacon, dramatic views over the rocks causing us to catch our breath in awe.

We paused for a breather on the "Green Ranger Bench," made from bits of shipwreck, near the sign commemorating the wreck of the Royal Fleet Auxiliary Tanker Green Ranger, wrecked on the Gunpath Rock on 17th November 1962, remnants of which can still be seen on the beach below.

Spekes Mill was wonderful, a flat sheer rock with a waterfall, a sideways flow then another waterfall down towards the sea. I resolved to come back sometime with grandchildren. On leaving this stunning location, we climbed up from the valley to some magnificent views and St Catherine's Tor, before the rocky beach of Hartland Quay came into sight, one of my favourite places; the rocks are great for exploring and crabbing and can be a great family day out. We just made it to the Hartland Quay Hotel for lunch at 2.30pm, before returning to Morwenstow to collect my car.

Lara

I swear Seb has walked Hartland at least four times. What's going on? Of course, I know it's fabulous, with its sweeping Atlantic coastline boasting spectacular views and rocky shore that's great for rock pools and crabbing. We've spent a couple of enjoyable afternoons there with kids, scrambling about the rock pools and searching for crabs. The shop has ice creams, fishing nets, buckets and spades and gifts, and the pub serves family-friendly pub grub.

I'm beginning to wonder if Rosa has a secret pied-a-terre somewhere nearby and they skive off for a few hours. Surely they cannot keep repeating the same old walk. Actually, how well do I know Rosa? We only met, what? Two and a half years ago or thereabouts. I hardly know anything about her past. I think she had a brief marriage, which ended in divorce, and I'm guessing she came out of it with enough to buy her cottage as she doesn't appear to be short of money. She hasn't any children but loves her niece and nephew. She doesn't talk much about herself but seems happy to listen to me rabbiting on about farm and family and, of course, she and Seb spend hours discussing the coast path.

Chapter Twelve

Birthday Surprise

Lara

It's Seb's birthday and I've booked a surprise. We rarely go out together so I booked us a meal in Ilfracombe, and as an extra treat, booked a room in a B and B so we can both have a drink and not worry about driving. I've already warned him he's in for a surprise and to expect the unexpected, so when I hand over my small parcel containing a pair of novelty socks depicting a gardener with a labrador at his heels he looks puzzled, until he spots the postcard of Ilfracombe on which I have written "Dinner at 8pm at The Tapas Bar and Overnight B and B in Fore Street."

He drops the card in consternation. "What today?"

"Yes of course today. It's all fine. I've arranged everything. We can check in at 3pm, have a relaxing evening with a good dinner, then tomorrow after breakfast, I thought we could stroll along the harbour and Capstan Hill before having a late lunch and coming home before dark. What? Aren't you pleased?"

Seb looks distinctly uncomfortable. "I didn't realise. I didn't know you'd booked anything. I didn't dream you'd book a night away."

"I know. It's great isn't it. It'll be fun. We haven't been out for ages and this way no one has to drive." I stare at him "What's the matter?"

"Well, you see." Seb swallows hard. "I've already arranged to go for a walk tomorrow."

"What! With Rosa? But it's not Monday."

"I know." Seb looks miserable. "She asked me what I wanted for my birthday and I jokingly said a walk. So she said, 'Okay, we'll go for a walk the day after your birthday and I'll treat you to lunch.' I wish I hadn't said a walk now."

"I see. Well, obviously, Sebastian, if that's what you wanted, joke or no joke, then that's what you must do. Are you still free for tonight? Or does your busy schedule not allow for dinner with your wife?"

"If I'd known I wouldn't have agreed. It is a lovely idea, staying overnight. I'll speak to Rosa, see if we can come up with a plan. I'm not sure where she had in mind. Thanks, love, it's a great present." He pecks me on the cheek and disappears with his phone.

We arrive in Ilfracombe at 3pm, Seb's phone pinging constantly. We check in then walk around Capstan Hill, which Seb has already done with Rosa of course. I have a hankering to visit the museum so we pop in for an hour. What a fascinating place: lots of treasures and exhibits, maritime history artefacts and information, and a very interesting display about the old railway line.

Back in the room, Michael Portillo is on the tv, walking the South West Coast Path with a camera crew. Seb is gripped. I have a long hot shower and wash my hair, then try to wrap the towel seductively around my chest but it drops to the floor immediately. I've never got the hang of it. I stick on my old dressing gown instead.

Seb has a shower and I channel hop until he returns.

"Come and join me, birthday boy, let's have a cuddle before we go out. We have time."

His phone pings. "Hang on a sec."

To what? I frown. He turns his phone sideways but I'm sure I spot an R.

"Okay as there's nothing to hang on to, I'll get my face on in the bathroom." My voice is thick with sarcasm but he takes no notice. He's too busy on his phone. I swipe the mascara wand so hard I poke my eye with the tip. Tears blurring my eyes, I nevertheless see frown lines, hard mouth and sagging jowls looking back at me. Just as I thought I had Seb's attention for the first time in a month, he'd rather see Rosa's plan for tomorrow. "Lara," I say to myself in the mirror. "Get a grip. Get your slap on. Smile. The night is young. Forget Rosa and the stupid walks."

We have a lovely meal and an excellent bottle of wine, and stroll back to the B and B arm in arm. "Thanks, Lara," whispers Seb. "It's been great. Totally unexpected and a real treat."

"The night's not over yet." I snuggle into his arm.

On our return the landlady is waiting for us. "You've had a delivery," she says to Seb, beaming. "Happy Birthday. I took the liberty of putting it in your room. Good night."

We look at each other. What can it be? Have the kids done something? On the table by the window there's a wine cooler with a bottle of Moet nestled in ice.

"Wow, Lara. Really?"

"Umm no, not me. Wait, there's a card. 'Happy birthday, Walking Partner. See you tomorrow. R x'."

After breakfast, we pack our bags, then, hearing a toot at 10am, Seb dashes to the window to see Rosa parked outside. "Bye, love, see you later. I shouldn't be too late. Rosa will drive me home."

I wave at Rosa's car from the window, but I don't think she sees me. Seb jumps into the passenger seat and they're gone. I sit on the bed to reflect. What should I do? Botox? A facelift? Lose weight? I do try but I tend to eat chocolate if I'm out of sorts. Also, I haven't even bothered about our makeshift gym lately. I wonder if I could do something with my hair. Maybe go blonde and straight. I hate my frizzy mop. I resolve to go to Boots for hair dye and straighteners.

Chapter Thirteen

Morwenstow to Boscastle

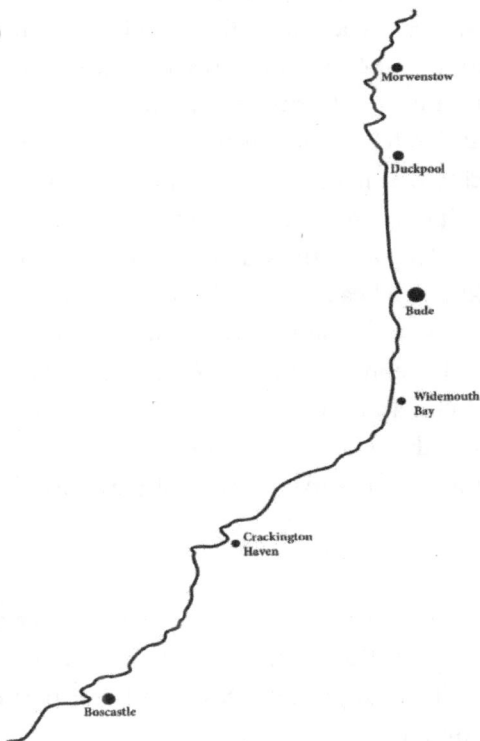

Seb

Morwenstow to Bude. Rosa and I drove to Bude, where Rosa has a friend who kindly offered to drive us to Morwenstow to save our bringing two cars. We had thought she might join us but she had other plans. She dropped us off at Morwenstow

Church and we set off in good spirits, enjoying the clement weather, ready to savour our seven-plus-mile challenge and which the app described as "severe." We passed Hawkers Hut, a hut buried into the cliff side overlooking the sea, made of timber with lots of messages etched into the wood. We wrote our initials with a sharp stone. A little further on we came to the GCHQ (Government Communications Headquarters intelligence service) satellites at Cleave Common, surrounded by high wire fencing. The path wound round a narrow headland and Rosa nearly slipped when a sudden gust of wind threw her off balance. After a steep and tricky descent down Steeple Point, we came to Duckpool, a beautiful sandy beach with many rock pools, then it was up again before another descent to Sandymouth, mostly pebbles but miles of sand if the tide is out, with awesome rocks and twisted high cliffs. It even has a waterfall; we loved this place. Northcott is another National Trust beach, a smaller cove, also rocky but with expanses of sand at low tide.

On our way home we marvelled at length about the gorgeous beaches and rocks along this coastline and we both agreed there is only one way to truly appreciate this wonderful part of the world and that is on foot.

Lara

Seb arrives home just in time for supper. He's been gone hours! He gabbles on about rock pools and cliffs and Rosa's friend, as I plate up the toad in the hole. "How long was the walk?" I enquire when I can get a word in edgewise. "You've had a long day."

"The walk was about six hours, or just over, but we had a short chat with Susie, Rosa's friend. She lives on the outskirts of Bude, and I popped briefly into Rosa's for a quick cup of tea and to fill in our walking diaries."

"How nice," I remark. "Bobby's been cleaning the chicken shed and I've been scrubbing the outside toilet."

Lara

We have booked a short stay away for Seb and Rosa to walk Widemouth to Boscastle.

Saturday morning and I have been up all night, sick and diarrhoea. I feel like death. "It's no good, Seb. I can't go. I can't even get out of bed except to dash to the loo."

"Oh no, you poor thing," Seb says distantly. Through my slitted eyes I can see what he is thinking. What about the walks? What about the holiday?

I wait, propped up on three pillows, teeth chattering. I have a temperature. "Seb, do you think you could bring me up a cup of weak hot tea please?"

"Of course." He disappears, but not before I see him slip his phone from his pocket. I'm too weak to follow him but guess he's speaking to Rosa.

He reappears after ten minutes with the tea and a packet of paracetamol. "You've been ages. How long does it take to boil a kettle?"

"Sorry. The thing is, I called Rosa to tell her about you. What do you think we should do? The accommodation is booked. Shall we wait till later to see how you are?"

"Sebastian, I have a temperature, my guts are inside out. There's no way I'm going anywhere today."

"Oh." Disappointment oozes from every pore. "Well…" He hesitates.

"Yes?" I sigh. I know what's coming.

"I suppose…well…how would you feel…well, erm…you know, I suppose…"

"Seb, spit it out. What are you trying to say?"

"Would you mind? Obviously if you do, we wouldn't go, but…erm…I suppose Rosa and I could still go. We need to do that stretch of walk. We won't need any food. There's bound to be a shop or a takeaway." He's starting to gabble.

"Stop." I cannot bear it another second. I have an intense headache coming on. "Stop gabbling and just leave me to die. I don't care what you do."

"You're the best." He leans in to kiss me but I wave him away. "Go away, Seb. Believe me you do not want to catch this."

"You're an angel." He dashes out and I can hear him dabbing on his phone.

I awake three hours later to find his suitcase gone and a scribbled note: "Didn't want to wake you. Will phone later, x."

Seb

Crackington Haven to Widemouth. Just over seven miles. Unfortunately, Lara was too ill with a severe tummy bug to come away as planned, but as the Airbnb was already booked, Rosa and I decided to go ahead on our own. Lara said she was fine with it, so I left her asleep in bed whilst I drove to Rosa's early to collect her, prior to driving to Widemouth car park, £3.50 for the day winter rate, which has toilets and a bus stop.

We caught the 95 single decker at 9.20am to reach Crackington Haven about 9.40. Crackington Haven is a small fishing village with a sand and shingle beach, nestled in a deep valley with a pub and the Cabin Café.

We started the steep ascent from the village, and looking down over the cliffs, we could see the stunning rock formations for which it is famous. We also spotted a waterfall.

After an acorn sign "Dizzard" we went through a very muddy gateway, then down to sea level via steps and across a small footbridge before another steep ascent. Some of the rock faces were so smooth they looked like glass. Looking across we could see a long zigzag path but first we went down to sea level again via wide, deep steps with wooden strips, which looked as if they would take you straight into the sea. This was scary but quite incredible and we took lots of photos. After another small cove and waterfall, the zigzag path took us up to another summit where we could look across and see Hartland and Morwenstow in the distance.

The path levelled out for a while but it was extremely muddy after all the recent rainfall, and in some places so narrow we had to cling on to hawthorn and brambles alongside, to avoid getting ankle deep in mud. The path ended abruptly and we were on a stretch of tarmac road leading to the hamlet of Millook Haven, then ascending again on the footpath. We met three ladies who had walked from Bude, on their way to Crackington Haven, lamenting about the mud they had encountered. We warned them of the excessive mud we had just come through.

Looking ahead, we could see Widemouth's lovely sandy beach with the tide going out. We decided to drive to the Life's a Beach Café in Bude, which fortunately serves lunch until 3pm.

We just made it in time and we had a wonderful fish lunch for a reasonable price. Rosa said it is one of her favourite places.

All in all, an arduous walk but totally stunning with glorious views and fantastic rock formations. A great day.

Lara

I awake briefly to read a text "Arrived. Great walk. Heading to accommodation. X."

Seb and Rosa have a small two-bedroomed apartment, one double, one single, with a shared bathroom that boasts a walk-in shower. Rosa steps out of the bathroom, damp tendrils framing her face, and a pink towel artfully knotted across her bosom. Seb comes around the corner, head down looking at his phone and bumps into her. The towel comes undone. "Whoops, sorry, Rosa." His eyes pop at her exquisite figure, smooth and flawless with a hint of gold. "Wow," he stutters and licks his lips.

"Seb, it's okay. No harm done." She takes his hand and places it on her waist. "Are you having a shower now? Or later?"

Seb cannot speak but reaches forward, groans, hesitates, then grabs the towel from the floor and thrusts it at her before flinging himself into the bathroom and bolting the door.

I awake and struggle to the loo for another bout of sickness. Returning to bed I am chilled but sweating. I'm sure my temperature has risen even higher. I'm hot, cold and possibly delirious. I wish I had the strength to go downstairs, but it's as much as I can do to get to the bathroom holding on to the wall. I check my phone. Three missed calls from Seb, and a text,

"Guess you are asleep. Hope you are feeling better. Rooms okay. Watching a dvd and having a pizza."

Back in bed I pick up a novel but it's no good, I cannot focus.

Seb emerges from the shower, scolding himself but unable to get the picture of Rosa's naked beauty from his mind.

"Good shower isn't it?" Rosa is now dressed in grey tracksuit bottoms and a minuscule white vest top with no bra.

"Mm yes," Seb mumbles. "Rosa, about before, I'm sorry. It was a mistake. I should have looked where I was going."

"It was an accident, Seb, not a mistake." Rosa looks into his eyes. "No problem for me. In fact absolutely fine with me, but if you're not comfortable, let's not talk about it. When shall we eat? Shall we have a prosecco first? I have a bottle in the fridge." She hands him the bottle whilst reaching into the wall cupboard for two flutes. "This is cosy isn't it." She leads him to the two-seater settee and flicks on the music channel, which is playing love songs.

"Rosa." Seb turns it down a notch. "I really am sorry. I wouldn't want anything to jeopardise our walks."

"Seb, it was a dropped towel, that's all. Forget it. Let's watch a dvd. I see there's Basic Instinct. *Shall we watch half and then think about food? I brought a pizza this morning in case there was nothing nearby. Happy with that?"*

"That sounds good." They settle back on the small settee, thighs touching. After watching Sharon Stone seduce Michael Douglas, Rosa announces, "I'll pop the pizza in the oven, okay? Are you ready for it? Perhaps you could uncork the red wine. I'm just going to change into something cooler; these trackies are too hot."

Seb continues watching Michael Douglas and Sharon Stone and Rosa reappears after ten minutes in a tiny pink and white camisole, barely covering her taut golden thighs. *"Cheers. Happy walking."* She waves her glass of red wine towards him. *"The pizza must be nearly ready. I'll just check."* She reaches down, her camisole riding up to reveal smooth bare buttocks, not a hint of cellulite in sight. *"Ready?"* She turns around. Seb nods, his mouth dry, and swigs a humungous gulp of wine. Rosa places the pizza on the coffee table and leans back against the arm of the settee. *"Be an angel and pass me a slice."* She reaches forward and Seb gulps.

"Mm, delicious, lovely and cheesy." Rosa licks her lips and sighs contentedly. *"You're not eating, Seb, help me out here."*

Seb reaches for a slice but is unable to tear his eyes from Rosa and cannot manage a nibble.

Rosa takes his plate and holds out her hand. *"What are we waiting for? I've been patient and I don't want much. Just one night. There's only the two of us here. Come on."* She grabs the wine bottle...

"I'm out of practice. I don't think I can."

"Of course you can. Look I'll just top your glass up and we'll give it a go, okay? I'll put some music on. Michael Bublé 'Can't Help Falling in Love' would be perfect, I think. I have it on my phone." She takes his hand. *"Ready? I'll help you, Slow, quick, quick. See? You're getting it already. The waltz is my favourite dance."*

I awake drenched in sweat with the duvet in a heap. Bobby has obviously looked in on me as the curtains are drawn, my water replenished, and there are a couple of plain biscuits on the bedside cabinet. I manage to send a text to Seb, "Still alive – just. Phone in the morning."

Seb

Crackington Haven to Boscastle. About seven miles. We had a quick breakfast, tidied up, packed our overnight bags and left the car in Boscastle car park to get the 9.46am bus to arrive at Crackington Haven at 10.06.

The bus dropped us off at the cove and we took the immediate steep ascent to the cliff top to look over the wonderful views. We came across the strange sight of a fence dangling in mid-air with posts waving over an open void where the fence would have been originally, and thought perhaps there had been a landslide leaving a deep cleft along the cliff edge. We crossed over a wooden bridge, the first of many on this walk, to a sign "Please use zigzag path to help prevent erosion." Another ascent and we could look back over to Cambeak, the promontory rocks at the bottom of the cliff looking like a giant turtle's head.

We passed a sign "Strangles Beach" but carried on following the sign to "High Cliff," which at over 700 feet is the highest in Cornwall. The path was in good condition, doubling back on itself and zigzagging up the hill.

We stopped briefly for a snack, (Rosa had brought a packet of M & S cookies) near the sign "Beeny Cliff" and looking forward we could see rocks offshore, which I think are called The Sisters.

Reaching Pentargon waterfall, we avoided the temptation to take the muddy offshoot for a better view and continued on an ascent of many, many steps stopping intermittently for a few breathers, until we could look back over the spectacular 120-foot-high waterfall. We took lots of photos then continued across yet another bridge to pass through a field of Red Devon cattle, peacefully grazing.

We were glad to see Boscastle ahead and descended to the harbour and into the village, one of Rosa's favourite places in Cornwall. Spoilt for choice, with several excellent places to eat, we opted for the Cobweb Inn to relax and discuss the morning over prosecco and tasty toasties with salad and chips.

A great walk, mostly along the cliff top, strenuous in places and with some challenging steps. There were several stopping points and benches to rest on and enjoy the outstanding views over the magnificent coastline.

Lara

I still feel weak but not nearly as bad as yesterday so I decide to change the bedding, which is singularly unpleasant. I'm struggling with the pillowcases when Seb appears with his overnight bag.

"I'm home. How are you? Any better? You still look pale."

"I'm okay. Do you mind finishing making the bed while I have a quick flannel wash? I cannot face a shower but I really must freshen up."

In the bathroom I look in the mirror to see a drawn white face with sunken eyes, hair in wild tufts and some itchy spots emerging on my arms. Ugh.

"Here you are. Lovely, clean sheets." Seb folds back the duvet. "I'll unpack, check on the ponies and grab something for me and Bobby from the freezer. Can I get you anything?"

"Just tea and toast please. Later will do. Can you give Ben a piece of carrot as a treat and a pat from me?"

"Okay. I won't be long. I'll show you a few photos of the walks, which were wonderful, then we could watch a film in bed if you like. I see *Kinky Boots* is on. Oh, I nearly forgot; we stopped on our way back to buy you some grapes. I'll bring them up with the tea." He goes out whistling.

Seb and I are lying side *by side on the floor, trussed and tied with ropes. Music is playing, Nancy Sinatra, "These Boots are Made for Walkin'".*

The door opens. Enter Rosa dressed in a black leather leotard, sheer black tights and thigh-high black leather boots with five-inch heels. She's wearing a black, diamond-studded eye mask and brandishing a silver-topped cane. Her boots start walking. They are ready...

She saunters towards us, me first. The heels sink down into my soft flesh. Total agony. Then she steps over to Seb and playfully strokes the cane along his mouth, before walking up and down his taut body. He doesn't flinch.

I'm on fire.

"Lara, you awake?" Seb nudges me.

"Ow, I am now," I grumble. "Ouch." I scratch my arms. I'm covered in tiny red itchy spots. "Oh no, I have hives, my skin's burning."

Chapter Fourteen

Boscastle to Port Isaac. Widemouth to Bude

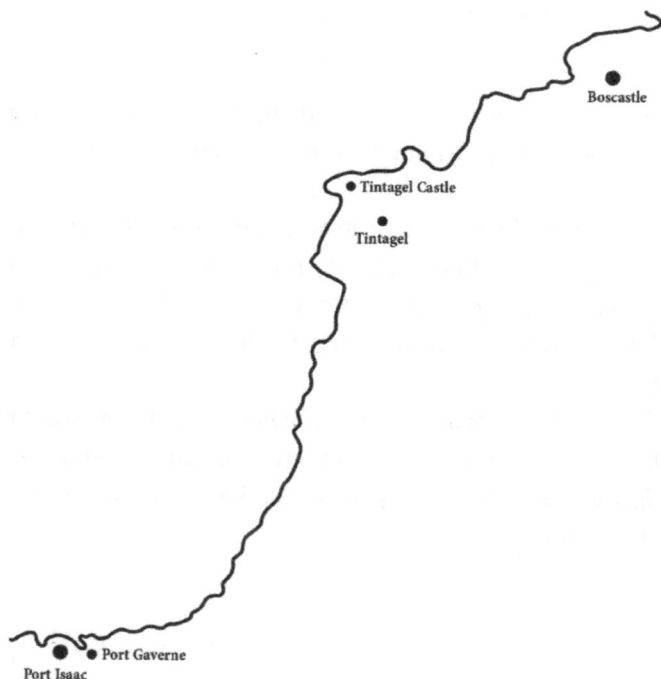

Seb

I'm really excited about this weekend. Rosa and I have completed all the walks now on day trips around the North Devon coast, and we had the one-night stay in Crackington Haven, but this will be the first proper weekend away in Cornwall with three walks planned. Let's hope for good weather. On Saturday I'm hoping we can do Boscastle to Tintagel, about three hours I think, so Lara can kill some time looking in the shops, she'll like that, and then it's only a short drive for her to Tintagel to the King Arthur's Arms. Sunday will be the test. I've googled Port Isaac to Tintagel and apparently it is strenuous, one of the toughest routes in the whole South West. I must remember extra socks.

Lara

"Lara," says Sebastian the minute he walks in on Friday evening after work, "have you googled Port Isaac to Tintagel, and the Boscastle walk? It looks amazing. I'm worried about the weather, though, and whether it will be too strenuous. So I have a Plan B." He takes a breath. "You could drive us to Port Gaverne about a mile or so from Port Isaac. It would shorten our route; that stretch is mostly along the road anyway. If the weather's bad we could get a taxi from Tre…" He breaks off and looks at me expectantly.

I stare back, unsmiling. "That sounds like a plan. I suppose I could come and fetch you, but I may have had a drink by then and, also, I hate driving on those little coastal hills."

I grit my teeth as he replies, "Of course, I wouldn't expect you to fetch us unless it was desperate. We'll probably be okay."

Saturday. I spend a leisurely couple of hours in Boscastle on my own, having waved off Sebastian and Rosa in a howling gale and lashing rain interspersed with hailstones. The National Trust lady in the shop looks at me as I mouth "Nuts" and says, "I don't get why people do it."

"Me neither," I reply. "I'm having a nice hot coffee and doing some serious shopping."

She nods her approval as I head for the café.

There are some very nice books, ornaments and gifts in the shop. So, refreshed after coffee and cake, I buy a couple of books and some sturdy gardening gloves, suitable for birthday or Christmas presents.

Boscastle is very pretty with its wonderful harbour and the river flowing into the sea where the rocks and coastline turn dramatic. The great flood of 2004 caused massive damage to the village when cars were washed out to sea, villagers were trapped in their houses – some clambered onto roofs awaiting rescue by helicopter, properties suffered severe damage, trees were uprooted, the visitor centre washed away, shops ruined. It took nearly a year for the village to rebuild, recover and prepare to welcome tourists again, but it is now as picturesque and attractive as ever with the harbour being a natural wonder, and some unusual shops selling interesting artefacts, pottery and gifts.

The walk to Tintagel is said to be one of the top five walks in Cornwall, possibly the UK, but I wonder how the two walkers will see anything in this weather, hoods over two thirds of their faces and battling against the wind. I chat to the postman and a couple of shop owners and the consensus is that I am the sensible one and those two are idiots.

It takes about ten minutes to drive carefully to Tintagel, and I am relieved to find the accommodation ready even though I'm over an hour early. It's great, with three double bedrooms, a living room, bathroom and hallway complete with electric boot warmers. After a brief recce I treat myself to a small glass of wine from the cool box I brought with us, before venturing out to inspect Tintagel's delights. There are several shops to browse in, cafés, pubs and tea rooms, a bakery and pasty shop, but it's not a big place, so I soon return to await the two drenched but satisfied explorers who arrive back in good time.

I have to sit through a thousand photos of waves crashing against rocks, rugged cliffs, mud, pictures of Sebastian clutching his walking stick whilst bravely posing against a precipitous cliff edge and Rosa smiling serenely at the horizon. I pour myself another glass of wine and head off for a shower whilst they open the prosecco and reminisce over the photos for the tenth time.

We have an excellent dinner in the pub and spend a riveting evening talking about tomorrow's trek. I long for some live music to stop them wittering on.

Seb

Boscastle to Tintagel. Just under five miles. What a fantastic walk. The weather was awful at first but cleared up enough for us to get some great views. Cornwall is spectacular and this walk must be one of the best. We made good time even though there was challenging terrain to cover, we are both getting so fit now that we can stride it out and still have time for photos and reflection. I'm already thinking we may do it again in better weather to really enjoy the wonderful views. Rosa was great; she remembered to bring two ham rolls, a large slab of chocolate and some water. I had a hip flask of spiced rum so we took shelter and indulged in some hefty swigs to warm us up. Soon we almost forgot the wind and posed against the cliff edge for photos.

There were many hills and valleys to master, but the joy of striding along this spectacular coast is indescribable; you can see the edge of the country with its coves and secret caves, the rocks and cliffs that are not visible or accessible by road, and experience the unspoilt countryside in all its beauty.

The boot warmers here are a godsend as ours were soaked. We'll have warm and dry feet tomorrow. Port Isaac to Tintagel is going to be a real challenge, one of the longest we've done so we'll need to set off early to get back before dark.

Lara

We breakfast early to allow for the possibility of a seven hour walk before dusk. Dutifully I drive to Port Gaverne, drop Seb and Rosa off on a hairpin bend then head off to Port Isaac car park. I reckon two hours will be enough as I put the cash in the Pay and Display.

Amazingly it's a beautiful sunny day after yesterday's storm, and the pretty fishing village is heaving with folk visiting *Doc Martin* locations and exclaiming over the views and the sweet little painted cottages. By the time I return to the car, I've almost completed my early Christmas shopping, there being several independent shops with plenty to choose from. The drive back to Tintagel seems quite long; goodness knows how far it must be for the two intrepids on the coast path.

Having bought myself a pasty and a yoghurt, I make a cuppa back in the hotel room, intending to go out again for a walk down to the newly built Tintagel bridge, after I've eaten. Two housekeeping staff knock on the door to clean the rooms and we have a brief chat.

"Oh, they'll need to be careful," says the chap, when I explain about the two hikers. "The coast path here is tricky. It can get muddy and slippery after all the rain we've had. I hope they have proper footwear; I've known some people to slide down quite a way if they just have ordinary trainers on."

"Don't worry," I reassure him. "They know what they're doing. Besides, I've warned them I'm not rescuing them if they get into difficulties, so it's up to them to take care."

Tintagel is busy with families enjoying a leisurely Sunday lunch, couples enjoying a welcome drink in the sunshine and many tourists visiting the castle and gazing at the Old Post Office with its sloping roof and tiny windows.

Seb

Port Gaverne to Tintagel. This was quite a long one, well over eight miles. What a glorious day. The sun was shining; the coast path was stunning. We scaled eight deep valleys; the cliff-top views were spectacular with the waves glinting in the sunlight, and the beaches at Tregardock and Trebarwith Strand were wonderful. Although we were conscious of the time (I text Lara to let her know where we were) we managed to soak in the dramatic scenes and explore the beaches and even some caves. We got back earlier than anticipated, about 4.45, where Lara was waiting for us with welcome coffees and glasses of rum. Rosa and I both collapsed on the settees exhausted but exuberant about having achieved our best walk so far.

Lara

"Night, Rosa," I call through her half-open bedroom door.

She is sitting at the dressing table, creaming her face. "Hi, Lara, you okay?"

"Yes, fine, how about you? You must be tired after your trek." I go in and perch on her bed.

"Just a little."

"I don't know how you do it. I'd be whacked, all that climbing steep hills."

"You get used to it. We're old hands now." She laughs. "You are okay with it aren't you, Lara? Seb says you've not been yourself lately."

I glower. Did he indeed? Recovering quickly, I reply, "Of course. Why wouldn't I be?"

"He wouldn't want to upset you, you know." Rosa's gentle voice continues. "He thinks the world of you."

Why are Seb and Rosa discussing me? Rosa's supposed to be MY friend and, if anything, WE should be having a laugh about Seb's shortcomings.

"Haha." I chortle madly. "I'm not surprised. He's lucky to have me slaving away and pandering to his every whim."

Rosa looks startled.

"I'm joking, Rosa. He loves walking the coast path. I don't know what he'll do when you complete it."

Rosa stares into space. "No, well we have a long way to go yet."

"Goodness it's late." I rise. "I'm off to bed. Sleep well. See you in the morning."

Seb is in bed. On his phone of course. I get into bed with a well-thumbed copy of *Mary Berry's Kitchen Favourites*, (I always take a cookbook away with me). "I was saying good night to Rosa. I wonder what it will be like to reach Poole."

"I have thought about it. We'll celebrate obviously." Seb looks up from his phone. "I'm not sure. I have mixed feelings, but there's a few miles to cover yet. I'm looking forward to the Jurassic Coast, but that's way off. I'm looking up our next stretch from here now; it looks great."

I open Mary. Yum, Sweet and Sour Chinese spareribs.

Seb and Rosa are walking the Jurassic Coast, staying at guest houses en route. The landlady at the Sunny Haven in Lyme Regis greets them with a smile. "Mr and Mrs Blog? Walking the coast path? A lot of our visitors do that. Two nights, that's right. Number 12, top of the stairs, turn right. A nice quiet corner room for writing your blogs." She grins and hands over the keys.

The room has a four poster and rose-coloured lamps. "I'll have a bath, Seb." Rosa wallows in petal-strewn bubbles, tealights flickering along the bath shelf. "This is heaven. Do you want to join me?"

Seb appears in the doorway, stark naked, brandishing two champagne flutes of bubbly. "Darling, we've done over 500 miles and every minute has been wonderful. I don't want to think about the end so let's enjoy the here and now."

"Even more heaven." Rosa sips the bubbly appreciatively. "Come on in." She raises herself slightly to allow Seb to get in.

I wake up in a pool of sweat. Seb is snoring beside me.

Lara

The third day, and the last few hours of our North Cornwall visit before heading home, follows the same pattern. Early breakfast followed by the drive to Widemouth Bay where Sebastian and Rosa don coats, hats, scarves and boots, and grab their sticks to set off in another howling gale. I wait for the rain to subside before driving to Bude, stopping at the first car park I see. Bude is very pleasant and, when the sun finally emerges, I wander around, immersed in its charm, browse several shops, and am quite taken aback when my phone rings and it's Sebastian. "We're nearly there. Which car park are you in?"

I give him directions and hasten to the car. They'll want to take off walking boots and dump their sticks in the boot. I reflect that by the time I've walked around Boscastle, Tintagel and Bude I've covered quite a few miles myself.

Do you know what I miss most? The long chats Rosa and I used to have over lunch and a coffee or wine. It doesn't really happen anymore as Sebastian is always with us. We do meet up at dancing classes sometimes but there again Seb is always there too. Mondays they are invariably off together on the stupid walk so that leaves no time for Rosa and I to meet up. By my reckoning they have walked all the North Devon coastline three times, if not four. We both work, I often have family commitments on Sundays, Sebastian meets up most Saturdays with kids and grandkids, often bringing them back to the farm and on a couple of afternoons a week I have my own granddaughter to collect from school. On the odd occasion when Rosa does come for lunch or tea, the talk always revolves around the stupid walks. Dull.

Seb

Widemouth Bay to Bude. This was a very short walk to complete the stretch of coastline that we didn't have time for when we stayed at Crackington Haven. Lara dropped us off at Widemouth car park and we set off along the beach, then climbed up the low cliffs, the path meandering along close to the nearby main road. We walked along the top of the cliffs and could see Morwenstow in the distance, then the sands of Bude ahead. Bude looked lovely in the sunlight, the sun dancing on the waves and we crossed the canal bridge sorry for the holiday to be almost over.

Chapter Fifteen

Port Isaac to Rock

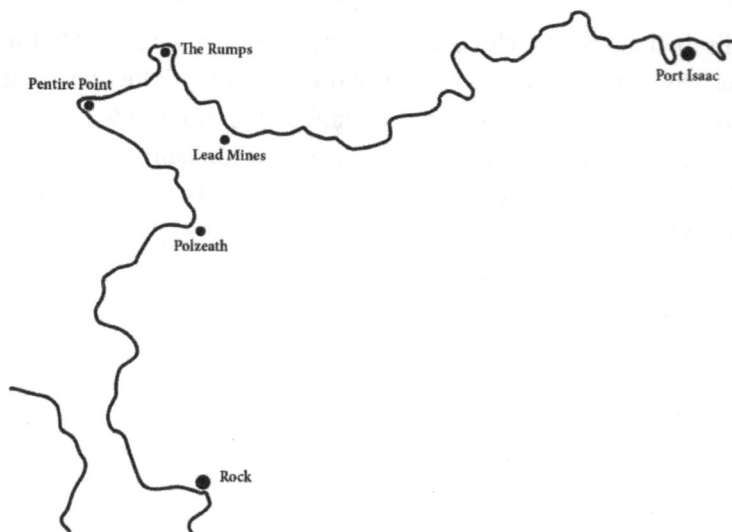

Lara

Back to Cornwall.

Muggins here is chauffeur again as being a Sunday there are no buses running to Rock. Fortunately I only have to drive about ten minutes from our accommodation on a good road so not much of a problem.

We are staying at the Oystercatcher in Polzeath, in a two-bedroomed apartment with fabulous panoramic views over the beach and surrounding countryside. The food is excellent, we had a delicious meal in the busy, bustling restaurant last night, obviously popular with locals and tourists alike. Seb had a huge bowl of mussels in a cream and cider sauce, which he raved over; Rosa had the paella and I had sea bass with a red pepper and chickpea salsa.

At 12.30 Seb texts me to say, "Can you see us? We are crossing the beach to go around Pentire Headland." Through the window I can see them approaching steps leading up to a row of great-looking properties perched on the curve rounding the cove. Maybe I'll watch their progress to the point of the headland as I can see the path quite well. Not for the first time I wish I had brought binoculars.

Seb

Rock to Polzeath. Six and a quarter miles. Lara dropped us off at Rock and we made our way towards the ferry point, past the Rock Inn to a fingerpost "Coast Path via The Ferry 100yd to Padstow" and "Polzeath 2 ½m".

We lost our way a little and clambered over rocks and along dunes, then found the path again at Brea Hill, the path being very wet because of the heavy overnight rain.

At Daymer Bay, known to be another of Cornwall's best beaches, we were unable to cross the sands because of a river of water running through, but by going inland slightly we discovered a bridge to take us on our way to Trebetherick. We had serious house envy at the substantial detached 1920s and 1930s properties with large gardens and access to the sandy cove. The path was easy going and flat; we could saunter along with ease, in the pleasant sunshine, overlooking the sea and having an occasional chat with the many other walkers taking advantage of the warm weather.

On reaching Polzeath along the beach, we followed the coast path sign "Port Isaac (via The Rumps) 7m". Climbing some steps at the far end of the beach we looked back over Polzeath and Trevose Lighthouse, then headed on to Pentire Point headland, owned by the National Trust. Again, there were many walkers, including a large group of eleven from Torquay, who we chatted to for several minutes.

The headland is beautiful with stunning views across to Padstow and as far as Morwenstow to the north.

We spent a long time admiring the Rumps at the tip of Pentire Point and the Mouls, which is an offshore island. There is a plaque in commemoration of the poet laureate Laurence Binyon who wrote "For the Fallen" at this wonderful location in 1914.

We tore ourselves away reluctantly to return to Polzeath via the Lead Mines and New Polzeath.

Lara

After boring me to death with their photos I am forced to go for "just a short way" along the path towards Rock, crossing the large car park on the hillside down to the cliff edge overlooking the fabulous huge beach. There are lots of families and surfers enjoying the good weather. I actually enjoy the walk along the cliff but I'm annoyed by Seb and Rosa educating me on points of interest and their constant references to their earlier walk. I wish they'd just let me enjoy the sunshine in peace and allow me to have opinions of my own.

I heat up a beef and ale pie I brought from home for supper and leave them to plan tomorrow's walk while I have an early night with Gillian Flynn's *Gone Girl*.

Seb

Port Isaac to the Lead Mines. Approx seven and a half miles. We caught the bus from Polzeath Beach car park to reach Port Isaac at 10.20am. As we started our previous walk at Port Gaverne, we walked quickly there and back in about fifteen minutes from Port Isaac car park, before walking down the path to the quay, up the hill past Doc Martin's house, where there were several people taking photos against the front door. We joined in the queue and did the same, before heading further up the hill to the field, location of many scenes from the tv programme, with low-rise cliffs and inset caves.

Going on to Port Quin, the path was arduous with many meandering ascents and descents, mostly with hundreds of wood strip steps. Looking back towards Tintagel we could see Port Isaac nestled between the two prominent headlands, very quaint and pretty in the sparkling sunshine.

Towards Port Quin the path had been fenced to one side, presumably to prevent cattle straying. Port Quin is tiny and unspoilt, a National Trust property, and we could see a fishing tractor and trailer on the small sandy beach. A sign informed us "Port Isaac, inland 2m, Coast Path route 3m."

After clambering up a few huge, deep granite steps towards Pentire, the path became easier and we could see a fascinating-looking folly on a headland (NT Doyden Castle). We passed some deep holes fenced off, which we presumed to be old mine shafts.

Rosa had a lengthy chat with a lady doing the circular walk, and she agreed that Port Isaac to Port Quin was gruelling. She said she makes a day of her walks, takes her time and enjoys a leisurely picnic, and told us we would soon reach Lundy Bay with its natural archway looking through to the sea.

Lundy Bay looked wonderful, a tiny, sheltered cove with a fantastic collapsed sea cave. We took advantage of a good photo opportunity. We resumed our walk, following the sign to Carnweather Point, and stopping for a chat with a man and his son who said this was their favourite section of the SW Coast Path. Rosa and I both agreed he could be right as, after a slight inland incursion, we suddenly saw the Mouls again, then Pentire Point and Polzeath, before reaching the Lead Mines. This was a truly spectacular stretch of coastline and we decided we must get Lara to see it.

Lara

Peace. I pour myself a coffee, tidy up the papers and chocolate box from the floor and notice with puzzlement a pair of Rosa's pink heart socks by our bed.

It is a lovely day so I decide to explore Polzeath. It is small but beautifully situated in a valley; the large sandy beach framed by cliffs. There is a Spar, a takeaway pasty and sandwich shop, bars, restaurants, a boutique, surf shops and a large store, Fusion, selling candles, gifts and clothes. The beach lies between two headlands and is busy with dog walkers, surfers and children with buckets and spades.

Trudging up the steep hill back to the apartment, I get a call from Seb: "Lara, can you pick us up from the Lead Mines? It's only a few miles and it's beautiful. You must see it." Rats! I was going to treat myself with a glass of white wine but now I've got to drive somewhere I have no idea how to find. I ask at the hotel reception and the helpful lady assures me it's easy. "Just drive out of Polzeath along the main road and you'll see a signpost on your left."

The two irritants are waiting for me in the car park and drag me through a kissing gate to look at the view to the Mouls and Pentire Point. I must agree it's breathtaking. I can see why people would want to walk along the coast on a day like this, but not when it's wet and windy.

When we get back to the hotel, they're actually grateful that I picked them up to avoid their having to trek the one and a half miles from the Lead Mines that they did yesterday. Even so, they are both waddling, with legs like jelly, and collapse comatose before exclaiming over the inevitable multitude of photos.

Rosa wanders into the bedroom, naked apart from a minuscule lacy thong. "Seb." She prods him awake. "I've lost my socks. Can you help me find them? I think I lost them last night." She pokes him in the ribs. They both crawl around the floor, giggling until they locate the socks. "Help me put them on." Rosa waggles a perfect leg while Seb reverently slides a sock over her equally perfect foot, then repeats with the other foot. Still giggling they tiptoe out of the room.

Chapter Sixteen

The Scarecrow

Lara

It is my birthday and Seb suggests we go to Westward Ho! and have lunch in the Pier House. This is a rare occurrence. We usually stay at home and I cook steak and chips for dinner. He must have a guilty conscience.

Even though we live only about twelve miles from Westward Ho! I have not been for ages, so I really enjoy visiting the golden sands and huge pebble ridge, and having a short stroll along the cliff top, past the "spooky house" and along the path towards Cornborough Cliffs with dramatic views across the ocean. Then browsing through the gift shops before tucking in to a great meal at the restaurant with a couple glasses of prosecco. Seb's booked a window table so we're able to appreciate the wonderful views stretching from Saunton to Hartland. Seb, of course, cannot resist droning on about landmarks and "Look, Lara, Rosa and I have walked all that way". The only thing to shut him up is eating. So after he pays the bill we wander around the town before spoiling ourselves with a Hockings ice cream.

Arriving home, I go upstairs to change into my old clothes, and reflect it's been a good day. But I got the feeling Seb would rather be striding along the cliff top than gazing longingly out of the Pier House window. I look at myself in the mirror and sigh. I haul logs, I lift bales, I've even been to the embarrassing dancing classes that Rosa recommended. It's not as if I sit down all day. I mow lawns, I clean the house (okay that's an exaggeration; I clean sketchily once a month). And yet I am squat, wide hipped, with a stocky build. I blame my genes: both parents were short and stocky.

It doesn't seem fair. I eat a boiled egg for breakfast (or two), not a fry up (well, not often). I think of Rosa. She's like a gazelle, endless long slim legs and a perfect body. Even if I paid to go on *Makeover Perfection*, or whatever it's called, on tv I'd never look like her. No wonder Seb loves walking with her; he's probably proud to be seen out with a tall blonde beauty.

I tried dying my hair blonde and straightening it. Disaster. I ended up with patchy dull yellow straw and singed ends. I looked like a sheep with yellow fever and had to wear a hat for a month. Seb and Bobby just laughed.

I try diets but they don't work. As soon as I think of a diet I'm immediately starving. I once tried a ridiculous box of fudge things supposed to repress your hunger. I ate the whole box and still wanted my dinner.

I think my hot flushes are getting worse too. Even the supermarket shop has me sweating. By the time I get to the checkout I cannot see the trolley handles for discarded coat, scarf and fleece. The cashiers look cool and neat and I'm a perspiring mess in a rumpled short-sleeved tee shirt, fanning myself with the newspaper. They probably take no notice though, as I think I'm becoming invisible. The cattle are the same and glance at me indifferently. Seb can stride into the shed and they all look up expectantly and know they're in for a TB test or a vet visit or some nasty occurrence. Me? They carry on munching as if I'm just an annoying fly.

If I stood in the middle of the corn field with my arms out like a scarecrow, not a hard stretch of imagination with my haystack hair, I don't think the crows would see me but perch on my arms and peck at my mop head disinterestedly.

Chapter Seventeen

Padstow to Newquay

Lara

Here we go again after a long pause. There's been so much going on with farm and family we haven't been able to get away for a while, so I'm looking forward to a few days' rest in Cornwall. Of course, Seb and Rosa haven't been too busy for their weekly jaunts, but I don't ask too many questions as I'm not sure I want to know the answers. It's beyond me to understand why anyone would want to repeat the same walk more than twice, but he says they always discover something new. He's stopped showing me the photos, although I know he still takes loads as he spends hours going through his files and deleting the rejects. He smiles, chuckles and sighs, hovers over the bin and I wonder what exactly he's deleting, but I can never see, as he's become even more private with his phone recently and never lets it out of his sight.

We've booked a two-bedroomed cottage for a week in Mawgan Porth, overlooking the sea, and I'm hoping the weather will be kind. Rosa is coming, of course, for the first four days. We set off in teeming rain, which doesn't cease all the way to Cornwall, and breathe a sigh of relief when we locate the cottage, with two parking spaces, along a small road off Tredragon Road in Trenance, a hamlet adjoining Mawgan Porth.

Although we stopped in Bude on the way and had a delicious lunch at the Life's A Beach waterfront café, by Summerleaze Beach, we're all beginning to feel hungry again. But first we must explore the cottage and unpack. Wow! The door opens to an incredible huge modern kitchen, open plan to the living area and overlooking the sea. It's too dark to see much but even in the dusk we can see that the view is amazing. There are two ensuite bedrooms.

We soon have the heating on and enjoy a snifter before I heat the Thai green curry I brought from home, along with spring rolls and prawn crackers. We finish the meal with a box of Dairy

Milk, although I don't like sharing, especially if someone snaffles the caramel heart before I do.

Seb

The cottage is great, with folding doors overlooking the sea and the coast path on the cliff. I am happy to be back in Cornwall with the prospect of four days' walking ahead. We will begin tomorrow with a short route starting from Constantine Bay. Being Sunday, the buses will be infrequent, so Lara will be the driver and she can enjoy the beaches too. For other walks there appears to be a Number 56 bus which stops at Mawgan Porth, so Rosa and I can go one way on the bus and walk back.

Lara

We are up early, the weather has cleared, so after a cooked breakfast we set off in the car for Harlyn Bay, just a few miles north towards Padstow. Having established that there is a huge car park there, we drive to Constantine to look for the start of the coast path near Trevose Golf Club. Parking up, Seb faffs about on his app for ten minutes trying to find the bus stop in preparation for tomorrow's walk from Constantine back to Mawgan Porth. At last they don walking boots and with a "Bye, Lara, see you in a couple of hours", they head off to the signed path, waving distractedly and beaming foolishly.

I drive back to Harlyn, creeping through some massive puddles accumulated from yesterday's rain. Harlyn car park is heaving with families, couples, dog walkers, surfers and sightseers. I park behind a van in a row of two, but after a few minutes, notice a third row being formed behind the cars adjacent to me, effectively blocking in the middle row. I hastily reverse and reposition myself to be first in a row. Sure enough, a party of four adults soon return from the Beach Box Café in the upper car park to find their car hemmed in. I watch with interest but they seem pretty blasé and wait patiently for over half an hour until the owner of the car behind turns up, apologising profusely. I walk around the car park for a while and look over the beach, but I'm thankful I brought a flask of coffee to sit in the car and people watch. We truly are a nation of dog lovers; there are dogs of many different breeds, several are wearing fancy dog jackets and most are in charge of the owners instead of vice versa.

Harlyn is obviously a big surfing beach and scores of surfers are struggling into wet suits or struggling out of them: standing, dripping in large plastic buckets, stripped to the waist before donning voluminous capes. Seb sends me a message after an hour: "Nearly there. We can see the beach and car park."

What? I don't think so. They haven't been long enough.

Half an hour later, "I got it wrong. We'll be a while yet."

I settle back with my crossword.

The two hours turns out to be over two and a half, and I'm ready to return to the cottage but: "Lara, shall we pop over to the next bay, Trevone? It's only a couple of miles and you know you said you wanted to see it." It's true, I did. The natural pool at Trevone is featured on the children's television series *Malory Towers*, based on the books by Enid Blyton, which I've been watching with my granddaughter.

"Okay." I sigh. "Let's not be long though, I'm hungry."

The beach at Trevone is pretty, surrounded by cliffs, but we stop only briefly before walking along the coastal path to the pool, which is quite a way. We spot the pool and wonder how the camera crew, actors and directors reach it. It's a mystery, as we can see no way to it apart from clambering over some slippery rocks to reach a flat shelf overlooking it. Seb and Rosa scramble down, and from my vantage point at the top, I can see them chatting to a couple of ladies sitting on towels with a picnic hamper. They seem to be having a laugh and Seb gets so excited he steps back and nearly falls in. Two young men pass me to descend to the pool, and a few minutes later, Seb and Rosa having returned, we watch them both swimming across the pool.

Seb spends the whole evening googling Constantine to Mawgan Porth and checks the bus app for the millionth time. "We'll get the 9.30 bus at the top of the road here. It's very handy, only five minutes' walk; that takes us to Constantine. The walk's about four hours, so we should be back for a late lunch."

We all fall asleep by the tv. Seb is awake at 6am checking his app again. I pull the duvet over my head and turn over. I'll be glad when it's 9.30 and I can get some peace.

Seb.

Constantine to Harlyn Bay. Lara dropped us off at Trevose Golf Club. I couldn't see where the path started at first, but Rosa, looking around, spotted the signpost just behind us, opposite the club. The sandy path took us to the actual coastal route via a narrow enclosed lane at the back of a row of houses, through some sand dunes, until we arrived at the beach, a sign saying "Winter Management 2018" obviously out of date. Constantine Bay is huge and was absolutely glorious in the winter sun; dog walkers were enjoying the mild weather with dogs racing around in circles and chasing each other. The water was running off the cliffs from yesterday's downpour, the sea rolling with big white crashing waves, we saw a blow hole with the sea rushing in and out and it was all so fabulous. I felt exhilarated to be back on the wonderful Cornish coast path again. After a flat stretch we mounted some steps, then a short tarmac path took us to Trevose Lighthouse, which is perched spectacularly on top of the cliffs. There is a large rock out at sea which I discovered is called the Bull. We thought we could see Harlyn Bay ahead of us but it turned out to be Polventon Bay, also known as Mother Ivey's Bay, derived from a legendary tale of a local white witch.

The coast path became very waterlogged at this point, so we decided to go down to the beach instead. Another walker told us it was possible to climb the rocks at the far end to rejoin our way, where we looked back over the lifeboat station, built in 1847, at Trevose Head.

Harlyn Bay was a magnificent sight, sheltered by sand dunes and low cliffs. The tide was out, the beach busy with families and children and many surfers enjoying the rolling waves. It had been a reasonably relaxed walk, not at all strenuous, and I had a moment of pure joy to be experiencing a new section of the coast path with Rosa. I grabbed her hand and said, "Thanks Rosa."

"No need, Seb." She understood immediately. "I love it too."

We'd looked down on some lovely secluded inaccessible coves, seen blow holes and caves, walked along miles of golden sand, wended our way past fields of cabbages and sprouts and looked enviously at some great properties overlooking the ocean and one particular treasure with its own boat shed and ramp.

Lara

O my goodness! Where's the fire? Just as I'm settling down with a steaming mug of coffee, having tidied away the breakfast things, Seb and Rosa storm back in through the door, Seb flinging his rucksack down and swearing.

"Calm down. Whatever's the matter?" I dare to whisper.

"Matter! Matter!" shouts Seb. "There was no bus, that's the matter." He swipes at his phone viciously, while Rosa subsides onto a kitchen chair. "I googled it precisely. The app says it went past but we didn't see it." He looks at Rosa for confirmation. "I do not understand it. You'll have to drive us, Lara."

"Wait, wait. Let's think about it." I don't want to drive when there's a perfectly convenient bus. One of the reasons for choosing this cottage was because of the handy bus route, meaning I don't have to drive them about so much. "Perhaps you could catch a later bus, go down to Betty's Newsagents in Mawgan Porth, there's a bus stop there."

Seb stamps his foot in frustration. "What do you think?" He looks at Rosa. After five minutes of debate, they decide to walk down to Mawgan Porth and see which bus turns up first.

Twenty minutes later a text appears from Seb: "On bus to Newquay." Thank goodness. I was afraid they'd come back and make me drive. I've switched on the tv, made another coffee and raided the biscuit tin. Also, I have a cold. I blame Seb, making me wait about in Harlyn and then trekking to the pool. Sneeze, sneeze, sneeze.

Seb

Newquay to Mawgan Porth. Approx five and a half miles. The day did not go as planned. I do not understand how we missed the bus to Constantine. We got to the stop in good time yet somehow it didn't show. We went back to the cottage, but as Lara was reluctant to drive us, Rosa and I decided to change our schedule and walk down to the bus stop near the shops at Mawgan Porth bridge and go for potluck about which bus showed up first. The 56 to Newquay appeared so we hopped on and enjoyed the journey while I rechecked the walking app for the route back to Trenance.

Having alighted at Newquay bus station, we strode back on the route into the town that the bus had taken, along pavements for about a mile and a half, being part of the coast path until we reached a footpath with a sign "Watergate Bay 2 ¼m."

A flat walk, then a short return to pavements took us to the privately owned Lusty Glaze Beach, boasting a restaurant and some very steep steps down to a small bay, but we opted to stay on the path towards Porth, where there is a bridge adjoining the next headland. We turned left towards two large mounds and took shelter by them briefly during a sudden heavy downpour. Googling the mounds, while waiting for the rain to cease, it seems they are Bronze Age Barrows. The path became so waterlogged that we nipped through the fence to a field to avoid it for a short section (obviously other folk have done the same).

Watergate Bay is a huge sandy beach and looked magnificent. Having passed the enormous hotel complex at the top I wanted to scramble down at the far end and explore some fine-looking caves, but Rosa wasn't keen so we stayed on the path, meandering to Bre-Pen, the sign saying "Mawgan Porth 1

½m" and, looking forward we could see Trenance visible in the distance.

We rested on a bench overlooking the beach and enjoyed our snack and the contents of my hip flask.

Around the headland, negotiating some wood and granite steps, we came to a bridge where there was a gushing stream, which turned into a waterfall over the cliff into the swirling waters of the sea. This was absolutely stunning and we took lots of photos. As we headed on to Mawgan Porth, we agreed this was a great walk overlooking secluded inaccessible coves with some tantalising caves. The views were fabulous, some of the best we have seen on the path so far.

Lara

I fail to see how they could have missed the bus when Seb has spent so many hours checking times. So having ascertained the times myself, I make the five-minute walk to the stop – except there is no bus stop. Just a phone box. What were those two doing? I investigate the phone box with suspicion but no clues are forthcoming, so I walk to Mawgan Porth, about a ten- or fifteen-minute stretch depending on which path you take. You cannot avoid the steepness though. At the bottom of the hill, by the bridge, there's Betty's Newsagents, the Catch Fish Restaurant, a couple of surf shops, a bead shop, a convenience store and the Merry Moor Inn which looks very inviting with a good menu.

From this point you can walk along the beach and up some steep paths to Trenance, or retrace your steps partway up the hill, turn left, up more steps towards the Scarlet Hotel and the Bedruthan Hotel.

They arrive back just before 3pm wanting nourishment. After a quick snack, Rosa, who looks exhausted, decides she'll have a rest in her room. Seb, even though he's walking like John Wayne, decides we must explore the beach for half an hour before dusk sets in, so we stroll down a long, winding path and reach the beach by some granite steps with a handrail, water cascading over, and we're glad to be wearing wellies. This beach is sensational. Seb skips around like a loon, huge grin on his face, seeing my reaction. He jumps a few waves and explores caves. The beach is vast as the tide is out and the surrounding cliffs boast some seriously fabulous properties. There seems to be a lot of construction work going on; the place appears to be booming and methinks you need serious money to live here. We pick out our cottage at the top of some terraces. We've visited several areas of Cornwall now and each has its merits, but Mawgan Porth is quite a gem. Reasonably unspoilt with breathtaking views.

***

Take two of the Constantine to Mawgan Porth walk. They forgo the near bus stop and walk down to Betty's Newsagents stop.

With a long day ahead of me, I decide to take myself to Newquay, a pretty thirty-minute bus ride away, explore the shops along the High Street and discover a small park by the harbour, which has some tiny wooden sheds selling jewellery, pottery and the like, then spend a pleasant half hour on a bench overlooking the sea, with a scrumptious toastie and coffee purchased from a cute little café tucked into a corner of the park.

Having consulted Seb's bus timetable notes, I decide to get the 2pm bus back, but after waiting twenty minutes it transpires that Seb has mistaken weekday times for Saturday times. I have been telling him for ages he needs to book a sight test but he ignores me, vain, vain, vain; for some stupid reason he will not admit he needs specs. For goodness' sake! I reschedule my departure for a later bus and return to the shops to look for *A Reading Guide for Five-Year-Olds* and a pair of extra-strength reading glasses.

The bus journey is unbelievable. A double decker travelling down the open curved steep hill to Watergate gives you a sense of a roller coaster, with the drop to the sea seemingly inches away and then the bus, returning a different route than the morning, travels along the tiny, cornered road through Mawgan with overhanging tree branches banging on the roof, before descending into Mawgan Porth along a long, narrow road, scraping the hedges, with very few passing places. A van driver coming towards us has to reverse for half a mile.

Seb

Constantine to Mawgan Porth. Nearly seven and a half miles. We caught the 9.30 bus to Constantine from Betty's Newsagents and arrived about 10am in lovely sunshine, another couple sporting bright blue matching anoraks, carrying rucksacks and walking sticks alighting at the same time. Rosa was eager to stop and chat but they looked rather slow, so I persuaded her to set off immediately to the beach.

The next bay along is Treyarnon and the coast path goes across the sand, but there was a wide stream of water at least six inches deep, running off the cliffs after last weekend's downpour, with no way to cross it without getting our feet thoroughly soaked. We noticed the blue anorak couple coming across the sand, looking perplexed. After a few head-scratching moments, we decided to go upstream to the shore edge and leap across at the narrowest point. Not easy but others had obviously done the same, judging by the worn and muddy bank.

Rounding the headland there were several deep inlets and some huge rocks just offshore, after which the path went past some fenced-off land with a notice: "RSPB Private Land." There were granite steps up to the next headland, where we looked down over several small rocky coves before reaching Porthcothan with its open sandy beach backed by grassy dunes and a row of properties, varying in style from old to modern. The acorn sign said "Mawgan Porth 4 ½m" so we decided to have our lunch at this point, sitting in a sheltered spot. We noticed blue anoraks some distance behind us. Nicely refreshed, we set off again, spotting a couple of fabulous blow holes near Park Head, then we were surprised to see about twenty cattle quite near the cliff edge and thought they must have broken through a nearby gate. They took no notice of us.

When we reached Bedruthan Steps, we were bitterly disappointed to read "Closed. No Entry, due to unstable cliffs." I was very tempted to try my luck anyway, but Rosa pointed out that it really did look dangerous. Bedruthan looked spectacular and reminiscent of Kynance Cove, which Lara and I visited a few years ago, with its beautiful beach and outstanding rock formations, and we could see there are walk-through caves that lead to the next beach, Carnewas. We left reluctantly then came across two signs, "Steps" and "No Steps". We took the steps. On looking back to Bedruthan, we noticed a large crack in the jutting cliff opposite, which looked alarmingly as if a big chunk of cliff is in danger of breaking off. Trenance and Mawgan Porth came into view, and again it was a flat walk before ascending the slope towards the cottage. We noticed the blue anoraks were now ahead of us. How did that happen?

Lara

I've nearly given up on their arriving back today when they eventually stumble in not long before 4.30pm. "Where have you been?" I accuse.

"What?" says Seb, kicking off his boots and collapsing on one end of the sofa while Rosa collapses on the other, "It was fabulous, Lara. You should have come with us. The views were some of the best I've ever seen."

"You said that yesterday."

"Well yes, it's true though. The views between Watergate and here, and from Constantine, are totally incredible. It helps, of course, that the sun has been shining both days." He rubs his calves, leans back his head and sighs. Rosa does the same. "Any chance of a glass of wine and some crisps."

The next hour drags interminably as five million photos are produced and exclaimed over.

"Did you see anyone else walking?" I always wonder if there are any other mugs intent on blisters, strained muscles and stitch, but it's been a beautiful day and I can see that some may be tempted.

"Oh yes, a few. Some young girls were striding it out around Constantine and soon got way ahead of us, and there was an older couple in blue anoraks who were plodding behind us most of the way, but somehow overtook us." Seb says before giving

Rosa a guilty glance. Rosa buries her head in her phone while Seb clears his throat and changes the subject. "Oh, Rosa, we saw some great blow holes, didn't we?" They then dissolve into helpless giggles.

Blow holes? What the hell? The mind boggles. I cannot imagine what a blow hole is and frankly I don't want to know. Finding their sniggering unbearable, I stomp off to the kitchen for toast and marmite, and when I return, Seb has gone to sleep with a smile on his face and Rosa is dozing with her feet up on my pouffe, next to my box of chocolates. I'm sure there's a distinct whiff in the air and I really wish they'd showered before relaxing in my space.

***

They caught the 9.30am bus towards Padstow to walk from Harlyn. I'm to meet them later in Padstow for a late lunch, so they won't be able to dawdle too much.

I'm still puzzling about the blue anorak couple who mysteriously overtook Seb and Rosa, even though they were older and less agile. What were Seb and Rosa doing? And how did a seven-mile walk take over five and a half hours? It doesn't add up.

At 12.30pm I'm waiting for the 12.39 bus to take me to Padstow, which doesn't arrive. I blame Seb; he's incapable of looking up a bus time on his app and this is the third time this week he has it wrong: the 9.30 to Constantine (I've since discovered they were waiting at the wrong end of Tredragon Road), the 2pm at Newquay and now today. On this occasion, though, it appears he's not the only one as the chap from the

Pitch 'n' Putt building emerges to wait with me and anxiously scans his phone and informs me that the bus should be running. After a very pleasant chat about Cornwall and buses, which we both think are quite dependable, although not today, we give up and I go to the newsagents for a paper before texting Seb to say I will not be meeting them for a pasty lunch in Padstow after all. I have a quick snack of soup and toast back at the cottage then decide to stroll along the beach, hoping the bracing air will clear my blocked nose and painful sinuses, when my phone pings: "Back in fifteen minutes." I do not understand as I thought the plan was to return on the 3.45 bus, so I hasten back to the cottage to let them in as I have locked up with the only key. They're both laughing and relaxed. "We're back earlier as we hired a taxi."

Seb.

Harlyn to Padstow. We caught the bus to Harlyn, which was very quiet today, a contrast to Sunday. There were just two couples walking as we approached Trevone, where we could not see the pool as the tide was in. The signpost said "Padstow 5m via Stepper Point". The path was a good surface and level, so the walking was easy, with fine views over the deep inlets, and the rock strata were particularly striking. There was a rock offshore with what looked like a spire and in the distance we could see a Daymark.

At a kissing gate there was a map of the headland mentioning Archway, Stepper Point, Old Boar and the Coastguard Station. We spent some time in the Daymark, a navigational aid built for sailors in 1830, looking through the arched windows, a cute little rock island visible from each window.

On to the Coastguard Lookout, Rosa went in search of a secluded spot desperate for a wee, while I was more than happy to chat to the friendly coastguard who invited me in to look around the impressive array of instruments and screens. The National Coastguard Institution is a charity and all seventy around the English Coast are manned by volunteers. Easy enough work on a day like today, explained the volunteer, inviting me to look out at the clear sky and calm sea, but very busy in stormy weather, swimmers, surfers, kayakers and the like in trouble, and in the summer when people take chances with inflatables.

"Ah here's your wife." The chap smiled as Rosa appeared brandishing her water bottle. "Nice to have a chat, enjoy the rest of your walk."

As we were looking across the Camel estuary towards Polzeath, a text came through from Lara: "Unable to meet for lunch as no show with bus. Don't feel like driving so I'll stay here."

Padstow is a charming harbour town and was very busy with pre-Christmas shoppers. There's a range of great places to eat and drink and we were happy to relax with a glass of wine and a seafood pasta.

We decided to take a taxi back, so I texted Lara to say we were on our way.

Lara

In answer to my query about why they decided on a taxi, Seb explains, "We thought it would be quicker, rather than wait for the 3.45 bus which would mean our getting back past 4.30, and Rosa is driving home this evening."

"Did you have any lunch?" I ask and they both nod, although decline to elaborate. I haven't the strength to pursue it as my head is throbbing, I'm coughing, sneezing, my sinuses are blocked and my eyes are streaming. "I've booked a table for us tonight remember," I tell Seb. "But I'm feeling rubbish."

Guess what! Rosa decides to stay; she says she'll drive back early tomorrow morning and get to work for 10am, so she and Seb go off to the Bedruthan Hotel for dinner a deux, which I had booked for me and Seb, while I retire to bed with a lemon toddy and a box of tissues. I dream of clinking glasses, sea bass fillets in romesco sauce, scallops, grilled halloumi, triple cooked chips and chocolate puddings.

"Good evening, sir. Table reserved for you and your wife, 8pm? This way." Seb and Rosa are shown to a table for two in the corner by the huge picture window. "This is lovely, Seb. The menu looks good. No wonder Lara said she'd been looking forward to it, poor thing. Shame to waste a reservation though." Rosa kicks off her heels under the table and runs her foot up Seb's calf.

The waiter arrives with their wine and sparkling water. "Having a good holiday?"

"Yes, it's great here. We're walking the South West Coast Path, aren't we, Rosa?"

"Good luck. You look fit on it. Bon appetit."

Rosa and Seb clink glasses. Their food arrives and is fabulous.

"This is wonderful." Rosa leans back for a breather. "I'm enjoying it so much I don't want to rush." She strokes Seb's leg again under the table.

"That's okay. Neither do I." Seb looks across at her. "You are beautiful, Rosa. You know that don't you?" He reaches across and puts his fingers to her lips. The couple on the next table avert their gaze and roll their eyes.

I sleep in till after 8am and note the brandy bottle and two glasses on the coffee table. Seb looks tired. I didn't hear him come in last night. He's just seen Rosa off and asks what I'd like to do. "Go to Padstow I think, as I missed the bus trip yesterday."

We catch the 9.30 bus but I change my mind after ten minutes as Seb prattles on and on about the stupid walk. "Oh look that's where Rosa and I…" Rosa this, Rosa that. I try to tune out; I just want to look at the wonderful scenery in peace from the front seat of the double decker bus. A double decker bus travelling along these small, picturesque roads seems remarkable and I wonder how on earth the driver manages in the summer when the roads are busy.

We pass a sprawling, fenced-off MOD area, which a neighbouring passenger informs us is an early warning system site, then through the charming town of Eval, marred by a huge array of turbines. The mesmerising route winds along, through Porthcothan, Treyarnon, St Merryn, Constantine and Harlyn, before descending the steep hill to Padstow Harbour. There are some lovely coastal properties on the way and I wonder how many are locally owned and how many are second homes for outsiders.

Padstow is a delight, and we browse the shops and have a mulled wine sitting on a bench overlooking the harbour until we return on the 1.30 bus for a quiet afternoon in the cottage. I note Seb does not suggest a lunch out and is keen to return for soup and toast, but I guess he's still full from yesterday's two splendid repasts. He spends the afternoon alternately browsing his archive of photos, texting and looking furtive, and planning further walks. I spend the afternoon sneezing, watching a film, (*The Other Woman*) and finishing the chocolates.

Chapter Eighteen

Christmas Again

Lara

It's not long until Christmas and Seb and Rosa have been out for the day on the coast path again. Why he can't keep fit by walking around the farm checking fences, I don't know.

Seb enters the kitchen. I glare at him. "Where have you been?" I sound shrewish to my own ears, but it's too late. I must say my piece. "Westward Ho! to Appledore is only three miles. What have you been doing all this time?"

Seb turns away. "Nothing."

"Nothing, nothing? How can you be doing nothing for five hours?"

"Well, we took a while walking. As we've done it before, we had more time to savour different aspects."

"Aspects?"

"It's a different time of year than when we last went so…" He pauses. "And I nipped into town to buy some shaving cream."

"Okay." I turn back to the cooker wearily. "There's beef goulash for supper, ready in a couple of hours. Do you want a cup of tea now?"

"No thanks. I had one with Rosa."

"Oh. Did she go to town with you? I suppose you popped into a café somewhere for tea and a toasted teacake."

Seb looks away guiltily. "We were hungry. We didn't stop for lunch, just a quick pasty. Are you all right, love? You seem tired."

"I'm fine," I lie. "I didn't have a good night, that's all."

"I realised." Seb heads towards the door. "I ended up with double the duvet on me. I suppose you were hot again. I'll go and help Bobby. You have a rest."

***

Christmas Day is tomorrow; how quickly it comes round each year. I've invited Rosa over for drinks and nibbles this evening. Everything is more or less prepared for the big day. The table is laid, presents wrapped, the ham glazed and roasted covered in the larder along with the turkey, stuffing, cranberry sauce and brandy butter. The spare beds are made up in readiness for family and relations turning up tomorrow morning for a two-night stay, and I have camp beds prepared for anyone who decides they can't drive home. Bobby is out this evening so the three of us sit in the living room, fire crackling, fairy lights twinkling on the tree, holly on the mantelpiece and all looks festive.

"Lara, this is lovely," sighs Rosa. "You're so good at it all: the family occasions and your wonderful cooking."

"I enjoy cooking. It's not a chore for me." We all look at the coffee table, where I've plated homemade quiche, mini Yorkshires with beef, cheese straws, sticky chipolatas, guacamole, tortilla crisps and chocolate profiteroles.

Seb opens the prosecco. "Happy Christmas." He hands a small glass to Rosa. "It's a shame you are not staying the night."

"I'm with my sister and family tomorrow." Rosa nods her thanks as I hand round the plates.

We pass a pleasant hour talking of Christmases past and present, then Rosa gets up. "I must go. It's been lovely, Lara."

She hands me a beautifully wrapped gift with trailing gold and blue ribbons and glances meaningfully at Seb, who reaches behind the curtains to produce a similarly wrapped parcel.

"Do you mind opening them now?" asks Seb. "We'll be so rushed tomorrow, we thought it would be nice to do it now."

I cringe at the "we" but say, "Of course. Gorgeous wrapping paper, too good to tear." Rosa's present is an exquisite navy and amber silk scarf and a personalised silver friendship bookmark. I give her a hug. "Thank you, both are just perfect. Shall I open yours too, Seb?"

"Do you mind?" Seb presses. I start to unwrap the paper and four eyes survey me anxiously as a pair of soft navy leather gloves appear and a small blue embossed box holding gorgeous gold and amber drop earrings.

"Wow, Seb. These are lovely."

"You deserve it. You're the best wife in the world. We both think you're wonderful, don't we, Rosa?" They nod in unison.

I actually feel quite sick. They look so earnest and so in tune. Symmetrical somehow. They've obviously spent time together choosing my gifts. Probably the week before last when I had a go at Seb for being out so long. I know he's giving me a waterproof jacket for the farm tomorrow as we chose it together, my old one being in shreds. He would never normally give me earrings. Perhaps I'm being paranoid. And ungrateful.

***

"Lara, Rosa and I would like to take you to dinner, our treat." Seb beams at me.

"Sebastian Sedgefield, what ARE you on about?"

"What I say. Take you out for a slap-up meal. It was Rosa's idea. And a good one. To say how much we appreciate your patience with our Mondays, and the walks."

"Do you know how ridiculous you sound, Seb? You and Rosa have decided to take out the long-suffering wife! You're my husband for heaven's sake! You and Rosa do not get to treat me like a pet or decide what I'd like." I stomp off.

Seb and Rosa are sitting side by side with large platters of steak and chips in front of them. A red candle in the centre of the table sends out a romantic glow and there's soft music playing in the background. I'm sitting opposite, unmistakably me but turned into a large dog, with soulful eyes and a brown shaggy coat, overweight and drooling, plumped on a squashy cushion, bib around my neck and an overflowing bowl of dog biscuits just out of my reach, with which they feed me intermittently along with chunks of steak.

Occasionally they reach across and pat my head. "Good doggy." Rosa feeds me most of her steak and smiles indulgently. "She is a good doggy, isn't she, Seb? I wonder if she would like an onion ring."

The plates are cleared away by the waiter, who then places a bowl of doggy chocolate drops on the table. I like the waiter and give him a lick. Everyone laughs, including the waiter who also pats me on the head.

I awake, hot, dribbling and itchy. My pyjama top has risen up and is wrapped around my neck like a collar. Seb must be up. I can hear doors banging downstairs.

Chapter Nineteen

Newquay to St Agnes

Lara

O my word, vertigo! The three of us are in Perranporth and we cannot believe our eyes, even though we had of course googled the top-floor apartment of the Victorian house before booking, we're still awestruck by the steep, thirty-step spiral staircase, the only access to our accommodation. No problem for Sebastian and Rosa, who sprint up, but vertiginous for me, clinging on to the handrail for dear life, before breathing a sigh of relief to reach the entrance door on a tiny decking area. The apartment is quirky, all floral patchwork sofas and cushions, white furniture, Cath Kidston accessories, pastel bunting, fairy lights and lanterns, the walls adorned with some good original paintings by the artist owner. I dash to the first ensuite double room, to use the toilet, Rosa not far behind, but Seb calls to her to help bring up the food bags from the car, so I discover that the next bedroom is larger. Seb grumbles that Rosa has the bigger shower, but both rooms are beautiful with crisp, white bedding and immaculate sweet-smelling shower rooms.

We unpack the food in the small well-equipped kitchen, then exclaim over the tiny turret room one step up with just room for a small dining table, with spectacular views over Perranporth and the beach.

After opening the wine and switching on the fake log burner, we leaf through the file of local places of interest and nearby restaurants.

"Kerching, kerching", Rosa's phone keeps ringing like a cash machine and she explains she's selling some items on eBay. "Kerching", she's made another sale. Between "kerchings" she and Seb discuss tomorrow's walk, starting from Newquay, and consult the bus timetable. There seems to be an excellent bus service, fortunately, as it gets me out of chauffeuring. They spend ages on the Bus Times website, heads together on the sofa, tracking and intermittently dashing to the window to see if they can spot a bus pulling in at the bus stop below.

8am. I've cooked scrambled eggs on toast and made coffee and we're exclaiming over the cuteness of the turret, when there's suddenly a mad panic to don boots and coats, grab provisions and hasten down the spiral stairs to catch the 8.35 bus.

I close the door on them thankfully. There is a cold easterly whistling and I want to relax with another coffee and my Jojo Moyes novel. I frown at the large bag of eBay parcels Rosa has asked if I would take to the Post Office, and chuck a blue crocheted throw over it. I'm not amused. I've got out of chauffeuring, but I still have errands to run. I fling another throw over the offending bag but it's no good; I cannot concentrate so I quickly slap on some make up, drag a brush through my frizzy mop then descend the steps gingerly with the bulky parcels. I wonder what they contain but I didn't think to ask. Perranporth is a delight. It's a cold but sunny day and the waves are glistening on the stunning huge beach, which is framed by sand dunes and low headlands, home to the stupid walk route. There's an island on the beach which looks intriguing. The charming town boasts many individual shops, a Post Office, Co-op and Premier store, several cafés, Indian, Chinese and Thai takeaways, fish and chip shops, pubs, inns, restaurants and a fabulous ice cream shop. There are a couple of pubs overlooking the beach and a bar, the Watering Hole, actually on the beach, unique as being the only bar on a beach in the UK. It looks great with live music shows advertised for the summer months.

I post the wretched parcels and inform the friendly lady I shall keep the £2 change from the £20 Rosa gave me as commission, then explore a few shops before finding the Boating Lake at the other end of the town. This is lovely, there being a circular path round the lake with a little island in the centre, ducks and geese calling merrily and several benches on which to sit and admire the well-kept gardens. I wonder for a moment where Seb and Rosa are, but not for long as I take my leave and head to the Co-op to stock up on chocolate, bread and wine. I'm not cooking tonight. We can either go out to one of the pubs or Seb can get us a takeaway.

Seb

Newquay to Perranporth. Approx ten miles. I studied the tide times in depth and unfortunately this week does not favour us, but that is the nature of the South West coast and we must adapt as best we can. Having caught the 8.35am U1A from Perranporth to Newquay, we waited a few minutes to go the short distance back to Crantock on the 9.25, the previous bus having bypassed it. The tide being in meant we were unable to cross the Gannel Estuary, and the walk around it would mean an extra hour, so we decided to leave it and see if we can do it separately the day after tomorrow.

The bus dropped us at the Crantock bus shelter and we set off in glorious, cold and crisp conditions. Passing a lovely thatched pub, the Old Albion, we reached the Crantock Beach car park with signposts saying, "Newquay Harbour via Summer Ferry 2 ½m" and "Newquay via Tidal Bridge 3 ¼m". We had a chat with a couple by the gate who were walking to Porth Joke, about an hour's walk, and they seemed impressed that we were going all the way to Perranporth. But we explained we are old hands now and it would take more miles than that to daunt us. They seemed puzzled when I said my wife would have a late lunch ready on our return and went on their way, scratching their heads. Overtaking them, we walked through sand dunes because of the high tide, and, looking back at the estuary, I noted that West Newquay has a lot of housing so I must do some research on how to reach the estuary from that side.

The walk was easy and flat; we could see an island offshore and, looking back, the lighthouse at Trevose Head in the distance. Rounding towards Pentire Headland there was a sign "Vugga Cove, 140yds", which Rosa was keen to explore, but as it's only accessible at low tide we carried on, looking down over deep inlets towards Porth Joke, which must be fabulous when the tide is out.

There were a few dog walkers and backpackers but mostly we had the path to ourselves. Having crossed the bridge to Porth Joke, we saw some twenty seals basking on the sand in an isolated cove and Rosa was enchanted. I leant over to take some photos but spotted a sign "Seals sleeping and being disturbed is bad for us", so I hastily withdrew. Rounding the next headland, Kelsey Head, we could see Holywell, so called because the well, St Cuthbert's, in one of the caves, was believed for many years to have healing powers and became a pilgrimage for sick people. Again, this is only accessible at low tide. There are two islands out at sea, Gull Rocks (or Carters Rocks). The sand dunes route was well signposted and easy walking. We were lucky enough to see a sizeable lizard on the sand which made Rosa gasp. Holywell looks an outstanding beach to explore and we agreed we would return sometime. As we progressed there were several signs, "MOD site", "Do not touch military debris. It may explode and kill you". We could see Perranporth ahead, so we paused for a while to take some welcome swigs from the hip flask and eat our chocolate bars. Rosa had also bought a couple of packs of nuts, so we had a companionable chat, admiring the view. I text Lara, "Can see Perranporth, took longer than we thought."

Perran Beach is huge with swirling clear water eddying up towards extensive dunes; we chatted to a couple of chaps walking towards Holywell and asked whether we should keep to the top path or descend to walk along the beach, and they said the beach would be fine as we had walking boots. The beach is so long that we took over half an hour to reach the car park and make our ascent up Cliff Road to the apartment. Looking west we could see Bawdens Rocks towards St Agnes, also known as Cow and Calf.

Lara

After breakfast we all three get on the 9.22am U1A bus to Truro, but Seb and Rosa get off at St Agnes at 9.35, discussing where they will buy a snack to take with them. I carry on to Truro bus station, arriving at 10.12. How the bus driver negotiates the narrow streets of St Agnes is a marvel.

After exploring the area around Lemon Quay, I stroll into the city centre with the magnificent, imposing cathedral at its heart, browse a few charity shops for books and cards, pop into Boots for a shower cap I forgot to bring and have a coffee and cake before returning to Perranporth.

Seb

St Agnes to Perranporth. Approx five miles. From St Agnes, we walked northwest to St Agnes Head, through some housing getting more isolated and remote until we saw a sign "To the Coast Path". The path hugs the edge of the headland here and we could clearly see the Cow and Calf rocks and, in the distance to the north, the vast expanse of Perran Beach. It looked deceptively near. Walking on, we looked down over some amazing rocky inlets until we reached a sign "Trevaunance Point", then went through the car park opposite the Driftwood Spars Hotel across the road leading to the beach, before climbing up through Downquay Gardens. Ascending a series of steep steps we could look back over the attractive cove, after which the path curved inland towards Blue Hills Tin and the area known as Jericho Valley, home to the Motorcycling Club. Curving back towards the coast to Trevellas Combe, the path then became a series of new-looking steps, running parallel to the old, worn path. The steps were hard going and we were thankful to reach the top with flat terrain that was home to many bunkers and old mine shafts. We could see the windsock of Perranporth Airport. The steep gullies to the sea looked wonderful, some with beautiful pink-stoned rock faces.

There were not many people about despite the clear, sunny weather but we chatted to a couple, obviously serious walkers with sticks and rucksacks, who commented on the relative ease of the walk. Reaching a sign "Hanover Cove North", Perran Beach now looked very close. We found a small track off the main path leading to a sheltered cave where we sat and ate our pasties and chocolate and discussed when we can get away to do the next leg of our journey around the Cornish Coast. Heading towards Perran Beach, we saw a sign "Cathedral Caverns" and, unable to resist, we almost had to crawl down a precarious path, not for the faint-hearted, but worth it to explore the fabulous caverns.

Lara

They finally stumble up the stairs just before 3pm. Where have they been? It's only five miles for goodness' sake!

"I've had my lunch," I tell them. "I couldn't wait. There's cold meat and cheese in the fridge if you want."

After they've had a snack and a large glass of prosecco each, they bore me rigid with paths, caves, cliffs and views. "Lara, you should have seen the Cathedral Caverns. They're incredible, look." Out come a million photos.

"I've visited a real cathedral today," I manage to squeeze in a word, but they're not listening.

"Let's go for a short walk, Lara. The path's only round the corner by the Youth Hostel and it's all flat." I'm longing for a cup of tea and an episode of *Murder She Wrote* but I find myself being dragged out like a six-year-old. How did this happen?

It is pleasant and bracing though. The path past the YHA is flat and the view over the bay is glorious but then, annoyingly, the track becomes narrow and trodden, alarmingly close to the cliff edge. They take no notice but I cannot look at the swirling sea without wobbling. Seb points out a teeny winding path down a precipitous drop to the Cathedral Caverns.

"What! Did you really go down there? It's lethal, not even a goat could manage it."

They look at me pityingly. "It's nothing." Seb smiles conspiratorially at Rosa, who nods.

"The path is slightly narrow it's true, but it's quite safe and the caverns are magical."

I shudder and resume my way along the normal path, but they overtake me and sprint up some steps to start chatting to a lady in pink. I'm puffing and panting up the last couple of steps when the pink lady passes by, nodding briefly with a sympathetic smile.

"Lara," laughs Seb when I catch up, "that lady has walked all the way from St Agnes and says she's scared of heights but it's okay if you don't look down."

I don't see how this is amusing but I have to admire the pink lady for her stoicism. It really is a steep drop. Besides, for all their smugness, I know they don't want me tagging along.

At the next rise, we agree to turn back as the other "amazing caves" are too far away, and I am painfully slow, only taking baby steps, afraid to look at the sea or the cliff edge. I'm glad to get back to the cottage for a reviving brandy.

Seb goes out for a takeaway for the three of us and they tuck into lemon chicken and king prawns as if they haven't seen food for a week. I suppose the invigorating walk must give them an appetite. I'm not sure I like the way they share a pancake roll though.

"Seb, can you help?" Rosa taps on our bedroom door. "I'm sorry to disturb you but there's something amiss with my shower. The knob seems stuck."

"Okay." Seb climbs out of bed. "Won't be a sec." He leans over me. "Lara, are you awake? Rosa needs help with her shower head."

Rosa is in her shower, naked. "Rosa, what are you doing?" Seb gasps. "I thought you said your shower was stuck."

"It seems to have righted itself, but can you just check the controls?" She reaches forward to remove his dressing gown.

"Actually, I think you need a good scrub. Look, I have some lovely Body Shop Almond shower gel that will sort you out. Turn around, I'll do your back." She slides his boxers off. "My, you do need a good going over. This could take a while."

I wake at 6.30am to Seb's lit-up phone screen. I turn over but half an hour later he's still dabbing. I sniff. I'm sure I can smell almonds. It reminds me of something, but I cannot recall what at the moment.

By 7.15 I can stand it no longer and go to the kitchen to make myself a cup of tea. His eyes don't leave the screen. At 7.45 he announces, "I think I've got it. If we get the 9.55 to Newquay and…"

I get up to make breakfast, leaving him wittering on and re-examining his phone. Over sausages, eggs and toast, Seb explains that as he and Rosa missed the short stretch of walk between Newquay and Crantock, he's worked out a quick route and we can all have a morning in Newquay.

Consequently, by 10am we are on the UA1 bus to Newquay, Seb pointing out various landmarks he and Rosa saw previously, although I question the ostrich farm. I can't see a pheasant, let alone an ostrich.

We alight near the town cemetery and walk along a footpath towards Fistral Beach. This is stunning and looks very inviting in the bright sunshine. They decide they must walk the length of the beach and back, so I wait on a bench whilst they go striding off, steps in unison. I almost expect them to hold hands. On their return we follow the path to Pentire car park to avail ourselves of the toilets, then, consulting the acorn signpost, continue towards Gannel Estuary (300yds). It's not 300yds; it's a long trek until we reach a likely-looking path which is locked and gated. A helpful builder repairing someone's driveway informs us that the path doesn't open until April and we'll need to walk a further ten minutes to gain access. After what seems like miles, we reach a winding slope down to the estuary but my feet are aching, so I wait at the top whilst those two skip down. After a while Seb messages, "Walk on along Pentire Crescent and we'll meet you in five minutes."

The five minutes is actually ten. They managed to cross the boardwalk, apparently, but I just want to get into the town centre for a coffee and a rest.

The little café on Killacourt Green is closed but we find a great Tapas style coffee shop, Mix, for a delicious coffee and cake, with great views of the harbour.

Seb

I am so pleased we managed to squeeze in the short walk we missed before, from Newquay to Crantock. We joined the coastal path near Fistral Beach, we did a quick walk along the sands and back, about a mile each way, then walked along the path to Pentire car park. The views over the beach towards the headland and beyond are breathtaking.

The path to Gannel was signposted but we had to walk quite a way past some waterside homes until we found the path down to sea level. I was hoping Lara could have a coffee in the Fern Pit Restaurant, but it was closed. The tide was rapidly coming in; we estimated we had about twenty minutes, so we hastened quickly across the boardwalk to Crantock and back. Mission accomplished.

Lara

I'm dragged out again before we go home as "we simply must explore the beach properly". This takes over two hours as the beach is wonderful and has everything a beach lover could possibly want. Huge expanses of golden sand, little pools for children to paddle, rocks to clamber over, caves to explore and Chapel Rock Island. This is the site of an ancient chapel, which was on the summit but has been eroded over the years, as have the cliffs. There is a natural swimming pool on the island rock created by the Parish Council in the 1950s.

After exploring the island, Seb and Rosa move on to the Arch Rock, a huge natural arch formed and weathered over the years, adjoining the cliff edge, then we all stroll along the enormous sandy beach for about two thirds of its length before heading back, Seb and Rosa darting in and out of the caves, exclaiming with delight.

"The caves are fabulous, Lara. You can go through some to other ones."

"I expect you can," I reply nonchalantly. "That's because they're not caves at all but old mine workings. Everything along these cliffs is manmade; this was a big mining territory years ago. You should study the Council Notice Board."

Three figures are walking along a cliff top, wearing boots and hoodies. One is slow and lagging behind the taller, fitter pair who are striding ahead and soon out of sight. The laggard cannot keep up and is soon out of breath, lost and disorientated. A heavy mist settles over the darkening sky and the rocks to the left loom menacingly. As the air deepens into a thick gloom, she stumbles on aimlessly, afraid of the cliff edge, heading blindly inland amongst the gorse, brambles and wire fencing. Her legs become leaden, and she has to drag herself forward until she can go no further and collapses in a heap.

Chapter Twenty

St Agnes to Hayle

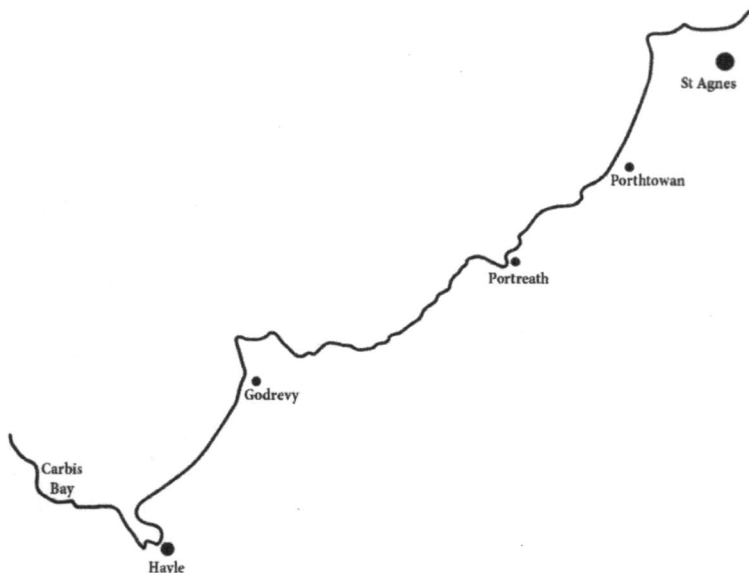

Lara

We've booked a holiday for a week in a self-catering cottage in Portreath, Cornwall. We haven't been away for quite a while and I'm really looking forward to getting away from the farm for a few days, catching up with reading, walking round some harbours, generally relaxing with takeaways and eating out at a nearby pub. It's all right for Seb, he's out practically every Monday, but my only time out is the supermarket shop. The cottage is perfect, a stone's throw from the beach and, of course, the South West Coast Path.

Oh yes, there's no let-up. Rosa's joining us halfway through the week, hence having to book a two-to-three-bedroomed property. Two would be fine, but three is a bonus as Seb likes to spread out his clothes in a second room if he can. The terraced house is beautifully clean and modern, and the kitchen is a dream with hi-tech machines which neither of us understand. Never mind. We've stocked the fridge with wine, prosecco, my homemade lasagne, meats, cheeses, smoked salmon and other goodies.

We have a couple of days to ourselves exploring the area, which is picturesque Cornwall at its best.

Seb meets Rosa at the station, and by the time we've ordered a Chinese takeaway and consumed two bottles of wine, those two are heads together on the sofa discussing their walk for tomorrow.

Seb

Lara and I have had a good couple of days exploring Portreath, walking on the beach (where there are some wonderful caves and walk-through rocks, which I spent over an hour enjoying), watching tv and lazing around, but I am getting excited about the walk now that Rosa is here. We are planning on an early start. Lara and I sussed out the route yesterday, driving to Godrevy so she could acquaint herself with the drive back on her own.

Lara

As usual, muggins is the driver. I drop them off at Godrevy in the rain – chocolate and hip flask safely stowed in Seb's rucksack, two pasties bought in Portreath bakery in Rosa's.

My drive back is good; it's quiet here out of season. I have a long day ahead of me but I'm used to my own company and have my time planned. I scroll through the photos on my tablet, deleting as I go back several years, in preparation to get the remainder printed, a job I've been meaning to do for a while. This takes far longer than I anticipated as there are a great many of Rosa and I together, usually with cake and hot chocolate or sitting in the garden with salmon bagels and wine, and several of us giggling and holding each other up. I keep a few but there's no point in keeping them all. These days of course it's photos of Seb and Rosa on their walks, which Seb has forwarded to me, posing against a cliff edge or a fingerpost. Delete, delete, delete.

Seb

Godrevy to Portreath, about seven miles. Godrevy is wonderful. There is a road up to the National Trust car park, where several surfers were getting kitted up. The walk was flat to start with, and easy going, and fortunately the rain eased off so we could appreciate the magnificent beach and rock formations. Godrevy Lighthouse, a beautiful and eye-catching white twenty-six-metre octagonal tower built by Trinity House in 1859 marking a dangerous reef known as the Stones, scene of several wrecks and cause of many casualties, is famous and has appeared in tv programmes and been mentioned in Virginia Woolfe's novel *To the Lighthouse*. The path went inland somewhat but still overlooked the sheltered, inaccessible sandy coves, spectacular rocks and the swirling, eddying water. We were looking for Deadman's Cove and retraced our steps when we realised we had passed it, but the tiny path was so slippery and overgrown with bracken that we abandoned the attempt, especially as the sky was turning grey again. By an immense stroke of luck, we came across a lovely little cave to take shelter in and eat our pasties, just as the heavens opened for a heavy shower. I was loath to leave it; I do love a cave. Nearing Portreath, there were some steep ascents and descents, making for an intense work-out for the thighs and feet.

Lara

Finally! At last they turn up. I'm sick of sneaking out to gaze up at the huge cliff to the left of Portreath Beach to see if they're sliding/slipping/ hobbling down. I've given up, poured myself a large glass of white wine, stuck *Place in the Sun* on tv, when there's a clatter by the front door and they stagger in, muddy boots and walking sticks discarded on the floor, grimacing and clutching thighs.

"Starving," gasps Seb.

"Exhausted" gasps Rosa.

For goodness' sake, are they fit or unfit? It's not supposed to be that strenuous a walk; the app said three hours, just over seven miles. Hmm, funny how they've taken six hours. And what's with the clutching of the thighs?

Sighing, I pour them a glass of wine (I know, stupid, I shouldn't wait on them but I need to distract them and shut them up before they embark endlessly on their memories of the day) and set out a few snacks. Meanwhile, Rosa has disappeared upstairs and Seb has stripped down to his underpants, throwing his jeans and tee shirt into the washing machine.

They both scoff down the food, regale me with a brief description of the walk and how they took shelter in a cave, then Seb drags himself upstairs for a quick shower, thank goodness.

I'm tired of him slumped in his pants. They then both subside on the two sofas. I wash up, perch on the pouffe watching the remainder of *The Professionals*, to which Seb has fallen asleep and Rosa is nodding off, eying Bodie's machine gun narrowly as Seb twitches in his sleep. It's unusual for them both to be so shattered. After all, this walk isn't strenuous like Hartland or Tintagel. I'm wondering how long exactly they were in that cave. Rosa looks quite flushed and her usually immaculate hair somewhat dishevelled. My own hair turns into a frizzy meltdown in two drops of rain but Rosa invariably maintains a sleek shining curtain.

Seb and Rosa are snuggled side by side under an overhanging rock, just out of reach of the heavy downpour obscuring the view. "Phew, this was a lucky find." Seb reaches into his pocket for his hip flask. "Fancy a nip?"

"Lovely. Shall we share a pasty? One is too much for me. Here." Rosa places the end of a large pasty in her mouth and pops the other end into Seb's. "Mmm." They munch away until Rosa has finished a third and Seb is coming to the end of his two thirds. "Haha," laughs Rosa. "I'll just check your lips for crumbs." She licks around his lips. "Mmm, tasty. Looks like the rain isn't going to stop for a while. What shall we do?"

***

Another day. Another stupid walk. When they finally roused themselves last evening, as I prepped an M & S ready meal, they spent eons looking over their photos, then at least an hour perusing the walking app for St Agnes to Portreath.

It looks as if the path could be hard going for them, I reflect, as I creep down the steep hill in second gear by the towering cliffs over Porthtowan, having dropped them off in St Agnes. The bay looks beautiful as I dare to risk a glance, sunlight glinting on the waves. Back at the cottage, after a coffee and clearing up the breakfast dishes I venture out for a walk around the harbour. Portreath was a busy working harbour in the eighteenth century, I gather from the information board, importing coal and exporting copper. I get chatting to a local chap taking his little terrier for a walk.

"It was heaving here in the summer," he informs me, waving the bag of dog poo he's just scooped up. "The Costcutters shop in the square had its shelves stripped bare on Bank Holiday Monday. Cars were parked everywhere, miles up the hill, and right across the harbour to the beach was a huge mass of smoking barbecues." He agitatedly swings the dog poo from hand to hand. We chat about Devon and Cornwall for a while and I mention that my husband and friend are on the coast path from St Agnes. "Oh dear." The dog poo bag swings ominously. "There are some very steep steps. They'll need to have good knees." He glances down at his own. "I wouldn't be able to do it with mine."

"I wouldn't want to either," I assure him. "Far too much hard work." We part company then I walk on to the pirate lookout, before popping into the convenience store for a paper and the bakery for some bread rolls.

Seb crawls up the stairs when they return. Rosa sinks onto the sofa, massaging her thighs. "There were some really steep bits," she explains.

Seb crawls down the stairs slowly and I pour them a glass of wine each before all three of us go through the usual million photos of beaches, cliffs, mines, bunkers. Apparently, they "bunked" down in a bunker to avoid a heavy rain shower, they laugh hysterically over this. "We had to crouch," sniggers Seb. "There was a huge puddle in the entrance."

I fail to see how this is remotely amusing but they're in convulsions again. "I'm going to make a sandwich to keep us going till dinner time." I retreat to the kitchen, leaving them to reminisce and giggle.

"By the way, how did you get on with all those steps?" I enquire from behind the fridge.

There is silence, then: "There were hundreds of steps, how did you know?"

Seb

St Agnes to Portreath. This was getting on for seven miles. Oh, the steps! The walk was fabulous. I just love the bunkers and the mines; this was a big mining area in the past. Most of the land is MOD. The path across the cliffs and down into Porthtowan was wonderful; you almost felt you were on top of the world, and Porthtowan itself is fabulous: sandy beach and rocks with towering cliffs either side, properties tucked into the hillside on terraces. We passed fields full of hundreds of cabbage plants. The walk itself was moderate apart from the many steep steps; there was just a small disappointment when the footpath descending into Portreath had a notice "Closed. Footpath foundered", meaning we had to walk along the lighthouse road instead.

Lara

Rosa treats us to a pub meal for our dinner. It is good fun, the three of us arm in arm, crossing the small bridge across the stream to a family-run pub, fairy lights twinkling. We all choose from the specials board and order a large glass of wine each. "A large merlot, a large shiraz and a large malbec." Seb smiles at the waitress.

"I'm sorry; I'm new here. I can't spell," she replies. Rosa, Seb and I stare at the waitress, speechless. I dare not meet their eyes. Seb recovers amazingly well and points out the wines on the menu. I love Cornwall, I really do. And the Cornish folk. You just get the feeling they're a law unto themselves and comfortable with life. Rosa's family came from Cornwall originally and we spend a good evening chatting about all things Cornish. The food is delicious, the wine going down nicely after the bottle we polished off earlier in the cottage over a game of Uno.

The waitress is friendly and efficient, the atmosphere mellow. Maybe stupid walks aren't so bad after all.

***

Don't ask me how but I've been sucked into walking to St Ives from Carbis Bay with them. Seb drives us to the car park I parked in previously and we walk down the hill to the station. I've only agreed because it's a mile and a half and supposedly easy. Seb, the liar: "It's nothing. No steps." Really! There are several steps going past the Carbis Bay Hotel (gorgeous by the way) before the path levels out past some fabulous properties alongside the railway track. I look enviously at a train whistling past.

St Ives is lovely. Long expanses of sand, sea rippling in the sunlight. We stop off at the first restaurant we see, Pedn Olva. It's right on the beach, spacious, light and airy and we secure a window seat overlooking the sea from two angles. We have a yummy light lunch and a glass of wine. Honestly, no wonder those two love their walks. I'm beginning to question whether they spend their time walking or visiting pubs and restaurants. Seb buys me and Rosa another medium wine each while he sticks to Coke. Makes a change for him to be the driver.

Seb

We managed to squeeze in the short walk from Godrevy to Hayle, about five miles, before coming home. We did Carbis Bay to St Ives yesterday with Lara. It was only about a mile but very pleasant walking along the top of the train track.

Lara dropped us off at Godrevy again, the tide was out so we walked along the beach. As we approached Hayle there were caravan parks and holiday resorts inland on our left. We could see Carbis Bay in the distance and wondered if we could risk carrying on but had to abort the idea when the water became too deep. It's been a good holiday; we've done St Agnes to Hayle, so on to Carbis Bay would have seen this stretch of the coastline completed but we shall have to wait for our next visit now.

Lara

Against my better judgement I've agreed to being a chauffeur again on our last day. Anything to stop them wittering on about missing a bit of valuable coast path. Back to Godrevy; they won't be long apparently as it's mostly beach. I drive on to Hayle and spend a pleasant half hour in Home Bargains, then stroll around the shops, popping into a couple of quirky little gift stores before retrieving the car from Home Bargains car park to drive to North Quay where we arranged to meet.

My phone pings. "Change of plan. Pick us up at Carbis Bay." What? I've just paid to park the car! Seethe. Gnash teeth. I might just refuse and go to the pub I spotted down the road. They can catch a bus.

Phone pings again. "Mission aborted. Back to Plan A. North Quay." I roll my eyes and start on the crossword. They turn up with wet shoes and socks and dripping ankles. After much jibber jabber and giggles, it emerges that they'd nearly reached Hayle along the beach when they saw the stretch going on to Carbis Bay and thought they may as well continue, until they realised that the river flows into the sea at that point. Soon they were ankle deep in water. They briefly considered wading through but even they're not quite that idiotic.

They change into dry socks and spend another annoying ten minutes giggling about it. It's even more annoying when I realise that, at some stage, they'll insist on coming back to that short stretch of path.

Chapter Twenty-One

Hayle to Land's End

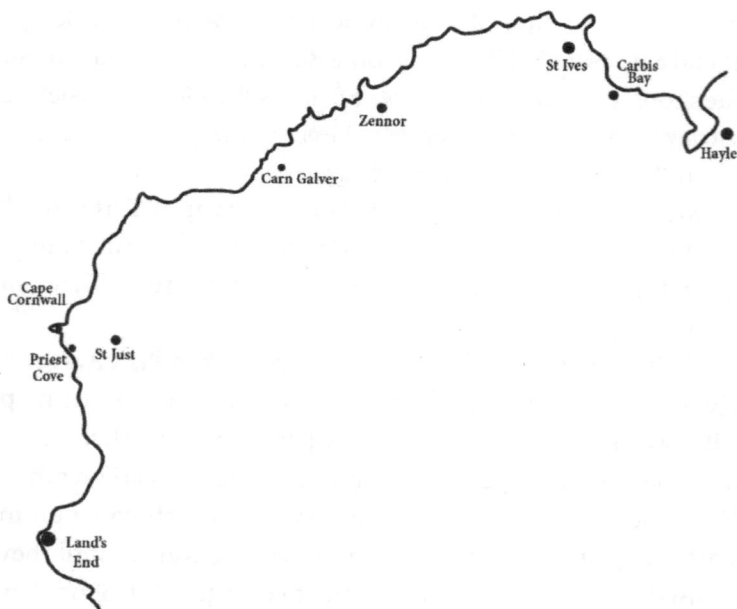

St Ives
Carbis Bay
Zennor
Hayle
Carn Galver
Cape Cornwall
Priest Cove
St Just
Land's End

Lara

We're off to Cornwall again. Three hours along the A30 to Hayle, mostly in pelting downpours of rain. However, the sun breaks through on reaching Hayle and it's soon warm enough for Seb to leave his coat in the car. We do a practice run of part of the route I will drive to on my own. Seb said he'll pace along at speed and won't be long, so I browse in an excellent toy shop along the front and buy some birthday gifts and cards.

All goes well on my drive to Carbis Bay although I have a slight panic at a large road sign "Long delays ahead. Find alternative route". Argh, how could I? I don't know an alternative route and we arranged to rendezvous in the church car park. Deciding to stay put, I'm fortunate in only having to wait about ten minutes. There's a huge tailback from the opposite direction so I hope I don't miss the turning, but it's easy enough and I have time to read the paper whilst waiting for Seb, trying to ignore the urgent need for a wee.

Seb

It was a short walk from Hayle to Carbis Bay and not particularly interesting, but it was the last stretch needed to be completed from St Agnes to St Ives. From Hayle it was mostly flat along the pavement by the road to Lelant, where you can see sand dunes across to Carbis Bay. I crossed the railway line and strode up the hill to the car park where Lara was waiting for me. Only about four and a half miles, just over an hour and fifteen minutes; I am quicker on my own. It is a shame Rosa had to miss this short section but she was unable to get away today.

Lara

Pebble Cottage in St Just is a little gem. Quite tiny, two up, two down, but immaculate and beautifully decorated, all you need in equipment including a cosy log burner with fuel provided.

We have a quiet evening with wine and a Chinese takeaway, the only irritant being Seb continually dabbing on his phone, looking up routes and times, and checking which train Rosa will be arriving on tomorrow.

We drive to Penzance to collect Rosa at the station. It's been a long journey for her and she's tired, so we spend the rest of the blustery afternoon by the log burner watching old episodes of our *Wycliffe* boxset, trying to recognise places we've visited. We retire early after a beef massaman curry I brought with me from home and hope the weather improves tomorrow.

It does. It's a glorious morning. After a good breakfast, we drive to Land's End. There is a £7 parking fee but the chap in the booth kindly waves us through when I explain the walkers are being dropped off and I'll be on my way in less than five minutes.

By the time those two faff about socks, boots (Seb's are developing a hole), whether or not to wear waterproof jackets, check their water bottles etc., it's more like ten minutes, but they're finally ready and I drive slowly out of the one-way system to the B road for my return to St Just, which has a large free car park.

St Just is lovely. There are a surprising number of shops, some small independent ones along with a Co-op and a Premier Stores. The Age Concern charity shop is great and I spend a very pleasant half hour chatting to the two friendly ladies running it and buy seven paperbacks for £1.50.

"You'll be all right, love, on your own." They smile. I've explained the situation to them. "You have your log burner, your wine and chocolate, and plenty of books."

"Bliss," I agree and promise to be back in a couple of days.

There's an interesting-looking bookshop café near our cottage, but it's closed today so I put that on my to do list as well.

Seb

Land's End to Cape Cornwall. Six and a half miles. What an exciting adventure. We took selfies near the iconic signpost at Land's End and set out for Sennen not far along the coast. It was a lovely day and there were several couples enjoying the sunshine. Rosa couldn't resist chatting, mostly they were dog walkers but a few keen coastal path followers too. At Penwith, very rocky with granite stones, there was a shipwreck jammed against the rocks, a sign explaining that the captain became unconscious and couldn't steer the ship. Intriguing. The signing along our route was varied, there were some posh granite signs near Land's End but then the normal acorn signs. I think we must have missed one, probably Rosa chatting again, as we went upward and lost the trail for a bit, then descended some very steep steps to the beach. Gwynver Beach is a pretty little cove and again there were many dog walkers enjoying the weather.

We got lost again, and clambered through some huge granite rocks, which was fine as we are both sure footed. I do not think Lara would be so fleet. It was all quite exciting with many notices, "Danger Mine Shafts. Keep to Footpath". We did lose the path again but eventually found a tiny trail to the top of a hill, all the time aiming for the Brisons, the two offshore rocks at Cape Cornwall, filmed for the *Poldark* tv series.

Lara

They arrive back from Land's End full of their adventure. We have a glass of prosecco each and I zone out, but actually the shipwreck which Seb photographed did look interesting, so I google "Shipwreck Penwith" and it transpires the ship, a German cargo vessel, was wrecked in 2003 when the chief officer caught his trousers in the lever of his chair, causing him to fall, bang his head and pass out. The six-man Polish crew were rescued, the chief officer came round, but it was too late to save the ship. I can't help thinking he wore the wrong trousers, poor chap.

After refreshments, Seb and Rosa decide "it will be good for you to get some fresh air, Lara. Let's go to Cape Cornwall." Naturally I succumb. It's only a mile or so from the cottage, there's a large National Trust car park, free as it's after 4pm, and I must say the coastline is truly majestic. We walk down the slipway to Priests Cove and gaze at *Poldark*'s the Brisons, glinting in the sunlight against the enormous crashing waves. Rosa and Seb are busy snapping away on their mobiles again, they must have unlimited storage. I shall refuse to look at the photos on our return though, I've been there, done it, gazed in awe; I don't need to look again.

***

Seb and Rosa have arranged to catch a Number 18 bus from St Just bus station to St Ives, via Penzance, at 9.07am. We have agreed to rendezvous in the kitchen at 8am.

At 5am Seb gets up to use the bathroom, then comes back to bed flicking through his phone. I turn over. At 6am Rosa is in the bathroom. I sigh. Is there no peace?

At 6.30 the entire cottage seems to be awake. "Lara," whispers Seb, "I think Rosa is awake." An unnecessary comment. "I'm thinking we could catch an earlier bus so we can have a longer day out. It's quite a difficult route, the app says."

"Fine. Whatever," I grumble. "We're all awake anyway. Are you sure there's an earlier bus?"

He starts to show me the bus timetable on his phone but I cannot be bothered and go downstairs to make tea.

"Don't worry about breakfast," says Seb magnanimously, when I return to bed, nursing my mug. "I've had a word with Rosa and she's all for it. We'll grab a bowl of cereal and some toast." I imagine Seb walking in on Rosa attired in either a black lacy vest top or a red and gold kimono and pull my trusty grey dressing gown tighter while I sip my tea.

Seb

St Ives to Carn Galver. Approx ten miles. Oh, my word! Rosa and I are totally shattered. This has been the most strenuous walk we have done, mainly because of the unforgiving terrain, the path being almost non existent for a large chunk of the way and the route being made up of rocks, stones and granite boulders.

Starting off from St Ives was easy, along a tarmac path. We spotted Godrevy Lighthouse in the distance behind us. After a while we paused for a rest on a bench, where there was a man with five golden labradors on leads. "Lovely day." He patted one of the dogs.

"Looks like you have your hands full," I replied, nodding towards his entourage. Rosa was cooing and patting them of course.

"On the walk then? The path to Zennor's dreadful. You'll need stamina. I'm an ex-para trooper and, believe me, it's tough going. Good luck."

The coastline is certainly rocky with fantastic views and the path is uneven; we had to climb over some huge boulders when the path disappeared completely, and on a few occasions we had to inch backwards because of the sheer steepness, clinging on almost vertically.

Rosa got chatting to a couple; the man was educating his female companion on the joys of the South West Coast Path. "I've walked the whole 630 miles" – he was naturally proud of the fact – "and this is the most arduous stretch of the entire route, because of the difficult terrain. We're doing a short walk today, as Lucy here is a novice."

Lucy, meanwhile, was examining Rosa and me closely. "I know you!" she cried. "Do you live near Barnstaple?" Soon she and Rosa were deep in conversation, but I knew we had no time to lose if we were to reach Carn Galver today.

We squelched through some boggy ground. I wished I had thought to wear my waterproof socks, which Rosa gave me for Christmas. There were some boardwalks over the worst of the bogs, but even so my feet got soaked. After clambering up a twenty-five-foot bridge of steep stone steps, we sank down to have our lunch by a rock overlooking the sea. Absolutely gorgeous. Worth the aches and pains.

On our way again, we passed Tregerthen and Zennor Head but decided we didn't have time to loiter and would aim to return another day. Two elderly men with walking sticks enquired, "Is it an easy path?"

We replied that it was only easy at that point, the rest was very hard going.

"There's a pub in Zennor if you fancy a pint," they chortled, but at this stage both Rosa and I realised we had to keep going or we would collapse.

I sent Lara a quick text and we staggered onward before heading inland to Carn Galver where she was waiting for us as planned. Our legs were aching but we had achieved nearly ten miles, our longest yet.

Lara

I receive a message at 4.15pm, having hovered around my phone for two hours. No signal before, so he says. Huh! They're nearly at Carn Galver Engine House (wherever that is) and can I drive along the road until I see them. It's not far and the road is passable for two cars most of the way. They're both in a state of collapse when I drop them off at the cottage before parking in the car park around the corner.

Seb just manages to light the log burner on his hands and knees, groaning. They've padded about in wet socks leaving damp patches. I grab the kitchen roll and mop up. What AM I doing!

They crawl upstairs for showers leaving the wet socks in a heap by the front door.

Now I've done my duty as chauffeur, I pour myself a hefty white wine, take a large slug, then follow them upstairs to shower and dress for the evening meal. I'm looking forward to the delights of the Kings Arms or the Commercial Inn, both of which have good menus. Mouth watering, I head downstairs to the kitchen only to be assailed by a pong. Oh no, the bin must need emptying from the Chinese takeaway remains. I hastily tie up the bag and deposit it in the wheelie bin outside. Grabbing my wine, I enter the living room where Seb is asleep, snoring on the sofa, one foot on the pouffe. The two pairs of walking boots are steaming by the hearth. My throat constricts, the boots are causing the pong! I pick them up gingerly by their laces and hastily sling them outside.

Rosa comes down, having had an hour's rest on her bed. She looks tired but attractively flushed with her blonde hair knotted in a loose ponytail. Seb looks quite grey and exhausted and is rubbing his left ankle. "I've twisted my ankle on the boulders. The steps were so irregular, we had to twist our feet sideways." He and Rosa grimace at each other and rub their ankles in unison.

"Well, you'll just have to hop to the Chinese takeaway won't you." I'm determined to show no leniency. No one's thought to ask me what I've been doing all day in solitude. "I presume we're having takeaway as you two are obviously in no fit state to go to the Kings Arms as planned."

They have the grace to look guilty but nod acquiescence. They're simply too shattered.

After supper they reminisce about their day and show me a multitude of pictures, including one of some cute labradors. "They were show dogs," explains Seb. "The owner let us take a photo of them, I knew you'd like them."

I'm particularly interested in the photo of Gurnard's Head. I've googled the inn there and it looks fabulous. I wouldn't be surprised if they nipped in for a lunch of sole meuniere and prosecco. No signal, my foot! Also, methinks there is too much rubbing of ankles. I shall see what they're like in the morning. If they're that bad, can they seriously be up for another walk?

Rosa relates an account of meeting a woman from Barnstaple, Lucy someone, who recognised her and Seb from our dancing classes. I'm not pleased. Does Lucy think Seb has moved on from his plain, dumpy wife to a new glamorous partner, or am I so insignificant that Lucy doesn't remember me anyway?

I throw the takeaway cartons angrily into the sink. There must be hundreds of folk on the coastal path thinking Seb and Rosa are a couple. There are probably loads of photos of them on Instagram or Snapchat or whatever people have on their devices. I'm not savvy with any of them and absolutely refuse to even have Facebook.

"I'm sorry, I'm going to bed," says Rosa about 9.30pm. "Is that okay? I'm shattered."

As Seb is nodding sleepily again, I'm glad for an early night myself. "Yes, you go on. We'll be up ourselves in a few minutes. See you in the morning." I have plans for Seb. I prod him awake. "Time to go up. Rosa's already gone."

"Uh oh." He staggers to his feet, wincing.

I'm quite wide awake now. This is a holiday after all, worries about ploughing, calving, shortage of red diesel pushed to the back of my mind. I've had a good day browsing in St Just, eaten half a tub of mini cheddars and two bars of Crunchie for lunch, read one of my charity shop paperbacks and relaxed. Okay, it was annoying having to collect them late afternoon, but after three glasses of wine, I feel a surge of affection for the old codger. He's not so bad, and although he can be an irritant, he's MY irritant. I stroke his little paunch. There's a slight snore. I stroke harder. "Uhh." Seb jerks. "Oh, hello, where are we? Have we reached Zennor yet?"

I recoil. What is he on about? He's already snoring again. Comatose. Sighing, I turn on my tablet to watch *Naked Attraction* on All 4, at least there'll be a wiggle or two.

Seb

I researched the rest of the walk on my app and it looked much easier from Carn Galver to Cape Cornwall.

After a good night's sleep, I was looking forward to completing the last section. I wasn't sure we would be up to it after yesterday's marathon, but Rosa was keen not to waste the day so Lara drove us to the Engine House about 11am, pausing briefly for us to pick up a couple of pasties from Warrens Bakery.

We walked from Porthmoina Cove towards Morvah along some narrow tracks with a steep cliff edge, almost having to walk sideways in places. Some of it was more a muddy trail than a path. The coastline here is very rugged and the waves were crashing against the rocks. I was envious of Rosa's pink bobble hat as the wind was whistling past my ears. Looking across, we saw Pendeen Lighthouse, which looks fairly new, gleaming white against the blue sky, but having done my research, I know it was built in 1900 as an aid for vessels around Pendeen and Gurnard's Head. We had to negotiate a series of steep descents and ascents before reaching a small deserted sandy beach. I think this was Portheras Cove, isolated with no obvious road access and a "No Lifeguards" sign.

The path towards Pendeen was very wet and our feet got soaked again. I must get a new pair of boots. Past the lighthouse there is a big inlet, so we walked inland where there was a car park and several sightseers. From thereon, it was real *Poldark* country with lots of old mine workings. Funny to imagine how busy it must have been back in the mining heyday. The Geevor Tin Mine, the largest preserved mining site in the UK, closed in 1990 and is now a visitors centre.

The path improved greatly towards Levant Mine, although there was one tricky steep descent and a near impossible climb over rocks; there were footholds but it was almost like abseiling without a safety rope.

We got back to the cottage just after 4pm. A lot later than I had anticipated, but it was seven miles and we would have been quicker if Rosa had not chatted to so many people. We spotted one lone red glove on the path, which we popped onto a gorse bush after looking vainly for its owner, then Rosa was on a mission to find its missing partner. She stopped countless people, enquiring if they had lost a glove and, convinced she had found the right lady who was sporting a red hat, lingered for over five minutes laughing about lost gloves, hats and scarves.

We knew we were nearly back when we saw St Just, Cape Cornwall and the Brisons beckoning us in the near distance.

Lara

Neither of them can walk in a straight line when they fall through the door. They do at least whip off their soaking socks and boots and leave them dripping outside before wobbling crabwise into the living room. "Drink," rasps Seb.

Rosa opens her mouth but no sound comes out.

I wonder why they're so exhausted? You'd think they'd be used to it by now. I pour them a large glass of prosecco, avoiding looking at their bare, damp feet snuggled together on the mat.

"Hungry?"

They nod feebly.

I prepare a tray of cheese, biscuits, salmon pate and olives, wondering why the two pasties didn't fill them up.

"It was strenuous," mumbles Seb through a mouthful of Cornish brie. "I didn't think it would take so long today, but there were many obstacles along the way."

After they've recovered slightly, we go through the whole interminable monotony of the endless photos of rocks, cliffs, coves, steps, signs, mines, lighthouses, stiles, car parks, Seb posing on the cliff edge, Rosa smiling out to sea, etc. etc. etc.

I'm not letting them get away with staying in again tonight, so I've booked the Kings Arms for 8pm. I've googled the menu and it looks good, lots of choice, burgers, loin of hake, gammon steak and so on. They're still doing their crabwalk when we venture to the pub just before 8pm, but manage to relax in the mellow atmosphere, perusing the wine list. We've already quaffed a bottle in the cottage, so settle on just a glass each, large of course. I order a shiraz, Seb a merlot, Rosa a rosé. When the wine arrives we all take a sip. "Oh dear," says Rosa. "I'm not sure I like this."

"I'll swap." Seb's response is instant.

"I'm not sure I like mine either." I throw in my two pennyworth for good measure, to gauge Seb's reaction.

He doesn't flinch, in fairness. Somehow we all end up swapping glasses; Rosa has my shiraz (I look at it longingly), I have the merlot, Seb (the loser) has the rosé. Actually, it's quite funny and we're soon giggling. At least, I'm giggling, those two are on the verge of manic hysterics. It's not THAT funny.

I hope we don't swap dinners. Or swap anything, come to think of it. I'm not into swapping. I've suddenly sobered up.

Back at the cottage, they stumble upstairs while I pour myself a nightcap with the intent of consummating the holiday. Seb had two glasses of rosé (what's wrong with him?) in the pub; he must be mellow. Rosa's falling asleep after two large shirazes, so she'll be oblivious to the thin walls. I march purposefully into the bedroom, seductively loosening the shoulder of my Primark tee shirt.

Seb's in bed, flat on his back, eyes closed.

"Lara, is that you?"

Who else would it be? "Do you fancy a nip of my nightcap?" I whisper in his ear.

"No thanks, love," he slurs sleepily. "I can't move. I think I've sprained something. It might be my back. I can't feel anything from the waist down."

"I'm sure I can do something about that," I murmur, stroking his chest.

Silence. Snore. No go AGAIN. Good thing I have *Naked Attraction* on repeat.

Abba is belting out "Dancing Queen" at a 1970s fancy dress party. Disco lights are flashing and the overhead lighting is dim. I'm sitting on a captain's chair in turquoise flares and a pink kaftan, sipping a glass of rosé. Seb and Rosa are dancing with a group of friends, and everyone is having a great time, bopping, shimmying and jiving. Rosa looks like Agnetha in a white satin jumpsuit and

Seb's wearing flares and a tight orange shirt with a huge hang-glider collar and a gold medallion.

I drink half my wine and decide to join them, but my flares are stuck around the chair legs. No matter how much I struggle I cannot move, and my bottom is wedged between the chair arms. I try to wave at Seb but he's in a large circle of dancers and cannot see me. A labrador comes along, gives me a sniff and jumps onto my lap, settling down for a comfortable snooze, his head on my chest.

The music changes to "Sailing" by Rod Stewart and by peering over the dog's ears I can just make out Seb and Rosa smooching and swaying to the music, eyes closed. Another labrador comes along and jumps up on my chest to join his companion.

I wake with cramp in my leg and two pillows over my face. I can't breathe. Flinging off the pillows I gingerly sidle off the bed to stretch my leg.

Seb is already up and I can hear voices downstairs.

Our last day. AND I've done it again: allowed myself to be pressured into going for "a little walk with us, Lara. It's gorgeous".

We're on the top path out of Cape Cornwall towards Sennen. Apparently, I must see the mine shafts and open expanses of ocean. It's lovely, admittedly, but I have thin trainers, not state-of-the-art hiking boots, and can feel every pebble and stone. I sympathise when a lady approaching us stumbles on her black low-heeled shoes. "I know," I murmur, "wrong shoes."

Rosa and Seb are striding ahead. Strange really as they agreed they were too tired to do another long stretch today. They toyed with the idea of walking a section from Land's End towards Penzance but decided to leave it for our next visit. Obviously, I wasn't going to argue as it would have meant my being chauffeur again. Tired or not, they seem pretty fit to me as I puff up the hill. "Come on, Lara, the view's great." There's a large parking area at the top of the trail, several people are walking dogs, children are playing and there's a horse rider in the distance. I sit on a bench whilst they go off looking for mines. If they fall in, they've brought it on themselves.

We walk back more slowly. The path is quite narrow in places for folk to pass and I sense a reluctance in Rosa for the holiday to end. She picks a few daffodils growing wild along the hedge. "These will look nice on the kitchen table."

On our return we shower, open the wine and peruse the Chinese takeaway menu. Having decided on lemon chicken, king prawns with cashews, sweet and sour pork and an extra large fried rice, Seb places the order. Great. Rosa and I start laying the table and open a second bottle of wine. She snips the ends off the daffodils and pops the blooms in a small jug at the centre of the table. By the time Seb returns with the food, we're quite giggly.

"Oh lovely. We've warmed the plates. I'll lay a teacloth over the table mats to save any drips from the Chinese; you know how it can stain."

Rosa busies herself with serving spoons while Seb starts chopping spring onions. "Here," he announces, proud of the fact he has helped with the preparation.

"What?" Rosa and I look at the chopping board on the worktop with the "spring onions" then at each other before bursting into uncontrollable laughter.

Seb looks bemused.

Rosa and I cannot speak. The tears are streaming down our faces. I think I may have wet myself! We finally splutter, "That's not spring onions, they're daffodil stems."

I escape upstairs to change my knickers whilst Rosa explains to Seb that she left the daffodil stems on the worktop. We have a delicious meal, minus spring onions, chortling every few minutes.

Chapter Twenty-Two

Land's End to Porthleven

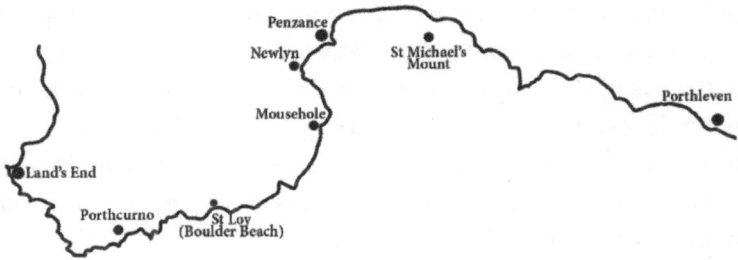

Lara

The long anticipated adventure around Land's End and Penzance has arrived and Seb's determined to make the most of it. He's talked nonstop about bus times, walk times, tide times, weather conditions and cottages by the coast until my mind is completely timed out and I shut out his incessant wittering. We arrive in Penzance and, even though he's checked the bus app a thousand times, we must park by the bus station to double check the situation.

Instead of going straight to our rented cottage we drive to the Merry Maidens Stone Circle for a recce prior to tomorrow's big event. There's a very long congested hill out of Newlyn so I sincerely hope the bus route fits as I don't fancy weaving between the parked cars and steady flow of traffic myself. Merry Maidens Stone Circle (first recorded in the seventeenth century) consists of nineteen granite stones forming a circle, in a field south of St Buryan. Local folklore being that nineteen maidens were turned into stone there for dancing on a Sunday.

We find the bus stop with the footpath to St Loy, the bus route turning inland at this point to St Buryan.

It's well past 4 o'clock when we eventually locate our cottage in Penzance overlooking the harbour, with great views across to St Michael's Mount. We're lucky enough to find a parking space right outside, so we unload our bags with minimum effort. The cottage is upside down with two bedrooms and a bathroom off the hallway, a spacious living/dining room and a tiny kitchen upstairs. There's only enough room for one person in the kitchen but that's okay, I doubt I shall be cooking much with so many restaurants and takeaways nearby.

Seb

St Loy to Land's End. Approx eight miles. Rosa and I caught the 9.03 Land's End coaster at the Jubilee Pool bus stop and paid £4 for return tickets to Land's End. The driver agreed to drop us off at the St Buryan turn off, just up the road from the Merry Maiden stone circle, near a layby with the footpath to St Loy, signed "To the Coast Path". After about twenty minutes of walking through a field, a path, a road and a track, the acorn sign with yellow arrows came into view and we could see the sea through the trees. At a right turn the path continued through a woodland trail before opening out with a vista to the sea with bobbing fishing boats aplenty. The track narrowed through a tangle of overgrown gorse and brambles, so we were glad we wore jeans, then we scrambled over huge granite rocks before steps down to sea level, over a small wooden bridge, then ascending again. Looking back we could see a small waterfall at the base of the steps.

A steep downhill drop took us to Penberth Cove, National Trust property, quiet, lovely and unspoilt.

Up another set of steps, with a sign "Ponies grazing", we came across four ponies, they took no notice of us and quietly continued munching. We paused for a chat with a lone walker who had taken a very early taxi ride to Land's End from Penzance and was proposing to achieve the entire walk in one day! Naturally he was in a hurry; sixteen plus miles is not something Rosa and I would contemplate. We saw several walkers heading towards us. We appeared to be the only ones going towards Land's End.

After "Treryn Dinas", the site of an Iron Age castle, the path became easier. We were fascinated to see a white stone pyramid monument that marked the place where the wooden hut that housed the end of the submarine telegraph cable used to be; the first cable station in Porthcurno being built in 1870 and closed in 1970.

Porthcurno Beach is stunningly beautiful, an idyllic semicircular bay of golden sands and crystal clear water surrounded by rugged cliffs, sheltered and unspoilt; the famous Minack outdoor theatre being a short way up the cliff.

Continuing along the path, we came across St Levan's Well, legendarily reputed to have medicinal qualities, before reaching Porthgwarra Cove, a charming, tranquil, and very picturesque little gem of a place and boasting a café where we were thankful to stop for a snack and make use of the toilets.

Resuming the path after our welcome break we passed Gwennap Head National Coastwatch Institution, then along the top we walked through a herd of Red Devon cattle with calves and a bull. They were sitting quietly enjoying the sun on their backs and took no notice of us. I took a photo to show Lara.

After pausing briefly on some granite rocks overlooking a bay with interesting-looking caves, we could soon see Land's End ahead and the Longships Lighthouse (1875).

On reaching our destination we checked out the bus times, which ran hourly back to Penzance and found we had time for lunch and a cocktail in the Land's End Hotel.

Lara

I watch from the window to make sure they get on the bus and do not skive off to the Scilly Isles for the day, have a coffee, then decide to explore Penzance in the sunshine. Walking past the harbour, I traverse the swing bridge and see signs for the Scillonian Ferry day trips to the Scilly Isles.

There are some gift shops along the front, opposite the large car park and the bus station, the usual chain stores in Market Jew Street: Boots, Smiths, Poundland etc. but also many interesting boutiques and shops, pasty cafés, antique stores, charity shops. These continue up the High Street with more clothes shops, greengrocers, knick-knack shops and stalls along with a bakery, cafés and more. Walking back down I treat myself to a coffee and teacake before heading back to the cottage via a shortcut through the churchyard with spectacular views over the sea.

They finally straggle in about 4.45pm. I'd practically given up on their returning at all by this time so I bang down two glasses of prosecco before they can speak and stomp into the kitchen for a bowl of Kettle crisps. Have they eaten or not? Frankly I don't care. Seb has not kept me informed except an odd text: "Waiting for bus".

After a shower and change of clothes, I'm regaled with their adventures of the day, which seem to consist of rock climbing, scenic coves and the views to Land's End, and subjected to hundreds of photos, although I note that Seb whips past the last one of Land's End Hotel, so I only catch a glimpse.

They're too exhausted to go out to eat, even though I've researched several great-sounding restaurants nearby: the Dolphin, Admiral Benbow, the Boatshed and a Thai among others, so we end up having a Chinese takeaway from the Sea Palace just round the corner.

Seb

Praa Sands to Porthleven. Approx four and a half miles. We decided on this short stretch today, as the weather forecast didn't bode well, before we return to St Loy to finish the Land's End to Penzance section tomorrow. It was easy going. The three of us caught the U4 bus at Penzance bus station to Porthleven. Saying goodbye to Lara, Rosa and I got off the bus near the car park in Praa Sands, a short stretch from the beach, after which we walked up some steps, past a Lifeguard Hut, and along the cliff-top path overlooking the sea before the path turned to tarmac past some 1930s bungalows with views across the Atlantic.

A sign informed us "Porthleven via Rinsey Head 4 ¼m". This was old mining territory again, with signs "Caution Mineshaft". The prominent house on the headland of Rinsey is privately owned and has been a setting for television programmes. The cliffs and beach are National Trust.

The path at this point was triple wired, presumably to prevent cattle from straying. We were prevented from the walkway to the beach as "Danger No Access".

Being a very blustery day, the waves were pounding and the gusts nearly blew Rosa off her feet. After Trewavas Head and Beacon Crag, we came across a memorial in memory of twenty-two Porthleven fishermen and mariners drowned on this part of the coast. We were soon heading towards Porthleven and into the area known as Breageside.

Lara

Seb and Rosa get off the U4 bus from Penzance at Praa Sands, while I continue to Porthleven, the bus driver skilfully negotiating the narrow roads out of Praa village. After a quick browse through the shops I take refuge in a café, the Nauti, for a welcome coffee and share my table with a couple on holiday, having a very pleasant chat about stupid walks, books, Agatha Christie, *Poldark* and *Wycliffe*. My phone pings, Seb: "Making good progress. Have you found anywhere for lunch?" And do I want to meet them on the path? No, I do not. It's blowing a gale and I haven't got a hat.

I order another coffee and take out my crossword before meeting them along the curve on the opposite side of the double harbour. The harbour itself is magnificent and surely one of the best in Cornwall. There are many great places to eat but the fabulous Kota Kai is closed, boo hoo. The Mussel Shoal shack looks good, but it's too blustery to eat outside so we end up in the Harbour Inn, finding a table for three near a window. It's comfortable and cosy with charming low beams and William Morris wallpaper. When Seb comes back from the bar he complains, "£30 for three drinks. I didn't ask the price. But I suppose this is Cornwall; North Devon's cheaper." The extensive menu offers a large range of tasty dishes and the service is prompt so we're soon relaxing in the pleasant ambience.

We get swept back to the bus stop in a howling gale and are thankful to reach the cottage upright, although Seb and Rosa are not upright; they seem to have jelly legs and are wobbling around.

After collapsing on the settees with a large glass of wine each (thank you Asda, 25% off six deal), they start to recover and warble on about scenery, mine shafts, engine houses and rocks, until Seb announces, "I'm off for a shower. I really fancy a relaxing soak in the bath though."

Rosa nods in agreement. They both wobble downstairs. I frown. What's going on? Is Seb having a shower while Rosa's in the bath? After five minutes of doors banging and muttered oaths echoing up the stairs, I can stand it no longer and go to investigate.

Even though I had a glass of wine in the Harbour Inn and another half a one here, I'm only mildly tipsy, but I blink my eyes in disbelief as I round the bottom of the stairs to see Rosa on her hands and knees in the hallway fiddling with Seb's lower half! In his dressing gown! What the hell? Seb's standing legs akimbo with a glazed expression on his face; Rosa's working hard at something just down from his stomach. I gasp.

"Oh, Lara," Seb grimaces. "My dressing gown cord's knotted itself and I'm stuck. Rosa's trying to undo it."

What, with her teeth?

I turn on the light, it's dim in the hallway. Rosa stands up, smiling triumphantly. "Great," says Seb, "I can have my shower now."

Rosa disappears into her room whilst I reel upstairs for a strong cup of tea with a shot of brandy.

Seb

St Loy to Penzance. Over eight and a half miles. We caught the 9.03 Land's End coaster again to the St Buryan turn off at the Merry Maidens Stone Circle and started off down the footpath, which we soon realised was very wet after yesterday's storm.

The path took us over the beach at St Loy, colloquially called Boulder Beach and we could see why. There are massive boulders which apparently fell off the cliffs before the Ice Age, and the process of thawing, freezing and being washed by the sea produced the smooth, large boulders present today.

Leaving the beach, the acorn sign pointed up the cliff where the path was sodden and muddy, due to the heavy overnight rain, and our boots and socks soon became soaked.

We clambered over some large rocks very close to the cliff edge; this was rather an endurance test, reminiscent of St Ives to Carn Galver, before squelching through a long meandering track on a descent. We paused to look at the memorial for the shipwreck of the cargo ship, Union Star and the Penlee Lifeboat, 19th December 1981, wrecked in hurricane force conditions with loss of all lives.

Steps up again took us to where we could look down over Tater Du Lighthouse, constructed in the 1960s to be fully automatic. The track narrowed with high growth on each side before we reached a huge boulder perched on top of a cliff, where the path disappeared to become steep boulders to climb over, a brief return to a short path then back to rock climbing.

We met a couple with no rucksacks or warm clothing who said they were walking from Penzance to Land's End. Rosa and I looked at each other aghast. "You won't do it in a day without having set off really early unless you're Olympic athletes. It's strenuous."

"Oh, we'll be fine." They waved airily.

Rosa and I slid down some steep rocks to Lamorna Cove, a lovely, peaceful spot, and rested for a while before ascending more rocks to reach a reasonable path. "Porthcurno 4 ¼m, Marazion 9m."

After a while there was more rock climbing and we came across a couple attempting to scale a three-foot-high granite rock. The man heaved himself over, but the poor lady could not manage it. "Try backwards dear, and grab that branch of gorse," he encouraged.

After several attempts she managed to haul herself over backwards and nodded to us. "It's going to get worse," we sympathised, wondering if they could keep going.

"Oh I know, dears. I couldn't do the St Ives walk at all and I only just managed Zennor, but I'm going to give it a go."

Rosa and I agreed that South West walkers are determined characters.

After they had disappeared, we leapt over a boulder just to prove we could.

After a sign "Kemyel Crease, Nature Reserve", a conifer plantation by the Cornwall Wildlife Trust, we rounded a corner to see Penzance ahead with the path becoming the road through

Mousehole, past the Penlee Lifeboat Station (closed 1983), along the harbour with the small St Clements Isle just offshore and then easy walking through Newlyn.

Lara

"I'm not sure what time we'll be back," says Seb. "The walking app seems to suggest it's difficult and easy in equal parts. We'll probably have a snack lunch somewhere, maybe Mousehole, so don't worry about food."

I notice that he and Rosa exchange a glance. Pecking me on the cheek, he and Rosa hasten to the corner for the Land's End coaster.

I settle down with a coffee and ponder my day, spotting Seb's printout of the bus timetables on the floor. Hmm, maybe I'll leave it an hour or so then set off to Mousehole myself. I may even spot them having a crafty drink somewhere.

The bus takes about ten minutes to reach Mousehole fishing port, which is part of the South West Coastal Path I see, noting the yellow arrows and acorns. It's a lovely little harbour village with quaint, narrow winding streets, cafés, galleries and gift shops with postcards and ice cream. I note the Ship Inn and the Old Coastguard Inn and wonder if Seb and Rosa will eat there; they both look great.

On my return, I stop off at Newlyn, a busy fishing port with many art galleries, fantastic fish shops with amazing arrays of fresh fish of every description, pasty shops, cafés and restaurants. I spot a Michelin star restaurant, the Tolcarne Inn, which seems busy with people sitting outside on benches with dogs at their feet.

I buy a pasty from Aunty May's Pasty Company to take home and wonder again where Seb and Rosa are.

They stagger in at 4.40, giggling, and as I plonk down a couple glasses of prosecco, I'm sure I can smell a whiff of alcohol. I bring out some crisps, crackers and cheese but they don't touch it. "We had a snack lunch, Lara. We're fine thanks."

Seb

Praa Sands to Penzance. Approx nine and a half miles. We caught the bus to Praa, getting off at the stop round the corner from the general store, and walked to the footpath past a row of modern houses on our right. The huge, sandy beach already had several dog walkers out and about.

The path was relatively easy to walk for the whole route. We admired Sydney Cove (National Trust), a delightful secluded beach, and caught a glimpse of a large property built on the cliff edge. After traversing a wooden walkway, we saw a grand-looking entrance and I found out later it is Porth-en-Alls at Prussia Cove.

After passing an ancient-looking winch, presumably used originally for winching boats, we took a small optional detour to HMS Warspite with fabulous views across the Atlantic. Hugging the coast all the way through Cudden Point, we could see St Michael's Mount ahead. The path became a series of steps but no steep climbs. We were in a hurry to beat the brewing storm, dark clouds gathering overhead, so we pressed on, only loitering slightly through Perranuthnoe, a gorgeous beach and village, quite unspoilt and not over developed, with cabbage fields right next to the coast. We had serious location envy.

A sign informed us "Marazion 2 ¼m".

Boat Cove was a small rocky bay and then we came to Trenow Cove where there was a sign "Danger. Footpath closed for Public Safety" so we headed up to the main road at Marazion. We chatted to a lone walker with a European accent, who was walking the entire route from Minehead to Poole and was today walking as far as he could before getting a bus back to Penzance Youth Hostel. It seems the South West Coast Path really is internationally famous, as since we started we have met and chatted to many walkers of all nationalities.

We walked through Marazion with its gift shops and cafés, used the handy loos, then hastened on towards St Michael's Mount, looking imposing with its causeway visible at low tide. St Michael's Mount is a tidal island and a civil parish, managed by both the National Trust and the St Aubyn family, open to the public and, as well as the castle, perched magnificently atop the rocky gardens, home to islanders living in the village cottages.

We walked through the spacious car park, across a footbridge over the sand to a concrete six-foot path/cycle track which took us back to Penzance past the impressive train depot, waves crashing against Penzance harbour as the storm accelerated.

Lara

Sebastian and Rosa crawl up the stairs groaning, "We pegged it out to beat the storm. It was easy walking but long. We've walked nine miles in a short time."

I interpret this as meaning they have walked the route in one go this time instead of stopping for snacks/drinks/food/prosecco/rests/caves/rum/chocolate/goodness knows what else.

Seb, exhausted, subsides onto the settee and without speaking indicates he wants me to bring the wine glass to his mouth! This is above and beyond, so I ignore him and place two drinks on the table between him and Rosa. I'm not providing food as we've already arranged to go to Wetherspoons for a late lunch.

After a while they recover and descend to have a shower and change into dry clothes. Seb's dropped his backpack on the floor, with water bottle, tissues and papers spilling out. So, tidying up, I obviously have a quick look to discover a tiny packet of blue pills and a receipt for £85 for the Tolcarne Inn in the bottom of the bag. I'm puzzled by the pills and cannot think what they can be, but I'm furious about the receipt. Snack my foot! They had a Michelin star lunch in Newlyn!

Seb comes upstairs. "Ready for Wetherspoons? I'm starving."

Wetherspoons is heaving but we find a tiny table stuck behind a pillar and Seb goes to the bar to order fish and chips, a Tennessee burger and a pasta bowl. I reckon my meal including a large glass of wine has cost £9, and it's good. I'm not complaining; the fish is tasty and the chips are hot but Michelin star it's not. I resist the urge to spit into his rum and Coke.

On our return we go through the inevitable photos, then Rosa retires to her room for "a quick rest" before Seb decides to do the same. Four hours later they reappear but I've had enough. I've given up on going to the Dolphin, made myself cheese on toast, watched three episodes of *Wycliffe* and am going to bed to plan a strategy. If Seb thinks he's getting away with a Michelin star lunch, he can think again. I've hidden his blue pills.

Leaving them in the living room watching Film Four, I get into bed with Mary Berry and a notebook and pen. I mark various recipes and make bullet points of a revenge plan forming in my mind. However, I need a cup of tea so put on my dressing gown and go upstairs to boil the kettle.

Seb and Rosa are talking about me I know. They both stop speaking abruptly when I enter the room and Seb quickly and inexpertly squeaks, "Oh yes that stretch was arduous wasn't it?"

What's going on? What were they saying? I'm sure I heard Rosa say "Bless". Bless really aggravates me. I know it's supposed to be akin to "Ahh, how sweet" but somehow it always sounds so condescending. Seb said it the other day when I inadvertently put a box of tissues in the fridge. And the Tesco cashier said it when I tried to pay for my groceries with the loyalty card instead of my bank card. Honestly! It's an easy enough mistake. I can't be the first person to have done it. I also have a feeling it's aimed at older people. You don't say "Bless" to a child when they've put a box of tissues in the fridge and left the door open. You don't say "Bless" to a child if they're snappy or forgetful. Now I know I'm snappy. It's nothing new although I do seem to be worse lately. Seb looks at me quite warily sometimes, as if he thinks I'm about to fly off the handle. Well, I haven't been the one sneaking off to Michelin star restaurants for hours on end or having huddled conversations on my mobile at the bottom of the garden.

I can just make out Seb by the bed, illuminated dimly by the streetlight through the window blinds. Rosa's on her knees tugging at his boxer shorts until they reach his knees. There's a row of small blue pills lined up neatly along his groin area. "Let's not waste time," whispers Rosa and drags him, hopping, into the wardrobe.

"Lara, Lara." Seb nudges me. "Are you awake? You've been talking in your sleep again. Something about wardrobes."

"What? I'm fine. Can you make me a cup of tea please? While I have a quick shower. I'm awfully hot." After he's gone upstairs, I investigate the wardrobe but it all seems normal, my hoody, two jumpers and spare jeans hanging neatly as before. I'm about to close the door when I spy a single long blonde hair on a coat hanger.

Seb comes back and puts down the tea. "Are you still having a shower? Your tea will get cold."

It's almost time to return home. They've been out together for four consecutive days and I think it's about time I asserted myself. "Seb, I've not been out much since we've been here. Shall we go on the Land's End coaster round trip?"

Seb seems reluctant but cannot wriggle out of it, so at 9.35am we're on the top outside deck of the bus, hanging on to our hoods in the cool breeze. Rosa has decided to spend the morning looking around Penzance.

We allow ourselves an hour at Land's End to look at the views, but the sharp gusts of wind are cold so I suggest a coffee in the Land's End Hotel. "Are you sure?" asks Seb, "There are other coffee shops."

"No. I fancy the hotel." I march towards the door.

"Hello again, sir," says the barman, presiding over the coffee machine and some tempting-looking cakes.

Seb smiles grimly. "Just an Americano and a hot chocolate please."

"I'll bring them over to your table, sir. The one you had the other day is free."

We sit in a window seat overlooking the sea and I peruse the menu. "Good menu, Seb." I look at him to gauge his reaction. "Lots of delicious-sounding salads, scampi in the basket with chips and slaw looks good and, ooh, some great cocktails."

Seb looks discomfited but I persist. "I suppose you and Rosa sampled one or two?"

"We had one and a salad. Shall we go? I need the loo."

I wait for Seb outside the loos but seeing him stuff something in his pocket, say, "You go on out, I'll just be a minute. I think I left my gloves in the Ladies."

Seeing him disappear to admire the view I quickly dash into the Gents and discover a machine selling little blue pills. Viagra? What's going on?

We rejoin the bus and head around the coast via Sennen, St Just, Zennor, St Ives, Carbis Bay, Marazion and back to Penzance.

Chapter Twenty-Three

A Friendly Chat

Lara

I'm out for a coffee with a friend. More of an acquaintance really. She text me out of the blue and suggested we meet for a catch-up. We both have a steaming mug of coffee and a slice of carrot cake and chat desultorily for a while about family and work, but I can see she's building up to something. Sure enough: "Lara," she says casually, "don't take this the wrong way but Seb and Rosa were seen together in the Land's End Hotel, looking rather cosy. I thought you should know. Joanne was on holiday there for a few days but they didn't see her. You remember Joanne, don't you?"

"Yes, of course. I was in Cornwall too."

"Really? I thought she said it was just the two of them."

"It would have been. They were having lunch, I expect, after walking the coast path. I was in Penzance. I don't do the walks. Anyway, how is Joanne? I haven't seen her for ages."

"She's fine. Sends her love to you. Shall we do this again soon? Maybe invite her too?"

"Yes, that would be great. I don't have a lot of spare time but we can squeeze in a coffee together," I prevaricate.

"Okay, Lara." My friend picks up her bag. "Are you sure everything's okay?" She squeezes my arm, hesitates then pats my hand. "I'm just concerned for you. It's not the first time they've been seen together. Someone said they saw them a few times in Hartland." She looks so anxious that I give her a hug.

"Thanks, Anne, you're a real friend, but don't worry. Seb and I are fine, honestly. See you soon. I must dash to the supermarket. Good to see you."

I escape, nearly tripping over in my rush. I abandon the supermarket and sit in the car. I cannot bear the thought of whispered gossip circulating and I'm certainly not going to add fuel to the fire by divulging anything to Anne or Joanne.

Chapter Twenty-Four

Porthleven to the Lizard

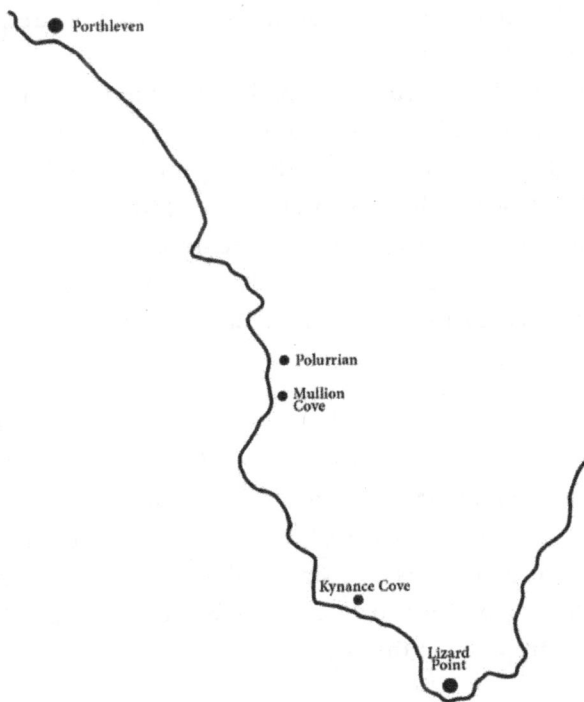

Lara

Sebastian and I are having a leisurely Saturday evening dinner after a hectic day of seeing grandchildren, logging trees in the far woods and other outside chores. I've prepared a Moroccan chicken dish, rice and vegetables with enough left over for another meal for Bobby tomorrow. We're sharing a bottle of wine and once we're replete, Seb says, "Will you be long? I'll just pack my bag and then we'll finish the bottle upstairs." He arms himself with the wine and glasses. "Don't be long."

I whizz round the kitchen, making sure the worktops are clean and clutter free, drape the wet washing on the airer, check the fridge and hasten upstairs.

"I'm so excited," Seb calls happily when I'm in the doorway, ready for wine, and some serious smooching. He's kneeling by the bed, gazing enraptured at the map of Cornwall. "I can't wait." His voice is thick with emotion. "Lizard to Mullion is going to be a fantastic experience." He traces the route lovingly then turns to his phone to double check the walking app.

"Great." I sigh and stomp off to have a long bath.

Next morning, we're up bright and early for the two-and-a-quarter-hour drive to Porthleven, waving goodbye to Bobby, who is no doubt looking forward to a couple of quiet days looking after the livestock and heating the meals I've left for him in the fridge. Rosa turns up at 8am and we set off with bags, wine box, wellies, boots, raincoats, etc. The forecast is good but it's as well to be prepared in the South West.

We park along the quay in Porthleven. It's mild but breezy so we don hats and scarves before setting off together. I start off with them for about ten minutes then wave them on their way before going back to the impressive harbour to visit one or two of the open gift shops prior to setting the satnav for the Polurrian Bay Hotel. It's relatively easy to find, though I panic slightly at the double roundabout outside Helston until I spot the sign "The Lizard". Mr Nav tries to direct me down a small road "unsuitable for motors" but I ignore him and stick to the main road; thank goodness, as I'm soon sailing through Mullion without a hitch.

The hotel is beautiful, perched right on top of the cliff overlooking the pounding waves of the Atlantic. It's too early to check in. "3pm," the receptionist informs me, "but I'll come and find you when it's ready." I grab a novel from the car, order a glass of Sauvignon blanc from the bar and plonk myself down in a window seat in the enormous lounge overlooking the sea.

It's about an hour before my phone starts pinging with messages from Sebastian saying they can see the hotel and will soon be with me. It's a good half hour before they turn up, but I'm kept amused by a trio of musicians setting up their gear in front of the window and tuning their guitars, ready for an afternoon jam session. I've restrained myself from ordering the afternoon tea and prosecco that comes with our deal, even though my stomach's rumbling as I haven't eaten anything other than a paltry breakfast at 7.30am and a quick stop for a coffee and bun en route. I didn't want to order on my own and didn't think to bring a sandwich, and besides, the deal comes with afternoon tea so it's hopefully worth waiting for.

At last, the windswept hikers arrive, but by the time Sebastian has booked us into our rooms, adjacent on the ground floor, unpacked the car and swapped hiking boots for trainers, it's getting on for 3.30pm.

Our afternoon tea is huge and delivered on three wooden platters: dainty crustless sandwiches, scones, cream and jam, various cakes and the welcome glass of prosecco. We tuck in with gusto before heaving a sigh of relief and relaxing. Seb and Rosa discuss their walk, informing me that they waved at the hotel from the monument half a mile along the coast as they were convinced I'd be watching from the window. Huh, I think, I was reading my book and watching the trio, not anxiously awaiting their return.

We spend an hour or so in the heated indoor pool and jacuzzi before returning to our rooms to rest and dress for dinner, booked for eight. Over dinner the talk is mostly of the next day's adventurous walk from the Lizard to Mullion and the wonders of Kynance Cove. Unfortunately, the weather forecast doesn't bode well. Rosa even suggests that they abandon the walk and stay in the hotel with me, as it's such a good place. Really! I thought we'd come for the stupid walks, not the three of us sharing a jolly.

Seb

Porthleven to Polurrian Cove. Approx six and a half miles. Leaving the car by the harbour, we walked around the corner on a cobbled road above Porthleven Sands. Lara came with us for a short distance. We turned right towards Loe Bar, went through a small car park, then a slight ascent up a zigzag path before descending to Loe Bar Beach which has a large freshwater lake.

We strolled on to Gunwalloe Cove and explored the church, which has featured in *Wycliffe* and *Poldark* and then hastened on along the cliff top past Poldhu Nursing Home and on to the Polurrian Hotel, perched magnificently over the sandy cove.

This was an easy walk with splendid views. We could have stopped at the Halzephron Inn for refreshments, but we knew Lara would be waiting for us to have the Polurrian afternoon tea.

Lara

Next morning the breakfast is excellent, the sun is shining, Sebastian is buoyant and looking forward to the challenge. Rosa and I both look at the dark clouds on the horizon and think this may be the calm before the storm. We drive the few miles to the Lizard and take photos of the adventurous pair, suitably booted and kitted, rations and water in rucksacks. The wind is fierce but as yet there's no rain.

As I wave them goodbye, I realise there's no phone signal and the sky is darkening. At the Lizard gift shop I buy a teacloth for Rosa to remind her of the day then set off back to Mullion. By now it's teeming with rain: the windscreen wipers are full blast and the headlights are on. Finding the car park easily, I hesitate before venturing out, but I've said I'll do a tour of Mullion and am determined to stick to the plan, even though it means getting drenched to the skin. I wish I'd brought a proper waterproof coat. The lady in the Spar shop where I buy a newspaper looks askance when I remark, "My husband and friend are out in this, on the South West Coastal Path."

"No! Do they have suitable gear? It's dreadful weather today."

"They're quite experienced," I reply, "but I think they're nuts."

I slosh back to the car, abandoning any attempt to look around the churchyard and try the satnav again to take me back to Polurrian Cove, less than a mile away. No joy. Oh well, how difficult can it be?

Twenty minutes later, having driven three times round the village, I heave a sigh of relief as the hotel comes into sight. The trouble is that everything looks different peering through the windscreen in thick gloom with wipers going full blast. I'm getting really worried about Seb and Rosa and consider several options: one, drive back to the Lizard and try to catch them up; two, drive to Kynance Cove to wait for them; three, call the coastguard to say two idiots are on the loose; four, go to our room and keep trying for a signal. I settle on option four, switch on *Escape to the Sun*, make a coffee, start on the crossword in the paper and try continually to get a signal. It's well past one o'clock when a WhatsApp message finally appears to say they're wet through but okay and the walking app is predicting one and a half hours further to go. I decide to take my book to the lounge and order a glass of white wine.

The rain ceases, the sun emerges and the afternoon is suddenly brighter. I toy with the idea of traipsing down the steep steps to meet them on the beach but decide my chair by the sunlit window and the chilled wine beats it, so stay put. After a few more texts, the weary pair finally arrive back. "It took longer than we thought." Seb shrugs off his coat whilst Rosa subsides into a chair, visibly shaken. She can barely speak but I soon realise she thinks she is lucky to be alive. "Oh, it wasn't that bad," Sebastian dismisses her attempts at a broken explanation.

"I'm guessing it was," I interrupt. "I was really worried. I nearly called the coastguard."

Rosa gasps, "I'm never doing that again. There was no signal, thick mist, we got lost and doubled back on ourselves, Seb slipped down a cliff, I fell over." She rubs her thigh. "I'm so thankful to be back. I thought at one point we wouldn't make it." She takes a huge gulp of the prosecco that the waiter has just brought to our table. She hasn't even bothered to take off her wet coat and the walking sticks are scattered willy-nilly. This is unlike her.

Seb chatters on about the adventure, trying to make light of the experience, while the tea platters are brought to our table. Rosa falls on the food eagerly and requests a strong coffee.

I manage several lengths in the pool but the walkers collapse in the jacuzzi for half an hour motionless and then decide "think we'll go back for a rest now". I sigh but comply. Remembering Seb left his trunks in the changing room yesterday, I ensure he's got them after his shower as we trudge back to our rooms. "Pass over the key, Lara." Seb's almost on his knees with exhaustion.

"Er, no, you have it."

"No, I don't."

"Yes, you do," Rosa pipes up. "I remember you had it when we went to the pool."

"Oh no." Seb searches his pockets. He stumbles back to the pool (quite a trek) but luckily returns with the key. The three of us decide to meet up in an hour for pre-dinner drinks in our room. I'm not joking, in less than two minutes Seb's sprawled on the bed, semi naked, snoring. I have a shower and slink into my new red cotton dressing gown. "We have half an hour," I breathe as I slide my leg across his back. No response. Hmm, this isn't going to be easy but I'm determined; I've not travelled all this way for another celibate weekend. I caress his back, note he's getting quite fit, then plant several long kisses, sighing with anticipation. After five minutes without as much as a quiver I give up, get dressed and switch on Corrie.

I'm in the pool swimming my slow granny-type breaststroke and pausing for rests at each end frequently.

Seb and Rosa are in the jacuzzi, jammed together, heads back, eyes closed, the bubbles swirling around them. They relax into the bliss of it and Rosa's hand slides under the water to caress Seb's thigh. Seb turns towards Rosa and they exchange a loving look. Rosa intensifies her stroking and Seb lies back with an ecstatic expression on his face.

There's a loud knocking at the door. "Are you ready?" Rosa's voice makes me jump.

"Yes, just a sec. Seb, wake up and get dressed. Rosa's waiting." I hastily hustle him into the bathroom, chucking his clothes in with him.

"Come in, sorry. We had a drink and lost track of the time."

Seb

The Lizard to Polurrian Cove via Mullion. About seven and a half miles. It's been a helluva day. I have adored every minute of it. Possibly one of the best days of my life.

Lara drove us to the Lizard, Rosa and I made use of the loos, we took some selfies then headed into a truly exhilarating clifftop walk. It was wild, wonderful and wicked. We got lost a couple of times but the climb, the view, the aspect was incredible. I felt on top of the world. Rosa was concerned we had no signal but what did it matter? We had the whole day, Lara was safe back in the hotel enjoying her solitude and we were experiencing this windswept wonder, battling against the elements like true adventurers. I slipped down a cliff and got my waterproofs muddy but it's all part of the fun. I want to do it all over again. Maybe with better weather to appreciate the spectacular views.

At Kynance Cove the path split into two walks, high tide and low tide; we decided to take the low but the stormy weather meant the waves were still beating up against the rocks. I gauged a leap across pebbles just before some crashing waves but realised on looking back that Rosa was stranded behind. She took a chance and leapt across but misjudged and got soaked up to her knees. We ate our lunch under an overhanging rock: soggy sandwiches and cake left over from yesterday's tea.

The storm showing no sign of abating, we didn't dawdle and soon resumed our way up a steep and stony path precariously close to the cliff edge. The howling gale was so strong that Rosa was momentarily lifted off her feet. So, scared to carry on that way, we decided to go inland and try to rejoin the cliff path somewhere ahead. Having battled our way through gorse and bracken which got more and more dense until we were surrounded by thicket, feeling completely lost and soaked through by the pelting rain, we eventually reached a footpath where we had to take a decision on turning left or right. After much deliberation we chose left and found our way back to the coast path. After that we couldn't get lost by keeping the sea to our left. We soon saw the Polurrian in the distance as the weather began to brighten up. It felt good to have something to aim for and even though we lost sight of it many times through several headlands and valleys, it was reassuring, especially for Rosa who was beginning to flag. On arriving back, the sun was so bright and warm I could scarcely believe the ordeal had occurred. Can't wait to do it again on a clear day.

Lara

At breakfast, Rosa announces, "There's a thick mist out there. I don't think we can walk today."

She's right. We're in a window seat but cannot see beyond a potted palm. The sea is obviously pounding on the cliffs but the mist obscures all.

"What?" Seb juts out his bottom lip. "We have to. That's why we're here. We'll be fine."

"No," insists Rosa. "It's not worth it. We can't see a hand in front of us. We could fall off the cliff edge. And we have no signal."

I tuck into my full English without comment even though I know she's right. Seb continues to sulk.

Rosa has her way. She's not going to risk her life. I absolutely agree with her but Seb pouts.

"We can be careful. What else are we going to do?"

Eventually I murmur, "You two can do the next walk, i.e., Lizard to Cadgwith Cove, next time we come to Cornwall. It could be a first-day short walk, prior to booking in to our accommodation, if we came early enough." See how I'm being sucked in! I'm appalled at myself.

"Mm," muses Seb, softening, "I suppose that would work."

We head home in dense fog and I think they're both thankful not to be doing the stupid walk, even though Seb cannot resist commenting, "We would have been okay."

Chapter Twenty-Five

The Lizard to Helford Passage

Helford Passage

Porthallow

Porthoustock

St Keverne

Coverack

Ruan Minor

Lizard
Point

Lara

Back in Cornwall. I loved the Polurrian, but we're staying in
Coverack in a self-catering apartment as there are four walks to
be achieved this time. Even as I'm saying this, I realise how

ridiculous I sound. The stupid walks have taken over my life now as well as Seb's. I don't think Seb and I have had a sensible conversation for months, without him reaching for his phone or getting a faraway look in his eyes, half listening when I mention cows, sheep or children.

The apartment is good, with two double bedrooms, a shared bathroom, an open plan living/kitchen area and a small enclosed patio. Coverack has a village shop, but the nearest large supermarket is in Helston, about eleven miles away, so I've come prepared with a couple of homemade frozen meals and the usual supply of eggs, bacon, sausages, cakes and biscuits. Just as well, as a couple of the restaurants are closed and there are no takeaways.

The apartment boasts uninterrupted views across the Atlantic. There are a couple of stationary ships, which Seb's Vessel Finder app reveals are a refrigerated cargo ship from Las Palmas and an oil carrier from New York, bearing a Maltese flag. We assume they must be waiting for entry to Falmouth harbour.

Seb

Cadgwith to the Lizard. Lara dropped us off at Ruan Minor. Buses from Coverack are only a couple of times a day to St Keverne and on to Helston. I knew this stay would involve Lara driving, but the roads are good so she will be fine.

The weather was unpredictable this morning, so we waited until just after 11am to start from Ruan Minor village shop down to Cadgwith. The road was steep and narrow but we diverted along a footpath for a short section before rejoining the road. There was a couple ahead of us in walking gear, carrying sticks, but suddenly the man's feet shot out from under him on the slippery tarmac and he came a cropper. Rosa was really concerned and hastened to help, but he assured us he was fine and soon back on his feet, grinning ruefully.

Cadgwith nestles in a deep valley and has charming thatched cottages and a small fishing cove, once famous for huge hauls of pilchards but, now the fishing industry is much reduced, it has become more of a tourist spot. We could not see much of the cove as it was obscured by boat sheds and covered with a great many fishing boats.

The path took us to the Devil's Frying Pan, a natural arch formed when the roof of a cave collapsed in 1868. In rough weather, the sea can appear to boil, hence the name, but not today as the sea was calm and the weather clement.

The path, although muddy after the downpour earlier, was easy terrain, making for a leisurely, meandering trek. Passing Church Cove (NT), small and deserted with just a couple of buildings, we came to Kilcobben Cove, home to the Lizard Lifeboat Station, the most southerly lifeboat station on mainland UK, opened in 1961, with the funicular railway leading to it opened in 1995. It is open to the public and a visitor attraction.

We continued along the cliff edge to Bass Point lookout station (a voluntary service) and on to the Lizard Wireless Station, set up originally by Marconi in the early 1900s, now National Trust, and from where he sent his first radio message to the Isle of Wight. After passing the Housel Bay hotel, where Rosa spent a time taking photos and saying she would like to stay there, we climbed steps nearing the Lizard, where we stopped to gaze down over the ocean and absorb the exhilaration and sheer joy of being on the edge of the world in this wonderful location. I think Rosa and I both had tears in our eyes when we finally tore ourselves away to finish the footpath to the Lizard Point. We were still on time for a late lunch and settled on the Wavecrest Café, with its inviting menu including lobster, hake, fresh fishcakes and king prawns.

Lara

I refuse to drive Seb and Rosa down to Cadgwith, which I know from experience is a charming fishing village, but the road is steep and narrow. Fine if you're visiting or staying but unnecessary for purely chauffeuring purposes. A few minutes' extra walk is nothing for them and frankly not my concern. They faff about because of the uncertainty of the weather, so when we finally reach Ruan Minor, having waited for a heavy downpour to cease, they are unprepared and dash into the shop for bottles of water.

"Bye, Lara. We'll be quick. It's only a short walk. See you in less than two hours." They set off in matching steps. As I drive to the Lizard, the rain starts spitting again and I wonder if they'll take shelter somewhere, but by the time I reach the village the sun is shining and it's a pleasant day. There are several souvenir and gift shops, a Cornish stone shop, a couple of pubs, a large pasty takeaway/restaurant, cafés and a marvellous-looking shellfish café/shop. I wander around, buy some souvenirs, grab a takeaway coffee and return to the car with a crossword.

My phone pings: "Can see Lizard." Another ping: "False alarm."

My stomach growls furiously. I'm starving but must wait, as the plan is to have lunch together on their return. I'm on the verge of giving in to a pasty when there's another ping: "Now can see Lizard. There in ten."

I drive carefully down to the NT lighthouse car park to find Seb already there. He gets in the passenger seat and says, "We need to drive down a bit to a lower car park." I negotiate the narrow road to a small car park, a few seconds walk from the Wavecrest Café, on the Lizard Point. Rosa is at a table near the window with a glass of prosecco. Seb slides in next to her, leaving me to lever myself into a small space opposite. The place is full of happy customers, and there are some diners outside in sheltered wooden booths. Seb pours me a small glass of prosecco and tops up Rosa's without asking. He glances at the menu. "I guess I know what you're having." He smiles.

"Yes, thanks Sebby." She smiles back and takes a sip of prosecco.

What! Is Seb a mind reader now? Also what's with the "Sebby".

"I'll have the hake please, Sebastian," I chip in. "Unless you already knew that."

Seb looks puzzled and goes off to place the order, whilst Rosa and I admire the stunning views of the swirling sea just yards from the window, the sun glistening and sparkling on the rolling white breakers. I have to crane my neck slightly as I'm stuck behind the wall.

After a delicious meal, we wander down to the tip of the point, the southernmost café, the Polpeor, perched just below the Wavecrest.

The dramatic coastline is spectacular, the rocks look like castles etched into the cliff face and the sea stretches endlessly all around. I'm instructed to take a few steps each side of the coast path but when I see smug glances passing to and fro, suggest we return to the car. I've been at the Lizard for hours and I need to go back to ponder how Seb can read Rosa's mind but still have no clue about my eating preferences after sixteen years of marriage.

Arriving back at the apartment, no one has much energy so the evening is spent looking at innumerable photos and exclaiming over the delights of the coastline. It's a beautiful night so while I'm washing up after our supper of quiche and salad, Seb and Rosa open the French doors onto the small patio area overlooking the sea. "Oh, Sebby," I can hear Rosa whisper, "It's so romantic."

"Come on out, Lara," calls Seb. "It's fabulous. The sound of the sea, the lights on the ships, the sky…"

I admit it's gorgeous. There's an almost-full moon; it's a calm clear, starry night and the lights twinkling on the two large vessels out at sea are magical. Rosa grabs Seb's arm and sighs, "This is lovely." After a while they start reminiscing again about the stupid walk, so I return to the living room to watch *Wycliffe* and finish the chocolates. They stay out for over an hour and a half.

Seb

Cadgwith to Coverack. Approx seven miles. Lara drove us to Ruan Minor again, but earlier than yesterday as this was a longer walk. We could not see the sign for the coast path at first but I used my app and we soon got going along a very wet, muddy path to find an acorn sign "Kennack Sands 1 ½m". We had a brief chat with four ladies, kitted out in style, who were walking from Coverack to Porthleven. Rosa and I could hardly believe it. It must be about twenty-five miles, how could they do it? We've taken four walks to do the same thing. There are certainly some intrepid walkers in the South West.

Looking across from the headland, the path looked deceptively flat. After traversing fields we came to Poltesco, site of the old South Wheal Copper Mine. Poltesco was also home to the Lizard Serpentine Company in the nineteenth century that gained royal approval when Prince Albert ordered mantelpieces and pedestals for Osborne House on the Isle of Wight.

We went over the wonderful curved Poltesco Bridge to a rocky cove, then along the side of a caravan park and golf course down to Kennack Sands, a family-friendly beach with extensive sands and numerous rock pools. There is also a large car park and toilets. A sudden rain squall caused us to run for shelter in some gaps in the wall at the top of the beach.

Carrying on, the path became barely existent, forcing us to almost crawl in places, grabbing the sides of rocks for safety, as well as clambering over some steep boulders. We looked down over an inaccessible unspoilt cove and Rosa was mesmerised by a seal flippering its way through the waves to the beach.

Walking on, and sighting another tempting inaccessible beach, some gusty winds nearly swept Rosa off her feet and we took shelter under a hawthorn hedge from a short intense downpour, squatting under Rosa's umbrella, which immediately turned inside out but did at least afford us some shelter.

The sun came out so we resumed our way, down some steps to sea level, then up again along a tiny steep and stony path to an upright single post with no hands but yellow arrows in four different directions. We followed the edge of the sea towards Beagles Point (NT) heaving a sigh of relief when the path became a field of grass.

At the Black Head Coastguard Hut, originally a naval signal station, we signed our names in the visitors book then headed on to Coverack, the path becoming rocky again, along Chynhalls Point to the apartment which is situated adjacent to the path.

Lara

Having dropped them off in Ruan Minor at 9.30am I return to Coverack and park in the free car park at the entrance to the village. I resolve to put a donation in the honesty box at the end of our stay. The apartment can be reached by a steep, narrow road with hairpin bends or by a long, winding three-mile inland detour off the main road. I don't fancy either and want to explore the village from end to end. Seb can collect the car later.

There are several people on the large sandy beach and two brave souls swimming. There are children exploring the rocky outcrops and people sitting on the large boulders near the sea wall. The long, winding street leads to the Paris Hotel and the Lifeboat Fish Restaurant at the tip of the village, near the lower coast path towards Cadgwith.

Along the way, I pass the Bay Hotel, a coffee shop and the village stores selling fruit, vegetables, provisions, dairy produce, papers and an array of interesting local books. After struggling to find my route back to the apartment and asking a couple if they knew where the upper footpath was in vain, as they were on holiday too, I find the steep School Hill and turn left along the footpath that leads to our small patio area, literally ten steps from the stupid walk coast path. I wonder if Seb arranged this on purpose? Even if he did, I'm still being chauffeur as there are barely any buses to and from Coverack and none along the coast except to St Keverne.

When they finally stagger in several hours later they're caked in mud. I refuse to let them in until they've taken off their boots and found some newspaper to dry them on. I toy with asking them to remove their dirty trousers too, but make do with, "You'll have to take off your jeans and socks and put them in the washing machine."

Seb takes his off and walks round in his pants. I roll my eyes but he takes no notice. I bet Rosa has a tiny lace thong just covering her toned bottom, but she reappears in a knee-length pink and white silk robe and matching pink silk ballet slippers. It's a gorgeous ensemble and I drool with envy. It would be no use for me though. I need a thick, serviceable granny type to withstand the cold trudge from bedroom to bathroom at home. Also I'd look ridiculous. Lace and pink hearts do not suit short, stocky, plain looks.

After a reviving drink and a snack of cheese on toast and fruit cake, they recover enough to get out the usual multitude of photos. They're nestled together on the sofa, dissecting each one, while I perch on the pouffe alongside, feigning interest. However, there's always something that catches my eye, and this time it's the Black Head Hut. "What's that?" I try to grab Seb's phone but he's too quick for me.

"Oh, nothing, just a hut." He snaps his phone shut, glancing guiltily at Rosa, who has bent to pick a piece of fluff from her slippers. "I don't know what I'm going to do tomorrow. My boots are falling apart." He picks his boots up from the newspaper and studies the flapping sole anxiously.

"Shame," I mutter insincerely, whilst resolving to google the Black Head Hut asap.

This is sooner than I think, as they both disappear to have a shower. I don't quite understand why they go together, as there's only one bathroom, but I cannot worry about that for a moment since I need to know the significance of the Black Head Hut. I reach for my tablet.

The Black Head Hut is deserted. Seb and Rosa have the place to themselves. Rosa gazes out at the grey sea. "Come here, Sebby." She wiggles her bottom. Seb joins Rosa by the lookout window, arms around her waist and Rosa gently twirls her ponytail to one side so their cheeks are touching. "This is heaven, Seb. I live for these walks."

"Oh so do I," Seb breathes. "I just love it all. The coastline, the landscape, the seclusion, the exhilaration, even the aching thighs."

"It's all that for me too, Sebby. I don't want it ever to end. It wouldn't be the same without you though. It's only you. You've changed my life." She turns round and caresses his cheek. "Let's sign the visitors book and make a pact." They reach for the pen simultaneously.

I must have dropped off for a while as I'm suddenly aware of a pervading pong. I realise instantly what it is. Seb has placed the two pairs of caked, damp walking boots inches from the electric fire and they're stinking the place out. Do people never learn! With my washing up gloves, I gingerly pick them up with my fingertips and throw them onto the patio.

Seb and Rosa stroll in from their showers, looking refreshed and glowing. Cats that got the cream springs to mind.

The weather forecast isn't good for tomorrow and Seb spends ages muttering, googling weather warnings and grumbling about his boots. Rosa seems unconcerned but says she does not want a repeat of the Kynance Cove walk; she'd rather come back another time. My eyes narrow at this. We cannot keep coming back to the Lizard just because Rosa's too delicate to withstand a bit of rain. She should try being a farmer.

Rosa has her way of course, and undoubtedly she's right. The forecast is horrendous, so they postpone the Helford Passage walk until tomorrow and instead we're going to Helston, "to take you out, Lara". I grit my teeth. I've gritted them so much in the last few months I've worn them down. And I think my hot flushes are getting worse. Is this because I'm in a permanent rage? Never mind, I'm a planner and I'll get my revenge somehow. I just haven't decided how yet. But no one puts this baby in a corner and gets away with it.

Helston, the most southerly town in Britain, and famous for the annual May Flora Day, is a charming small town with a good selection of shops, restaurants and cafés. We pop into some charity shops for a satisfying book-buying fix, then wander along until, by chance, we come across the Museum of Cornish

Life. This is fabulous, over three floors jampacked with thousands of interesting artefacts and relics from times past, "rooms" denoting kitchens, post office, veterinary equipment, musical instruments, along with a cider press, car, clothes and all sorts of paraphernalia. The building itself is fascinating, being the site of the old Butter and Meat Marketing Market.

When we emerge, the rain is hammering down so we hotfoot it to the nearest pub, a few doors away. As we peruse the menu, I wonder if Seb can read Rosa's mind again.

We spend an hour discussing where to find a new pair of walking boots for Seb, but give up the quest when we realise the rainstorm isn't abating and head back to the apartment, bootless, popping quickly into Sainsburys for provisions.

The weather eases up late afternoon, the storm clouds abate and the three of us stir ourselves after dozing in front of the television most of the afternoon. "Shall we go out to eat?" suggests Seb. "Give you a break from cooking, Lara."

"Great, I'll change while you have a shower and google where we can go."

After his shower, Seb comes into the living room dressed for dinner in a new shirt and a sweater knotted casually around his neck.

"You look good, Seb," says Rosa.

"Yes, you do." I gaze at him. "I don't think I've seen that shirt before. Is it new?"

Seb averts his eyes. "I thought I'd treat myself. My old ones are so worn." He self-consciously pats the sweater but I refrain from comment.

"I'll just get my bag." In the bedroom I check Seb's suitcase to discover two new tee shirts and an unopened pack of pants. Has he won the lottery? What's going on? I haven't bought myself as much as a pair of socks in three years. I've noticed, too, that he smells good lately. I check his washbag. A small bottle of Clinique's Happy for Men! Eau de dandelion it certainly is not. I grab my bag and survey myself in the mirror. My leggings have seen better days, my long black Asda tunic covers my muffin top and wide hips, but it's threadbare along the hem. I can never find clothes to suit or fit, even on the rare occasions I have time to look. Rosa, of course, always looks effortlessly chic. Tonight, she's wearing dark blue skinny jeans, a figure-hugging cream top and a pale blue cardigan knotted around her neck. Hold on! I grip the door handle as a thought strikes me. Seb's new shirt is cream and blue, his new sweater is a cornflower blue. Are they dressing alike now?

They walk ahead of me to the pub, steps in symmetry, whilst I study their backs. Seb has lost weight and looks trim; Rosa has always had an amazing figure. Someone on the opposite pavement stops to look at them. Perhaps he thinks they're a celebrity couple: Ben Affleck and Jennifer Lopez, with a bag lady trailing along behind.

We reach the pub and the waiter indicates a table for two in the corner until Seb stops him. "Table for three please. My wife's just closing the door." The waiter looks from Rosa to me in disbelief but quickly regains his professionalism and guides us to a booth along the wall. Rosa and Seb sink down on the plush upholstery and I perch on the chair opposite.

I'm sitting in a shop doorway with a filthy bag containing a flea-ridden tatty blanket and two shrunken dirty green jumpers, a half bottle of meths by my side. A golden couple with halos creating a shimmering aura around their heads, stroll past arm in arm. They are wearing expensive, exquisite clothes and ooze confidence and wealth. "Look, Ben," the lady whispers. "The poor dear, she looks so old and forlorn. Do you have any cash?"

The man reaches into his pocket and produces a fat wallet stuffed with cards. "Here, £20, that's all I have."

I snatch it and mumble through my broken black teeth and the golden couple smile and continue on their way, only to return after ten minutes with a soft navy and cream car blanket and a carton of hot coffee. "Here you are. Sleep well." They stroll off again, pleased with their caring solicitude.

Seb

Helford Passage to Coverack. This was a long walk, about twelve miles. We had several plans in place – Plan A: Helford Passage to St Keverne, using two buses to get there and then walking back to get the 2.10pm bus back to Coverack. Plan B: Same buses as before but getting Lara to collect us from St Keverne. Plan C: Ditto but Lara join us for lunch. Or Plan D: Do the whole route in one day using the buses in the morning but walking back to Coverack instead of splitting the walk into two. We decided on Plan D as yesterday's weather disrupted the first three plans.

Arising early, we walked down to the bus stop near Coverack's main car park. We were getting very anxious about the time but the 9.00am bus eventually turned up at 9.15. We needed to get to St Keverne to catch the 9.30am minibus to Helford Passage. A close shave! In my haste to dash onto the minibus which I feared would pull off, leaving us behind, I stumbled on the cobbles and ripped the rest of my flapping boot sole nearly off. The little red minibus took us down to Porthallow along very narrow, winding hills and had to reverse at one point for a goods lorry, but we reached Helford car park on time at 10am.

We started along a good path with the Helford Estuary on our left, then we turned inland slightly through some trees where we could still catch glimpses of the water with a plethora of sailing boats bobbing. After passing a sign "Permissive path, St Anthonys 2 ½m" the end of the passage opened out to the sea and we passed along several small beaches. The beauty and serenity of this beautiful location, sheltered and peaceful with calm waters, had us in awe and we took many photos.

Spying a small pile of rubbish, which looked as if a band of litter pickers had been clearing up, I found a piece of fishing cord to tie around my flapping sole. "That's not going to last," said Rosa, so I took another piece as a safeguard. It was better than nothing. I could barely go on otherwise.

Looking across, we could see the St Anthony Lighthouse and St Mawes. On reaching Dennis Head, at the head of the Helford Passage, we turned right for Gillan Creek, where there was a signpost "Flushing 1m/2 ¾m". Having googled this, I knew this meant 1 mile across the creek via stepping stones at low tide or a ferry if running. Or, if no ferry, 2 ¾ miles around the creek meaning an extra three-quarter-hour walk.

On reaching the creek, of course the tide was in, so I asked the lady in the kiosk if there was a ferry and she replied, "No, but I'll radio my husband."

Rosa wanted to investigate the kiosk, which looked as if it may have interesting things on sale, but hubby appeared and ushered us onto his small outboard motor boat. This was great, an adventure in itself and only cost a fiver saving us the long walk around the creek.

Resuming the path, a signpost informed us "Porthallow 3 ¼m". We walked along the coast, past an amazing house with a private beach, until we saw a sign: "Parbean Footbridge removed ½m ahead. No access to Nare Point or Head from this point via the SW Coast Path. Please use diversionary inland footpath network to rejoin SWCP west of Penare House".

This was disappointing, but not overly, as we could still see some great views. We walked inland for a while but were soon back on the original footpath down to Porthallow, with its shingle beach, large car park and pub.

After a steep incline out of the village we walked along the top of the cliffs but quickly became confused as to the correct route. After a debate we decided to descend to the coast again where we passed some large buildings, possibly quarry works and maybe ex MOD. Not sure we were on the right path, we hastened on to Porthkerris Divers Café (deserted) up a path, across a field, past some gates "Private No Entry. Blasting Area", then inland until thankfully we came across an acorn sign pointing us down to Porthoustock. This was similar to

Porthallow with a large shingle beach and car park and a cluster of pretty cottages with steep hills each side.

From there the path went inland, so seeing it was just after 2 o'clock we decided to pop up to St Keverne, only a ten-minute detour, for a pub lunch at the Three Tuns. We were famished, having finished our chocolate bars at 11am.

We didn't linger, being conscious of the time and daylight hours, so, after a satisfying lunch and a quick g and t, rejoined the path above Porthoustock, past "The Ponds", an area formed after the long hot summer of 1976.

The path was mostly inland with several signs "Stay on Footpath", until we went down several steps to sea level, from where we could look back over the quarry buildings. Conscious of my dilapidated boot, we picked our way along the wet, flat path with some handy stepping stones, along NT Lowland Point, until we could see Coverack ahead.

We walked along the harbour to the Paris Hotel and decided to pop in for a quick drink as neither of us wanted the holiday to end.

Lara

They eventually appear at 7pm. I've sent several messages, paced the floor and opened the wine, so when they walk in merrily, I'm relieved and furious.

"Where have you been? You didn't answer my texts. I was worried."

"Hi, Lara. We've had a great day. And look, my boot held up the entire walk thanks to a piece of fishing rope." Seb and Rosa giggle over the boot. "It was such a find. I discovered it in a pile of rubbish and it's lasted all day." He takes off the wondrous boot and points it towards me. I recoil. It's gross.

"Haha," he laughs. "Don't worry. I'll bin them now." He removes the other boot and bags them up.

Rosa takes off her boots, subsides onto the sofa and smiles at Seb hopping about and removing his waterproof socks.

"I take it you had a good day then," I spit out.

"It was great. Wasn't it Rosa?" Seb sinks down next to her. "Gillan Creek was fabulous. You'd love it. We got a lift in a boat across." He grins at Rosa. "We got lost a couple of times but it really was an excellent walk."

"How come you've been so long?" I decide to play it cool.

"Oh well…we had to eat so we popped into St Keverne. We were quick though as we were thinking of daylight hours."

"Really? So what time did you have lunch?"

"Erm, about 2ish." Seb glances at Rosa, who announces she is going to have a shower. "We popped into the Paris Hotel to look at the menu."

"We know the menu, Sebastian. You can't have forgotten."

He looks away. "I must take off these jeans and change."

I realise he and Rosa have scarcely given me a thought while they've been out gallivanting. I've spent hours worrying and looking at weather reports, while they've been swanning about in pubs without a care in the world. My heart hardens and my resolution strengthens.

I cannot sleep. Mainly because I'm furious. They spent the whole day out together without thinking of me alone at all. Could they not have text me at least to suggest "Meet at the Paris for a drink".

Seb and Rosa are lying on a tartan picnic blanket in a secluded quiet spot off the beaten track. They've just spent a pleasant half hour being punted across the creek and are now reclining in the dappled sunlight reflecting on the adventure. Seb produces two miniatures of prosecco, a punnet of strawberries and two chocolate flakes. They hold hands and sigh with ecstasy. "This is bliss."

Seb's boots are tied up with white wedding ribbon and Rosa is wearing a white floral coronet. They talk companionably and lie back, smiling, until Seb reluctantly gets to his feet and reaches for Rosa. "Come on, Mrs Lazybones. We'd better get going. We need to get to the pub for our nuptials."

The sun is shining, the sea is glistening and they barely notice the hills as they skip along hand in hand, Seb occasionally putting his hand protectively on Rosa's back to help her. At the pub, in a quiet corner nook, the landlord gives them two glasses of prosecco. "On the house, I hope you'll be very happy."

They linger over the delicious food with two glasses of gin and tonic each, then reluctantly resume their way along the footpath. The lights at Coverack are twinkling and romantic and with one accord they make their way to the Paris Hotel. "Hello again, Mr and Mrs…" The landlord beams. "Happy day, eh? What are you having?"

Chapter Twenty-Six

Helford Passage to Falmouth

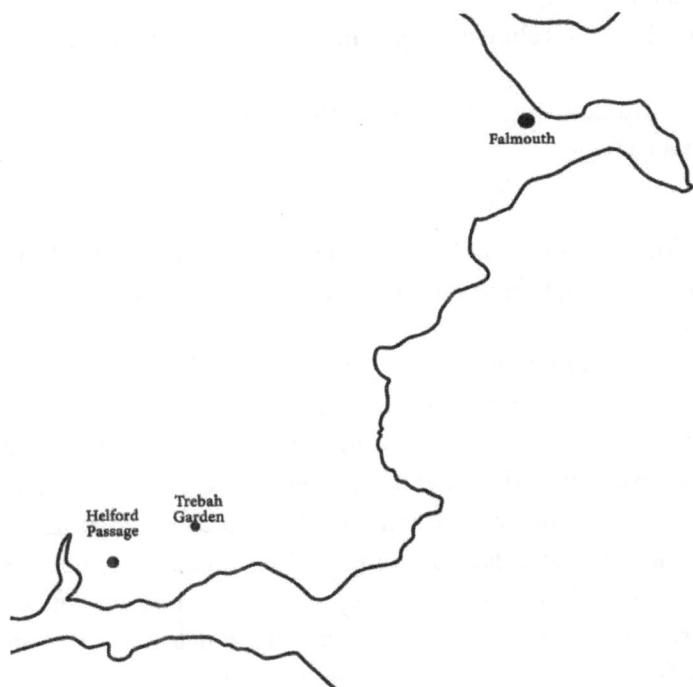

Lara

"Lara." Seb comes into the kitchen. "Has Rosa phoned? She's…"

Ping. "No. Wait, a voicemail. Hang on."

I listen to Rosa's dulcet tones for a couple of minutes. "Yes, that was her. Something about friends of hers in Falmouth going on holiday and wanting her to dogsit for a week and do we want to join her. The friends would be okay with it if we took our own bedding."

"Well?" Seb looks hopeful.

"I wonder what breed of dog it is. She didn't say. She prefers cats I know." I look at Ben, our old labrador, snoozing on his blanket by the Aga.

Seb himself is almost begging like a puppy for a treat. I ignore him.

"I'll think about it but I don't think we have time. Do you want a coffee?"

The dog is a labradoodle called Hermione and she and I are friends. "Let's go for a walk shall we?" I ruffle her neck and put on her lead.

The terraced house is not far from Gyllyngvase Beach, perfectly located for a stroll along the front which boasts many hotels and guest houses overlooking the wide sandy beach and near a small park, which has a large kiwi tree growing along the wall by the entrance and beds of agave, palms, agapanthus, echiums, fatsia and flax. Hermione is well acquainted with the park and leads me around. We admire the bog garden of towering gunnera and pause by the plaque, which reads "Queen Mary Gardens opened in 1912", then stroll through the far gate to return by the beach.

Seb and Rosa are on a walk, of course, so having given Hermione a couple of biscuits, filled her water bowl and told her I won't be long, I head towards the town centre, an area I know well as Seb and I have visited Falmouth a few times. It's one of my favourite places so I didn't put up too much of a fight about coming away for a couple of days. The High Street is very long with many different and quirky shops alongside the usual chains. The retro shop is packed with people picking up all sorts of bargains and I spend a pleasant fifteen minutes in the old-fashioned-style bookshop before browsing through Trago Mills superstore.

Back at the house, I settle myself comfortably on the sofa with Hermione to watch afternoon tv. She has two biscuits; I have a jam doughnut and a hot chocolate.

When Seb and Rosa arrive back they're full of their adventure as usual and burble on about Trebah Gardens and Swanpool. I pick up that they had lunch at Maenporth Beach Café but I'm not really interested and take Hermione out for a quick walk before getting ready to go to Gyllyngvase Beach Café for dinner. Rosa got in an M & S ready meal for us last evening, which was fine, but I want a meal out tonight. I'm certainly not cooking and Rosa can't.

The meal is great, as I knew it would be. Seb has mackerel, I have sea bass fillets, Rosa has a scallops and crab dish, and we share a bottle of wine. The three of us have a bop to the live trio playing '80s music and we stroll home arm in arm.

There's a shriek from next door. "Seb, can you come? There's something in my room."

"Okay." Seb shrugs on his dressing gown. "Coming."

He's gone hours! All sorts of noises come through the wall. Furniture moving, chairs scraping, long silences, shrieks, more scraping, rumble, repeat, repeat, repeat. Seb finally reappears, looking bedraggled, clutching a wad of loo paper in his right hand. "What on earth have you been doing? It sounded like a war zone."

"It was a spider. A huge one. Rosa was freaked. But it kept scuttling and hiding. Anyway I've got it now. I'll flush it away. Actually I may have a quick shower. I'm sweating."

"Yes, you do look flushed." Oh my word, what a fuss. I catch my own spiders, set my own mouse traps and put down rat poison. How does Rosa manage, living alone? I suppose she has her cat.

Seb is on his hands and knees stalking a tarantula, like a cat. He puts out a paw to tease the spider who waves her legs at him and hisses, "Loser." Rosa is sitting, hunched on the windowsill, wearing tiny pink pyjama shorts and a teeny top with lacey straps, hair piled loosely with a pink scrunchie. "Oh, you're so brave. You're like a lion." She covers her mouth with her hand in awe as Seb continues prowling around the room on all fours, his little bell on his neck collar tinkling merrily.

Seb

Helford Passage to Falmouth. Approx six and a half miles. Rosa and I walked to "The Moors" in the centre of Falmouth to catch the bus to Helford Passage, the 63 at 10.45am. The buses run every hour at quarter to, either a 63 or a 35.

We got off the bus at the Helford Passage turning, at 11.10am, and walked half a mile down the hill to Helford village to connect with the coast path. We looked back over to St Anthony's church, where the bus dropped us off last time, when we were walking to Coverack. The path was wet and muddy; thank goodness I had my new boots, although they got instantly covered in mud. Walking on a short way we could look down over Trebah Beach. Lara and I visited Trebah Gardens a couple of years ago and Rosa has visited twice with her friends so we spent some minutes comparing notes and reminiscing about the glorious grounds and gardens and the history of it. On 1st June 1944, 500 troops embarked from Trebah Beach to take part in the D Day Landings in Normandy.

Onwards we went, over a fenced bridge overlooking the estuary and then a tree-lined path to open country before seeing Falmouth ahead. After a NT sign "Nansidwell" the easy walk soon got us to Maenporth, a sheltered and tranquil sandy beach with rock pools and a beach café where we stopped for a very tasty ciabatta and coffee.

There was a digger and a small dumper truck, parked near the path, which we assumed had been used for repairing the surface and laying chippings. So, refreshed after our short break, we had a comfortable track to walk on. A sudden squall had us sheltering in a handy tunnel, just off the footpath, then we resumed on our way to Swanpool Beach and Nature Reserve. This was a very pretty picture-postcard place and we spent a while looking around. Rosa had been before but said she never gets tired of it. There was a beach café and a restaurant, Hooked on the Rocks, both looked tempting.

All too soon we reached Gyllyngvase Beach and decided to leave Pendennis for tomorrow so as not to leave Lara alone for too long.

Gyllyngvase Beach to Pendennis Castle and St Mawes Ferry. We walked to Pendennis Point, firstly along the pavement, then turned slightly left along a path adjacent to the road to reach the point, bypassing the castle. There were several cars parked and many people enjoying the all round views. The path then went along the coast past Falmouth Docks, the third deepest natural harbour in the world and a very impressive sight, before we came to the Prince of Wales pier and the pedestrian ferry to St Mawes, which runs frequently 364 days of the year.

Lara

Our last couple of hours before heading home. Hermione and I go for a long walk towards Pendennis castle and come back partway along the beach so she can have a good run around. I wish I could take her home.

Seb and Rosa return full of Pendennis Point and Falmouth Docks, so after a quick coffee and biscuits and a prolonged farewell to Rosa and Hermione, Seb drives to the point and along the coast so I can see for myself. I enthuse wholeheartedly as it is indeed impressive, but mostly because I want to persuade Seb to have a labradoodle.

Chapter Twenty-Seven

Brother Visit

Lara

Seb is visiting his brother Stephen in Salisbury for a couple of days. He's changed his usual format of leaving at 5am to arrive for breakfast, preferring instead to travel after work on Friday evening to get there for an 8pm dinner. This is unusual, he's always preferred morning driving. He text me last night to say he arrived safely and didn't know what the plans were for today.

I've caught up with work and Bobby's in the far field on his tractor, so I decide to call Rosa to see if she's free to come over and keep me company. No answer. Send a text, no reply. WhatsApp, ditto. I make a batch of shortbread, grab a tub of roasted red pepper soup from the freezer and send another text. "Guess you may be in the garden. Coming over on the off chance. See you in half an hour."

Rosa's place is deserted. The carport is carless and she's obviously not in. Hmm funny, she usually tells me if she's going away. Perhaps she's shopping and can't hear her phone? I pop into town to get a couple of salmon fillets and a bag of watercress for tonight's supper and head home. Seb sends me a text at 7pm. "Busy day. Going out to dinner. See you tomorrow. X." How strange. He normally phones me with an account of his day with Stephen and sends a couple of photos of them enjoying a drink. I try Rosa again but no reply.

Go to bed with a new Leigh Russell paperback and a large bar of Dairy Milk.

I awake to the dawn chorus and the usual day on the farm.

I'm expecting Seb home around 8pm so I save him a slice of chicken and ham pie. By 9.30pm I'm getting anxious and text, "Are you nearly home?" At 10pm I'm pacing the floor, but ping: "Soz, trouble with car. Stuck in Taunton."

"On no," I text back. "Are you okay?"

After half an hour I decide to have a shower and get ready for bed. When I return to the room, there's a message on 121. "Car in garage. Staying the night here. Boring. Hope to be home mid-morning. Hope all okay there."

I try phoning him back but there's no answer. Where is he, Premier Inn, Travelodge? On impulse I WhatsApp Rosa again but no reply. No blue ticks. I spend a sleepless night.

Seb and Rosa are in a cosy thatched pub on a country road, halfway to Salisbury, sitting in a secluded nook next to a roaring log fire. Rosa is glowing in the flickering light, dressed in a sparkling silver and black striped tunic top, figure-hugging tight black leggings and silver high heels. Her hair is pinned back in soft curls with silver combs. Seb is staring at her mesmerised. The waiter hovers with a bottle of Rioja. "Sir?"

"That looks fine, thank you. I'll pour." Seb fills their glasses and they clink, the ruby wine reflecting on their faces. Rosa relaxes back on the red plush chair and sighs contentedly. Seb wipes drool from his lips. The waiter hovers. "Your starter, madame, scallops."

"Lovely, thanks." Rosa smiles and the waiter nearly drops the plate. He too is drooling. He plonks down Seb's deep-fried brie and, with a last longing look at Rosa, disappears behind the bar, casting covert glances at the ravishing vision that she is.

"Fancy a scallop, Seb?" Rosa waves her fork enticingly.

"Mmm." Seb opens his mouth like a fish, eyes never leaving Rosa's face.

She smiles seductively and licks her lips. "Delicious."

Seb groans, "Amazing."

The waiter is doubled over in pain behind the bar and the landlady prods him. "Stop. She's taken. Though I do see your point." She looks across at the vision. "She is gorgeous." She drools as well. "Clear their plates," she says snappily, then looks at herself in the bar back mirror and sighs, depressingly, before returning her gaze to the couple in the nook. "They can't be married, that's for sure."

The waiter delivers Rosa's tarragon chicken with a flourish and bangs down Seb's pork loin with calvados apple slices. Rosa slips off her heels and caresses Seb's leg under the table with her foot. "What time do you have to be in Salisbury tomorrow?"

"I really should be there by 9am latest. I said I'd be there by 8am and Stephen may wonder where I am."

"Okay, well we'd better make the most of tonight then. Let's not bother about dessert."

Chapter Twenty-Eight

St Anthony's Head to Gorran Haven

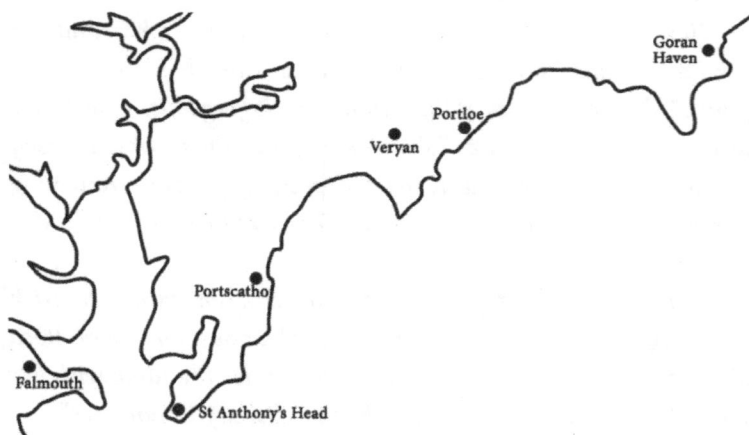

Seb

It is my birthday week, so we are treating ourselves to another Cornish break. Rosa is going to join us at some point so we can accomplish a couple of walks, possibly around the St Mawes area. Lara can have a day in Truro if she wants. I love my app, it's so useful.

Lara

We've booked the most amazing cottage in Portscatho, Cornwall on the Roseland Peninsula, huge windows just yards from the sea with a private terrace. The view is mesmerising, miles of sea meeting the horizon. A mild, dry week is forecast. Rosa's not coming for a couple of days, so Seb and I do a recce of the area.

We drive to Portloe via Veryan, several miles of narrow, steep single-lane tracks with no passing places. No thank you. If Seb thinks I'm negotiating these on my own, he can think again. "I don't want you to do anything you're uncomfortable with," he lies through his teeth.

Portloe is charming. Gorgeous homes overlooking the bay. It must be packed in the summer; I wonder about the parking. The Lugger Hotel right on the water's edge looks wonderful, but we don't have time to stop. We suss out a bus stop, but surely a bus cannot be possible on the small road. Fortunately for Seb, we discover another route to the main road, which I can manage without giving myself palpitations. It's not that I'm unfamiliar with small country lanes, obviously. We live on one. But it's the unfamiliarity of the steepness and sharp bends with little or no passing places that worries me. We drive to St Anthony's Head, and I can see Seb getting twitchy. "Lara, I know it's naughty as Rosa isn't here yet, but well… would you mind if I have a short walk on my own, maybe an hour? You could come with me if you like, but we'd have to return for the car."

The cheek of it. He's even wanting to do a stupid walk on one of the few days we have together on our own. Of course, I say yes. He's obviously itching to go and I don't want to spoil our time by one: him getting into a sulk; or two, me getting into a sulk. "Great, I won't be long." He nips out of the car to put on his walking boots, always kept in the boot "just in case".

The drive back is uneventful, St Anthony's Head to Portscatho via Gerrans being an easy ten-minute trip. My phone pings: "Sorry, I've just seen a sign saying Portscatho three miles. I thought it was only two. I'll stride it out though." Does he not realise there's a South West Coastal footpath sign just a few metres from the cottage that reads "St Anthony's Head 4.8 m"?

***

Rosa arrived last evening. By eight this morning Seb was in Portscatho Stores (a fabulous shop that sells everything you could possibly need) buying croissants for them. I stick to my two boiled eggs and soldiers. I know I'm being virtuous but it sickens me how much those two can stash away and still be so slim. Well, Rosa, maybe Seb not so much. They tuck into scrambled egg and smoked salmon plus a small glass of prosecco each. Seb seems to have developed more exotic tastes and has even bought a small jar of fake caviar from Sainsbury's. "Cheers." they clink glasses. "Here's to a great walk. The weather's perfect."

Indeed it is, I think, gloomily drinking my coffee as they stow chocolate bars and hip flask before piling into their chauffeur-driven car.

The journey isn't too bad; I memorised it the other day and all went well, apart from the embarrassment of a kindly South West Water engineer helping me park in the confined space outside the cottage on my return. "Come on." He beckons as I inch into a diagonal spot opposite their traffic cones, bollards and temporary fencing, trying not to look at his mate's bottom stuck in the air.

There's a sheer drop to the beach, with only some flimsy-looking railings, but I dutifully submit to his encouragement until I can stand no more of his arm waving and stop two inches from the railing. Thankfully, I get out of the car only to discover

I cannot sidle past, even sucking in my stomach to the utmost. "Haha," I chortle madly as I clamber over the railing. "That's a tight fit." I bet Seb and Rosa are strolling along carefree, munching their chocolate bars, as I escape red faced into the sanctuary of the cottage.

Seb sends a text four hours later: "Nearly back." Then he phones and asks, "Can you see us? We're by the WW2 nuclear fallout shelter opposite Portscatho." Is he insane? Why would I be looking out for them? As it happens, I've just gone for a stroll to the shop and taken a detour along the harbour path and, squinting, I eventually discern two obscure figures across the bay. We all wave frantically, although I'm not sure. Maybe it's only me waving; I cannot see anything other than two blobs.

Seb

Portloe to Portscatho. Seven and a half miles. Lara dropped us off at Portloe bus stop and we were on the coast path in a few minutes. It is great to be back in Cornwall walking with Rosa again. The first part of the path was somewhat hilly, very picturesque, then flatter and easy going. We looked out over Gull Rock. I love it, it reminded me of Kirrin Island of *Famous Five* fame, and there seemed to be a cave I'd like to explore. I wondered how you get there. There were some fields of sheep and some lovely little secluded beaches. Not many people about, we only saw two other couples and I'm not sure they were even serious walkers.

After the WW2 shelter, where we waved at Lara across the water, we came across the Hidden Hut at Rosevine, a shack-type restaurant, on the beach, serving rustic-type fare. Looked great.

Lara

They arrive back with filthy boots and socks. Seb takes off his socks by the front door and hands the stinking things to me. I nearly take them automatically but recoil in the nick of time. "Put them straight in the machine." I glare. "Rosa, you too."

Sockless, they sink onto the sofas in the living room, accepting a glass of wine gratefully.

"We've had a really good time." Seb takes his phone from his back pocket. "Look, this is where we waved at you. And this is the Hidden Hut, owned by the same people as Tatams here in Portscatho."

"I know," I interpose. "I walked around this morning and took a photo of Tatams. They do takeaway pizza Wednesday to Saturday."

We have a very late lunch, then, don't ask me how it happens, I find myself agreeing to walk to the Hidden Hut with them before darkness falls. "It's only a short walk, ten minutes max," enthuses Seb. "Rosevine's quicker to walk to than drive."

So, booted and hatted, I'm soon on the stupid walk with the two enthusiasts bobbing along next to me making encouraging sounds. It's a pleasant little jaunt but their jollity is seriously irritating.

We only see one other walker, a lady being dragged along by her dog, nearly bent double by its irrepressibility. I swear there's nobody sensible on the SW Coast Path.

***

It's Seb's birthday. I awake to find a note on his pillow: "Gone for a swim."

The weather is unseasonably mild and we've seen some brave folk swimming every morning. I turn over and go back to sleep.

Rosa, in a skimpy pink and white bikini, gold bangles on her slim wrists, is skipping along the beach. "Come on, Seb." Seb hurries to catch her up and they both plunge into the waves without hesitation, to emerge, heads bobbing, laughing, to join together in a clinch, arms entwined, before separating and swimming purposefully sideways before meeting up for another intense clinch, gazing into each other's eyes. When they emerge, dripping, they disappear hand in hand to the sheltered cliff overhang.

Seb comes back wrapped in a towel under his fleece, shivering. "That was great. It took some courage but I'm glad I did it."

"What?" I struggle awake.

"I've been for a swim. I left you a note."

"Oh yes, I know. Where's Rosa?"

"Er, in her room I think."

I get up to make the breakfast and Rosa appears looking immaculate. "Good morning. Happy Birthday, Seb." She kisses him on the cheek and hands him a gift-wrapped box and a card.

Did she go swimming or not? She looks incredible. Long shining curled hair cascading around her angular cheekbones, eyes huge with blue eyeshadow and curled lashes, lips smoothly glossed in understated pink. She's dressed in a pale grey tracksuit with a pink silk scarf artfully knotted around her slender neck, and both wrists jangle with several gold bangles.

Seb says, "You shouldn't have", before opening the card, which is a beautiful watercolour of Portreath Beach, painted by Rosa herself. The gift box contains a wine glass with "I love Land's End" inscribed on it.

Seb is beside himself with delight. I don't have a present for him as we agreed that his present would be the new pair of wellies we bought together last month.

I serve up my homemade pancakes with blueberries and maple syrup, followed by a fines herbes fluffy omelette and Bucks Fizz.

Seb and Rosa waffle on about Land's End and I zone out. I feel like an outsider; this cannot go on.

I look at Rosa's perfect pink toenails as I shove my broad Tesco slipper socks under the table and brood.

"Lara, Lara." Seb's voice is loud and I jump, startled.

"Have you nodded off again?" He looks annoyed.

"No, of course not. Don't be ridiculous." I snatch up the plates and march to the kitchen.

I can hear murmurs from the living room. No doubt they're dissecting my temporary lapse. I must concentrate. Smiling, I collect the rest of the dishes. "Well Sebastian, it's your day. What do you fancy doing?"

Seb scratches his head and shifts nervously, clearing his throat. I sense what's coming and intervene. "Ferry across to

Falmouth from St Mawes? I'll drive. I love St Mawes. We can have a coffee, get the ferry, look around the shops, have a good lunch somewhere and return at our leisure."

Seb swallows and dances from foot to foot, "I...we...I."

"Another Bucks Fizz?" I proffer the bubbly bottle, even though it's empty.

"No, I'm fine. Erm..." He glances at Rosa, who's collecting the salt and pepper. "Do you mind? I know it's not on really but..." He's stuttering. "I'd really like to walk from Gorran Haven today."

"Oh right. Silly me. I didn't know you had your day planned. Well, obviously that's fine. It's your day. You must do what you like."

Smiling, I turn my back and return to the kitchen to squirt Fairy Liquid into the bowl, furiously swishing the suds. "Do you need me to drive?" I chuck the cutlery into the bowl and stab my left hand washing up glove with the paring knife.

"Thanks, Lara, you are wonderful." Seb comes into the kitchen and kisses the top of my head before collecting his bag with boots, water bottle and the usual walking paraphernalia.

Grr! If it wasn't for this fabulous cottage smack on the beach I might be tempted to drive home and leave them to it. Seb sets the satnav for Gorran Haven. "It's not far. Only about thirty minutes or so." I don't believe him. I took twenty minutes driving from Portloe and I'm sure Gorran Haven's much further away. The road to Tregony and beyond is good, traffic is light, but I start getting anxious as we head towards Polmassick. The road is steep and narrow, descending into the lovely little hamlet, the ascent the other side is the same but at least there are a few passing places. We drive through Gorran Haven to the car park and have a quick look round. It's a typical small fishing port. I make Seb drive a mile back up the road before they leave me. I don't see why I should make it too easy for them. They'd be using taxis without me.

I meet three cars going down into Polmassick and a huge tractor and trailer the other side but luckily all at handy passing places. Back in Portscatho, I cut a large slice of cake, pour a mug of coffee and chat to a seagull, which has landed on the terrace, through the window, before grabbing my coat and going for a stroll around the harbour. The sun is shining, the place is beautiful and this is my holiday too, I remind myself, even though I've spent half of it alone. I may go to the shop and spend lots of money.

My phone pings: "We should be in Portloe about 2.45." To add insult to injury, I must pick them up. Why they couldn't complete the whole stretch from Gorran Haven to Portscatho in one day, I don't know.

I'm thinking of changing my name to Jeeves as I arrive at the appointed time and hold the boot open for them as they puff and pant and struggle out of their walking boots into trainers. "You can drive back." I hand the keys over to Seb. "I've had enough driving for one day."

Seb rubs his thighs with a pained expression but dare not refuse. However, after two miles of watching him drive with one hand on the steering wheel and the other rubbing his thigh, I can stand it no longer. "Pull in. I'll drive, so you can massage your thighs to your heart's content."

Rosa's very quiet in the back seat, but I can hear a lot of sighing. On arrival back at the cottage they both hobble indoors as if they have bunions and rheumatoid arthritis, then slump against the kitchen worktop, unable to stomach the stairs. (This is a three-level cottage). Are they having simultaneous spasms? They're both bent, knees apart, with glazed expressions, rubbing their thighs. Now I think about it, I wonder how long today's walk was? The app said three to four hours but they took over five. I dare not ask them for details.

We eat lunch in silence, before the hot soup, bread and cheese and prosecco revive them. "We should have started further down the road in Gorran Haven," Seb has an accusatory tone. "We had to walk half an hour to find the start of the path. You were probably home before we even began." After the third glass of prosecco each, they're soon in full swing. They produce the endless reel of photos, pick at olives and cheese straws, then giggle helplessly about East Portholland, West Portholland, Port this, Port that. I cannot see what's so amusing. When Seb starts droning on again about Gull Rock, I've had enough and announce, "I'm googling the pub to see what's on the menu."

Seb

Gorran Haven to Portloe. Nine miles. Lara dropped us off at Gorran Haven. We took a while to find the start of the path as she refused to drop us off at the harbour, and insisted on my driving back a mile, so we spent half an hour walking around until we spotted the acorn sign. We had a fine walk, climbing up at first then rounding the headlands. There were some great beaches with long stretches of sand and rocks, we spent time savouring the beauty of it all and gazing across at Dodman Point. Porthluney Cove is very inviting, the magnificent Caerhays Castle behind it with fabulous parkland and lake. The last stretch to Portloe was strenuous and our thighs got a good work-out before we were looking down over the Lugger Hotel, having passed East Portholland and West Portholland.

I wished I had asked Lara to meet us at the car park rather than the bus stop to save us walking a further three minutes up the hill. After seven and a half miles we were both ready to drop.

Lara

Our last day. We had a lovely dinner last night at the Plume of Feathers pub just a few metres from the cottage; warm and cosy, log fire blazing, fairy lights twinkling, comfortable seats. The menu was good, I had Catch of the Day, halibut in a cockle sauce, gorgeous. There was a funny moment when Seb ordered a bottle of wine, and the waiter asked, "Three glasses?"

I thought he had misinterpreted and was going to bring us three small glasses of wine already poured. "No," I corrected him, "just a bottle." Poor chap looked at me in astonishment. Probably thought I was going to neck it straight down. Rosa, Seb and I had a good laugh and I kept very quiet when Seb ordered a second bottle. I'm sure I'm becoming deaf. It's Seb's fault for prattling on about stupid walks; I've trained my ears to close down.

In the next room there were a bunch of Cornishmen singing sea shanties, unaccompanied by music. They were very good and Rosa and I couldn't resist joining in with "Sloop John B" by the Beach Boys. Rosa has a wonderful clear voice but kept it muted. All in all, a great evening, only marred by one thing. Whilst the three of us were getting ready to go out, Rosa spent about fifteen minutes in the shower, so I whispered to Seb, "Fancy a birthday quickie while she can't hear us?"

Seb rubbed his thighs (again) and whispered, "Okay, but I'm really stiff."

"Good," I whispered back. "That's what I was hoping for."

Seb looked contrite. "No, I mean my legs are stiff and aching."

"Never mind, let's be quick." But, much as I tried to turn Seb the sprout into Seb the courgette, it was no good and bathroom door opened before we got started.

"I'm out," Rosa called cheerfully. "Lovely hot water."

I'm driving a limousine, wearing a smart jacket and peaked cap. Seb and Rosa are in the back seat, rubbing their thighs. I try not to look but my eyes keep straying to the rear mirror. Is it thighs they're rubbing? Or not? I stiffen my back. I'm a professional chauffeur and good at my job. I will not look. I hear the cork pop on the magnum of champagne I put ready for them, and really hope they don't spill any. I'm getting bored with clearing up their mess. I drive on steadily, concentrating on the road. After a couple of miles of muted sounds and sighs coming from the rear, I dare to risk another glance in the mirror. Where are they? I can hear them but I cannot see them. A muddy boot appears on the back of the passenger seat next to me. It seems to be waving about. Is there a leg attached?

I'm on my own again this morning as they're traversing around St Anthony's Head. Yes, the very same walk Seb did four days ago on his own. "It was so good; I didn't want Rosa to miss out. You don't mind, do you? We won't be long and we can all have a nice lunch when we return. We'll do the circular route from here, which takes about an hour."

I bang the breakfast pans into the sink and mentally cross something off his Christmas list while adding something onto mine. At least I don't have to drive.

Seb

Rosa looked so disappointed when she learnt I had been around St Anthony's Head on my own, that I said I would love to do it again if Lara was okay with it.

It was a dry morning, although greyer and cloudier than yesterday. The waves were swelling against the rocks and the fresh breeze was bracing. Rosa wore a pink hat with a large bobble. I almost wished I had remembered my grey beanie but I like to feel the wind whipping around my head.

St Anthony's church is small and cute, and Rosa spent some time looking over it; the walk itself was marvellous with awesome vistas over St Mawes and Falmouth. We spotted a large tanker, stationary a little way from Falmouth, and on googling the vessel app discovered it was a gas tanker that had sailed from Cape Verde. We assumed it was waiting for customs before entering Falmouth harbour. Near the lighthouse there's a small hut, National Trust, with a sign "former paraffin store for lighthouse". Rosa perused this at length and I began to think this walk was taking much longer with the two of us than when I came alone.

Lara

Well, the "hour or so" has turned into almost four by the time they return. Also, if I see any more thigh clutching, I'm going to cut off arms, legs or both! They look flushed and exuberant, although Seb's obviously feeling somewhat guilty. "Are you okay? We were longer than I anticipated. It was glorious though. I think I missed some of the best bits the other day."

He and Rosa warble on about lighthouses and tankers, harbours and views for a good half hour while I brew the coffee. Out come the phones with a million photos again. Rosa has a giggling fit about the lighthouse, something about sheltering from the blustery wind and flashing lights from the window, but I zone out. It's so tedious.

The "nice lunch" we were supposed to be sharing turns out to be pasties from the shop, as it's getting late. "We'll just relax for half an hour," says Seb opening his Alexander Kent paperback *Stand into Danger*. Huh! After ten minutes he's sound asleep on one sofa and Rosa's nodding off on the other. I play Patience on my tablet in the small chair by the window and watch the seagulls swooping.

After refreshing naps, it seems both walkers feel the need to educate me on the delights of St Anthony's Head footpath. "Come on, Lara, we'll go a short distance. You'll love it." They're almost speaking in unison. Soon they'll be finishing each other's sentences, I think morosely. Why do I let myself be bullied? Don't ask me, but somehow I don wellies and tramp along the route that, by my reckoning, Seb has been on three times this week.

I must admit it's impressive, with the rolling waves crashing against the rocks in dramatic style. "Lara, you're doing the South West Coast Path," they shout against the wind, with glee. Do they even realise how glib and patronising they sound? My lunch pasty threatens to rise in my gullet. En route are two sets of granite steps to negotiate, about four or five in number and at least thirty centimetres high, they both scale them like goats, of course, while my short, fat legs don't stand a chance. I waddle through the adjoining gate, stamping on a muddy puddle whilst they go storming ahead.

There's a gorgeous small cove along the way, reached by a teeny winding path tucked into a precarious-looking cliff, on which they are set on persuading me to venture, but for once I stand firm. It's no bigger than a child's slide with no handrails and has a ninety-degree corner. No way! Undaunted, they skip down and spend twenty minutes exploring the rocks and crevices while Old Granny Coddles watches anxiously from the cliff top. Amend that, not anxious, I really hope the tide comes in and cuts them off. Serve them right if they have to spend twelve hours clinging to a rock face. We tramp back, me silent, them chortling over the adventure.

I heat the cottage pie I brought from home, and we spend a gripping evening discussing the next expedition to Cornwall. At least, they do; I try to tune out and concentrate on the *Wycliffe* dvd.

Rosa leaves early in the morning after a snatched breakfast, and Seb waves her off. "Phone you later."

We leave the cottage as clean and tidy as possible. I may be a bit slovenly at home, but I always clean up when we're away. Seb drives home complaining of a backache. Serves him right for cavorting about on cliffs, thinking he's a twenty-year-old instead of heading towards sixty. At home, there's lots to catch up on and we go to bed too tired to watch tv.

Seb and Rosa are in Rosa's living room looking at photos.

"This is the cave, Sebby."

"How could I forget," Seb rasps.

"And this is the bunker."

Seb shrinks down into a squat on Rosa's grey settee. "I remember."

"And this the Black Hut. Remember?"

"The Black Hut, omg. It was one of the best days of my life." *He reaches for Rosa.*

"Wait, Sebby." She playfully fans him away. "Here's the paraffin house at St Anthony's Head."

"Argh," groans Seb. "But we didn't."

"No of course not," whispers Rosa in his ear. "But we thought about it. Remember? What fun it would be to build a fire, cosy down and look out over the sea."

"Rosa. This has taken over my life. Come here." Panting. "Show me the rest."

"Sebby." Rosa wags her finger. "Patience. Oh look, Helford Passage, that was gorgeous, wasn't it? And look, The Paris Hotel."

"Wonderful," he sighs.

Rosa raises a beautiful long leg in the air and stretches. "We love the coast path, don't we, Sebby?"

"Oh yes we do, we do."

"Good morning, my sweet." Seb pops a cup of tea on my bedside cabinet and pecks me on the cheek. "You didn't have a good night, tossing and turning. You have a lie in. I'll help Bobby. Even though I didn't have a good night either." He rubs his back. "I think I've pulled a muscle. I had to take ibuprofen in the early hours, it was so painful. I hope I didn't disturb you."

Chapter Twenty-Nine

Freesias

Lara

Seb enters the kitchen, looking despondent. "Won't be walking today, after all. Rosa has text to say she's poorly."

"Oh shame. I'll WhatsApp her to see if she needs anything. Did she say what was wrong?"

"No, just that she's unwell."

I send Rosa a message: "What's up? Do you need anything? Chicken soup? I can come over."

Ping: "No thanks. I don't need company. I'm headachey and under the weather. A day in bed should set me straight."

I relay the message to Seb. "No walk today for you. We could fix the broken fence in Long Meadow? It'll only take a couple of hours."

After I've cleared up the lunch dishes and decided that Seb and I can drive around checking more fences, Seb goes upstairs, to reappear after five minutes, changed into clean jeans and tee shirt. "Where are you going?"

"I need to buy some wood to strengthen the stable doors. It's been on my to-do list for a while."

"Okay, I'll get on with some paperwork until you get back."

He's gone for two and a half hours. How long can it take to buy two planks of wood? "Where have you been?" I demand when he comes in at 4.30pm. "Where's the wood?"

"Wood?" He looks vague. "In the garage."

"What took you so long?"

"Erm, I popped in to see Rosa to make sure she was all right. I fed the cat."

"I thought she wanted to be on her own."

"She's okay. Just a bit of a temperature. She was in bed so I made her a cup of tea and some toast."

I have a vision of Rosa propped on three pillows, wearing a white frilly camisole and a pink cashmere throw around her shoulders, looking wan and pale, whilst Seb flaps around with tea. "Considerate of you." I cannot remember the last time he brought me tea and toast in bed without being prompted.

"Did you have tea as well?"

"Just a quick cup. I didn't stay long. I'll get changed and start on the stable doors."

At 6.30pm, as I'm stirring mushrooms into a pasta sauce, my phone pings: "Feeling better. Seb was an angel. The freesias are gorgeous. C u soon, R.x."

Chapter Thirty

Gorran Haven to Fowey

Lara

"Minehead to Mevagissey." Seb wanders into the kitchen, beaming. "It has a magical ring to it. A marvellous, melodious, magical ring."

"When did you become so poetic?" I mutter. "You'll be spouting Daphne du Maurier next."

"Who? Oh, I know Daphne du Maurier. She lived somewhere near Mevagissey, didn't she? Fowey, I think."

"You have done your research; that's why I mentioned her. I love her books." I drain the parboiled potatoes.

"I have. It's going to be great. I'm getting some things ready to take tomorrow." He grabs a can of Coke from the fridge and goes out humming "I'm Gonna Be (500 Miles)" by the Proclaimers.

I open the oven door to spoon the potatoes into the hot sizzling oil and burn my hand. Cursing, I hold it under the cold tap, stifle the threatening tears and harden my heart. Maybe I will write a book. *Murder in Mevagissey* by Lara du Morticia.

I pour myself a small wine from the Sauvignon in the fridge, to help ease the pain of my blistered hand, and think, perhaps *The Sedgefield Slaughter* by Lara du Sledgehammer, or *Casualty on the Coast Path* by Lara du Snuffit. Or even *Stuffit* by Lara du Sluggit. I giggle and feel better.

Back in Cornwall again. Not that I don't like Cornwall. I do. It's a fabulous county with a spectacular coastline and pretty villages, but I have a hankering for a change. I'd really like to go to Lanzarote again to a four-star all-inclusive hotel, sunbathe, read lots of books and hire a car to tour the island. It seems ages since Seb and I had a proper holiday together that didn't involve Rosa and stupid walks. I'm not sure how much longer I can put up with it, to be honest.

We're staying in a delightful two-bedroom, two-bathroom cottage in Pentewan, spacious yet cosy with a quirky "movie room", dark blue with dim lighting and huge surround sound tv – prosecco and popcorn thoughtfully provided by the owner. There's also a fantastic complimentary hamper containing a week's supply of fresh bacon, eggs, sausages, bread, milk, scones and cream, all from the local farm shop. While I unpack my food bag, wondering how we're going to eat all the eggs as, naturally, I've brought a couple of dozen from home, Seb and Rosa disappear to explore the terraced garden at the rear.

"Wow." They burst back in. "Lara, it's fantastic. There are two big terraces, one with a barbecue, table and chairs, and a higher one with a hot tub and sunbeds, private and sheltered."

"Bit chilly for a hot tub, isn't it?" I stack my prepped meals in the freezer.

"It's a wood-fired tub and they've provided logs. I suppose it's a bit chilly, but we'll see how the weather is in the next few days. I'll take our suitcases upstairs before I work out how the movie room tv works. You okay with your bag, Rosa?" They lug the cases upstairs and I can hear them exclaiming with delight about the bathrooms. I've already laid claim to the one with underfloor heating by leaving my handbag by the door, as it has a large walk-in shower and the bedroom has a king-size bed.

After a light supper of a chicken casserole and sauté potatoes, Seb and Rosa disappear into the blue movie room to watch *Double Jeopardy* while I sprawl on the living room settee to watch *Vera*. I'm not a huge film fan. Besides, the movie room has a small double sofa and the thought of Seb squashed in the middle between his two women is nauseating. I can imagine him putting his arms around our shoulders, Rosa's head nestled into his neck, while I sit stiff and upright in the corner. I try not to think of them and concentrate on *Vera*.

Seb

Gorran Haven to Pentewan. An easy walk of about five and a half miles. We caught the Number 23 red minibus at Pentewan

Turn at 9.07am to reach Gorran Haven at 9.37. On the way, the bus stopped at the Lost Gardens of Heligan for a couple of minutes. Lara and I spent a day there a few years ago, and Rosa said she has been on a couple of occasions. We agreed it is a great day out and has wonderful gardens. There were only five of us on the bus, three people got off in Mevagissey and we were the last two to alight at Gorran Haven car park.

We started from the harbour, as before, the fingerpost informing us "Portmellon 2 ½m". After going through a muddy gateway, avoiding a large puddle from the recent rain, we crossed several open fields with sheep grazing. Rosa gasped in delight at seeing a perfect rainbow before a sudden squall had us sheltering under an elder tree for a few minutes.

We soon carried on and had a brief chat with a man walking with his dog around the circular walk from Gorran Haven to Portmellon. He was also attempting the whole coastal path and had started from Poole, doing short sections a time, like us. He recommended the Ship Inn in Pentewan.

The path was easy going to Portmellon and became a tarmac road going into the village.

We saw some fabulous properties along the way, including Bodrugan and Chapels Point on a promontory with a boathouse. Henry Bodrugan was a controversial character in the fifteenth century and was rumoured either to have leapt, or pretended to leap, into the sea to escape being caught by King Henry VII's men for treason. The cliff is called Bodrugan's Leap.

Along the harbour at Portmellon there were numerous signs warning of waves crashing over the wall but we were lucky today with clement weather. We carried on walking along residential roads to Mevagissey, admiring the picturesque harbour. Rosa was enraptured with the narrow, winding streets and independent shops so we decided to explore for a while and have an early lunch before continuing up the zigzag ascent towards Pentewan. We crossed fields, then the footpath near the main road turned into pavement back to Pentewan Turn, across the bridge to the quay before a steep and muddy path at the end of the harbour led back to the cottage.

A lovely walk with wonderful views. I love being back in Cornwall.

Lara

After they have dashed out to catch the bus, I sit at the dining table with a large notepad and make a list.

1. Walks together most weeks over a period of nearly three years.
2. Night together alone in Crackington Haven.
3. Numerous lunches.
4. Michelin star lunch.
5. Drinks in many pubs and evening drinks in the Paris Hotel.
6. Dashing to Rosa's sick bed whilst abandoning me to mine.
7. Nearly two hours on the terrace in Coverack.
8. Walking ahead whilst leaving me to walk behind like a spare part.
9. Knowing Rosa's menu choice.
10. Buying new clothes.
11. Incessant texts, messages and phone calls.
12. Buying my Christmas present together.

I wander into the blue movie room and note two dents on the cushions, two discarded empty popcorn packs, two empty wine glasses and two pink and white socks. Why did Rosa take off her socks? Update list.

Walking down the hill to the pretty village I ponder on my life. This cannot go on. I work, I cook, I pander, I spend hours on my own. I'm not happy. I want to be happy. I'm fed up with Seb being constantly on his phone; if I could get my hands on it I'd throw it over a cliff into the sea. Whoa! An unbidden thought comes into my mind and I stop, gazing unseeingly across the river flowing towards Pentewan Beach. A car horn toots and I jump, twisting my ankle, before waving apologetically to the driver and continuing on my way to the Co-op across the small bridge over the St Austell river towards the main road. I buy a newspaper, a pack of bread rolls and a bag of popcorn.

Back in the cottage I dump the popcorn on the kitchen worktop in disbelief. Popcorn? What was I thinking? I never buy popcorn. I wince as I take off my trainers. I think I've hurt my ankle.

Seb and Rosa get back about 3.30pm. I cannot be bothered to ask why they've been so long. I know why. Obviously they had a leisurely lunch in Mevagissey. Out comes the inevitable reel of photos, but for once I'm interested – for research reasons. I pick out a few of high cliffs, with one or the other of them posing at the edge and enquire nonchalantly, "Where's that? Looks amazing." I soon have a small number of sites in my mind which I intend to google when they're out of the way, which is sooner than anticipated as the sun comes out. It's a beautiful afternoon and quite warm. Seb and Rosa skip up the steps to the top terrace to investigate the hot tub but soon reappear with Seb announcing, "Lara, we're going to have a go at lighting the hot tub. Do you fancy it? We'll just have a quick shower first."

"No, I don't. It's not warm enough. I haven't brought a swimsuit and I've sprained my ankle." I hop into the living room and prop my aching foot up on two cushions on the settee.

"It may not work but it seems a shame not to try. It's quite warm up there in the sunshine. Rosa's having a quick shower and I shall too, a very quick one as I don't want to waste time." He grabs a bottle of wine, two plastic glasses and the bag of popcorn. "Popcorn? Great. Do you want some?"

"No. I bought it by mistake. You have it."

Two hours later, he reappears, slurring his words. "What are we eating tonight? We cannot leave the hot tub while it's heating; there's a notice. It's almost hot enough though. Can we grab something quickly or...?"

"I'm cooking those lovely fat butchers' sausages from the hamper. I thought we'd have hot dogs with a mustard relish and salad."

"That sounds amazing. Rosa and I are starving. Do you mind if I come down in half an hour or so and take our plates up to the terrace? It's lovely up there with the candles and the lights of Pentewan twinkling below. Can you manage the steps to join us?"

I hop to the oven to check the sausages. "No, Seb. I've sprained my ankle, in case you've forgotten. Twenty minutes, okay. I'll have it ready."

"Great. You're a star." He kisses the back of my head.

Do you know what? I'm tired. Tired of being chief cook and bottle washer just to get a peck on the back of my head while he and Rosa sip wine and share popcorn.

I contemplate my list. It needs updating.

Dutifully, I plate the food and cover with tin foil to keep warm, but my mind's whirring. Seb comes in to collect the tray. "The tub's warming up nicely now. Are you sure you can't come up if I help you?"

"No, Seb. I can barely manage the few stairs to the bedroom, let alone the forty steep ones to the terrace."

"Shame." He picks up the tray but hesitates by the door. "Is it all right if I take the prosecco too?" He looks at the fridge.

"Go ahead. I don't want any."

"Great." He grabs the bottle. "We'll be about an hour I expect."

I stab my sausage viciously as he goes off laden with the bounty, and glare at his retreating back. I wonder if they've remembered towels, but reflect that no doubt they'll find a way to dry themselves. I stab my sausage again and dunk it in the mustard relish, but for once I'm not hungry. I need to plan. And google cliff tops around the Mevagissey area.

Rosa is lying back in the hot tub, sipping a glass of prosecco. Seb appears with a platter of crispy brown sausages, hot and sizzling. "Fancy a sausage?"

"Yes, I certainly do. I fancy a sausage very much. Put that plate down and come in here with me. It's warm but I think I need warming up some more."

Seb strips off his clothes.

"Oh lovely, lovely big fat juicy sausage." Rosa sits up and holds out her hand to help him in.

***

After yesterday's fine weather, the forecast today is for a few squally showers so Seb and Rosa decide to have a day off from walks. They disappear into the blue movie room again while I rest my ankle in the living room. Late morning, the sun comes out so we decide to explore Pentewan Beach. I manage to hobble down the steep footpath from the cottage to the harbour where you can still see the old lock gates, and then we cross a bridge to the extensive large clean sandy beach, privately owned by the Pentewan Sands Holiday Park. Pentewan at one time had a thriving china clay industry with the busy port shipping one third of the county's china clay production.

Seb and Rosa decide to walk along the Pentewan Trail for a while. "Don't bother about lunch for us, Lara; we may pop into the Ship for a sandwich. I can text you if you want to join us?"

"No, I'm going back to the cottage. My ankle's hurting again. I won't be able to walk down the hill again today."

They arrive back at 4 o'clock. How long can a lunch take? "We had a great stroll along the trail, the valley along the river is lovely. Then we popped into the pub; they do great sandwiches."

Seb

Fowey to Par. About seven miles. I drove the car to Par and we caught the 24 bus to Fowey, arriving about 10am. The bus driver stopped at the top of Fowey and did a three-point turn for the return journey; we were not sure at first how to join the coast path but headed for the sea, popping into a bakery on the way for a couple of pasties. Along the front we could look across to Polruan, which can be reached by ferry from Fowey.

An acorn sign informed us "Polkerris 4 ¼m" and then another sign "Gribbin Head 2m, St Catherine's Castle 290yds."

A climb took us up to the castle on the headland, a small artillery fort built in the sixteenth century by Henry VIII to defend the harbour, and we paused for a while to look at the stunning views. Onwards on the undulating path, muddy after the recent rain but not too strenuous, we approached Polridmouth. Beyond the privately owned lake, the valley goes up to Menabilly where Daphne du Maurier lived for some years. Polridmouth has two sheltered secluded coves, but we continued across a short boardwalk, up a steep grassy path to reach the Gribbin Daymark, a striking red and white tower standing twenty-six metres high, constructed by Trinity House in 1832. This was a great location and there were several people strolling with their dogs. We chatted to a couple who were walking to Polkerris for a pub lunch.

Leaving Gribbin Tower, we discussed going for a pub lunch and saving the pasties in Rosa's backpack for later. Perhaps because we were so busy chatting, somehow, Rosa suddenly slipped on the wet, muddy path; I sprang forward to save her but ended up slipping myself. We were both plastered in mud; legs, arms, hands, jeans and coats. We staggered to our feet, aghast at the mess we were in, then Rosa saw the funny side and soon we were almost falling over again in mirth. When we had calmed down, though, it was no joke. We tried to lessen the thick mud on our hands by wiping them on grass but soon realised the gorse prickles hiding amongst it were painful. Rosa had some wipes in her bag but we didn't want to risk getting mud on the pasties and the rest of the bag's contents, so we carried on until we found some clean gorse-free grass, then managed to get the wipes out, just as we approached the Rashleigh Inn at Polkerris. We were far too muddy to go into the pub so we sat on the beach and ate the pasties.

Afterwards we walked along the beach a short way, then up a tarmac road to rejoin the footpath, ascending some steep steps to the cliff towards Par, then down again to walk along the long, sandy beach to get back to the car. We took off our boots and coats, placed a couple of carrier bags on the car seats to sit on and noticed ruefully the walking sticks in the boot, which in our hurry not to miss the morning's bus we had inadvertently left behind.

Lara

As I didn't hear too much about Mevagissey the other day, I decide to go there myself. My ankle's still aching but I can walk, albeit with a slight limp, and I don't intend to sit around moping. The bus runs regularly from Pentewan Turn and it's only a couple of miles. I cannot believe that the little red minibus goes down through the winding narrow streets, and wonder what happens in the height of summer, when the village is busy with holidaymakers.

There are a good variety of shops along the narrow, quaint streets: clothes shops, gift and lifestyle stores, a bookshop and an antique shop selling some fascinating seafaring antiquities and I spend a pleasant hour browsing. There are also several pubs, cafés and restaurants, and I wonder where Seb and Rosa ate. The Sharksfin, the Harbour Tavern, the Ship, the Fountain?

I return on the bus and make myself a sandwich. Seb sends a text: "Back in couple hours."

They arrive back mid-afternoon, caked in mud. Mud on jeans, coats and faces and carrying their walking boots. I recoil in horror. "What happened? Never mind, tell me later. Stand on the mat and I'll take your coats and trousers. You cannot come in like that."

They strip off to tops and pants. Fortunately, Rosa has sensible black bikini knickers, but Seb is too busy handing me the dirty clothes to even notice. I sling the socks and jeans outside the back door. "You can hose them off before they go in the washing machine."

They disappear upstairs together, and I hear Seb saying, "Rosa, do you mind if I use your bathroom so I can have a soak in your tub. Our bathroom only has a shower and I really fancy a soak."

"Good idea. I think I'll do the same. Do you want some bubbles?"

Am I hearing things? Are they having a bath together? I give myself a shake and tell myself off. After a while I can hear Seb sighing loudly and calling out, "This is heaven." Has he left the bathroom door open? I think I can hear Rosa moving around in her bedroom and I'm sure I can hear music playing, "Heaven" by Bryan Adams, and possibly Rosa speaking, but it's muffled and I cannot be sure.

After an hour Seb reappears looking flushed and glowing. "The bath is lovely. You can relax against the curved back and almost drift off. Rosa had a bath too. Luckily there's plenty of hot water. Fancy a glass of wine?"

I think I actually need a large brandy to calm my racing mind but nod acquiescence. After a while, Rosa comes down, looking equally flushed and glowing, and they clink glasses before getting out the inevitable raft of photos.

Lara

Rosa is spending the whole of the holiday with us this time. When I think back to Portreath and Mawgan Porth, Seb and I had a few days to ourselves, but this time, as in Coverack and Penzance, we've all come together in one car for the duration. As there's no walk planned today, Seb and I decide to go to Fowey while Rosa spends some time in St Austell. Seb offers to drive but I want to go on the bus so I can experience some of what they do together. The bus from Pentewan takes over an hour to get to Fowey, stopping at St Austell bus station briefly, through the suburbs of St Blazey, around the one-way system in Par, then on to Fowey, stopping at the top of Brown's Hill. Fowey is gorgeous with many independent shops along its narrow, winding streets: a fabulous bookshop and a great choice of bakeries displaying delectable-looking pasties and artisan breads. There are great views across the estuary to Boddinick and Polruan; we can see the ferry crossing and boats bobbing on the water. We pop into the market above the Fowey Museum and buy a pot of chilli jam and a bottle of chilli sauce from the lady who owns the Cornish Chilli farm's stall.

We have a wide choice of great-looking places for lunch but we settle on Sam's, which proves to be a good decision, quirky with prints and artefacts covering the walls, a glowing wood burner, music playing in the background and, best of all, a great menu. Seb has Thai lemon mussels and I have the Thai red mullet. Delicious and with a glass of cold white wine, a real treat.

I reflect that this is probably the sort of lunch that Seb and Rosa have together frequently.

We stroll around some more but soon get the bus back as Seb is anxious about Rosa being on her own. Humph! Funny how he can go off for hours walking and visiting pubs without worrying about me.

***

Our last full day. "I wonder if there's a Michelin star restaurant anywhere near," I remark casually as Seb and Rosa are packing their backpacks.

"The pub in the village does good food." Seb nods at me. "You could google, I suppose, but someone would have to drive and, besides, I'm pretty sure Michelin star is out of our price range."

"Is it? How do you know? Have you ever been to a Michelin star restaurant?"

"Well, no. I've heard, though, that the portions might be slightly smaller than we're used to."

"How do you know if you've never been?"

"I don't. Google if you want, but I fancy the pub's steak and chips."

"We have steak and chips at home. Our own beef, remember?"

"Okay." He backs off. "See you later."

I WILL go to a Michelin star restaurant but not with Rosa. It has to be me and Seb on our own. I look at my nose in the mirror to ensure it hasn't grown into a trunk. An elephant never forgets, and neither does Lara Sedgefield. Action time.

Seb

Par to Pentewan. Approx eight and a half miles. We rose early to catch the 8.20am 24 bus at Pentewan Turn to reach Par at 9.08am. The weather was sunny and mild so we wore fleeces and left our muddy coats behind.

From the Par bus stop, we started by walking on pavements under the railway bridge to reach a shrubbed path behind a mass of industrial buildings, following the railway line until we reached the coast. Looking back we could see the prominent Gribbin Tower, and looking forward, a headland in the distance, which we thought could be Chapel Point. The footpath, muddy in places, went along the edge of the extensive golf course of the Carlyon Bay Hotel, and we were conscious of stray golf balls as there were several golfers out with trolleys.

Carlyon Bay itself is a lovely, long sandy beach and we could see lengths of fishing nets out at sea. There were several dog walkers on the beach and along the grassy area alongside properties. A sign warned "uneven ground", but the walk was easy and towards Charlestown a good gravel path made this a very pleasant stroll. We passed the Charlestown Lookout Station on Landrion Point then headed into Charlestown itself, which is a historic, unspoilt Georgian port and has been the location for many films and television programmes including *Poldark*, *Hornblower* and *Mansfield Park*. We walked around the fabulous harbour, admiring a couple of old boats moored there, and stopped to read the information board, which made for fascinating reading. Many centuries ago, the tiny fishing hamlet was known as Porthmeur and had just a very few dwellings until the entrepreneur Charles Rashleigh bought some land near the village and built a grand house for himself and his family in 1779. Realising the potential of the location, he and the engineer John Smeaton began building the impressive harbour, and by the turn of the century, the village was thriving with imports and exports, which led to other related industries and businesses and the building of cottages, shops and inns. The Gun Battery was built to protect the village, and the village was renamed Charlestown in 1799 in Charles Rashleigh's honour.

Leaving the harbour reluctantly, as there were several cafés and restaurants that looked very inviting, we went through a muddy gateway with a sign "Coast Path Porthpean 1m, Crinnis Cliff Battery 200yds." Having passed the Battery wall, we could look down over a small cove, then the path became gravel again to take us to Porthpean Beach where we sat on a blue-painted bench to eat our wraps that we had bought at the Co-op. We didn't linger as a sign displayed "Pentewan 3 ¼m" and we knew the hard part of the walk was about to begin. A short, muddy stretch, then some steps to a good path where we could overlook the sea soon became a descent on some steep steps and, looking ahead, we faced the prospect of ascending hundreds of steep steps. This was really hard going, and we had to stop frequently for breathers. At this point we couldn't see much of the coast as the path was mostly enclosed by shrubs. Pausing by another sign we looked in disbelief at "Pentewan 3 ¼m", the same as before. A descent took us to Ropehaven Nature Reserve, where we took several photos posed against the fabulous cliff edge. Resuming the path towards Black Head, we caught occasional glimpses of the sea, then more steep steps through woods until we could spot Pentewan ahead of us and we were thankful to be on a descent.

It was a great walk, easy at first, but very strenuous on the latter part with a punishing work-out for the thighs. We saw some incredible views, wonderful beaches, a waterfall with a natural arch, a rock just offshore with several black cormorants and, of course, the marvellous harbour at Charlestown.

Lara

When they return, exhausted and happy, I say cheerfully, "Have a glass of prosecco and a long shower before dinner. I have things to do." I lay the table, dim the lights, light the candles and put my homemade lamb tagine on the hob to heat, then slice a couple of avocados and make a Marie rose sauce for the prawns. The chocolate torte is defrosting and there's a large bowl of double cream in the fridge. Rick Astley is crooning "Never gonna give you up" softly in the background while I open a bottle of white wine and decant a bottle of red.

"Wow, Lara, this fabulous." They waft in together. Rosa has on tight black leggings and a sparkly top; Seb has on his new shirt and smells of Clinique.

"I thought, as this is our last night, I'd do something special." I pour the wine and sprinkle cayenne pepper on the prawns. "Tuck in, it could be a while until we return to Cornwall. How did today's walk go?"

They reminisce about steps and views whilst I steep some couscous and snip coriander. "Any really high cliffs overlooking the rocks?" I enquire nonchalantly.

"Oh yes, look." Seb produces his phone and I admire photos of him and Rosa posing against what look like some terrifyingly precipitous cliff edges.

I shudder.

"You'd never go near the edge, Lara," Seb laughs. He knows I hate heights and get wobbly even looking over a safe, high balcony.

"Mmm, this is heaven," Rosa mumbles through a mouthful of meltingly tender lamb, apricots and sweet potato. "I couldn't produce a meal like this if I read every cookery book available."

"It comes naturally to me. I'm not good at anything else. You're good at lots of things." I top up their glasses and sip mine slowly. I need a clear head. "What are your plans for tomorrow?"

Seb and Rosa glance at each other. "We thought we could squeeze in a very short section near those cliffs you were admiring. Only an hour. Not quite sure exactly where yet, but as you commented on the photos, it would be great to show you some of the views. Of course, we've already done the walks, but we don't need to rush home. You could come with us if you like?"

"Oh no, I'll be fine. I'd only hold you up. My ankle's still not fully recovered. I'll sit in the car with a book."

"Great, the weather forecast looks fine, so it would be a nice way to end the holiday." Seb smiles at Rosa and I swear he's tempted to reach across the table to hold her hand. I wonder if their knees are touching.

I top up their glasses again and plate the chocolate torte, stifling a smile. Looks like they've played straight into my hands.

***

We're up, breakfasted and packing the car by 9am, and ready to leave before the checkout time of 10am. Seb and Rosa are still discussing which short section they'd prefer to revisit, so I chip in, "As long as there's a small parking area round the corner from some great views of the sea, I'm sure we'll all be happy. Also, I'd like some high cliffs, although I have no intention of going anywhere near them."

They laugh and Seb says, "Typical you, Lara. Right, I know just the place."

We park in a small, deserted parking area and they don boots and coats, before striding off. "See you in an hour. The views just round the corner from here are amazing. I'll ring when we're almost back."

I look at their backs and sigh. They're so happy. But I'm not and neither of them seem to notice or care. In fact, they appear only to care about the stupid walks and each other's company. I wait ten minutes to make sure they'll be out of sight, then investigate the cliff top. It's perfect. There's no one else about, the cliff is high, and the sea below swirls and eddies onto the uneven, jagged rocks below. I return to the car but cannot settle with my book, and I have a severe stomach-ache. After half an hour, I stow my mobile under the passenger seat as far back as it will go, put on my hat and gloves, and venture back to the cliff top. After a while Seb and Rosa appear, chatting so closely that they don't notice me at first.

"Oh, Lara." Seb recovers himself. "There you are. You didn't answer your phone. Look, this view's great isn't it? Let's take a few last photos, Rosa. You don't mind do you, Lara? We're not in a hurry to get home."

"No, that's fine." I pat my pockets. "Oh no, I must have left my phone in the car. Do you mind getting it for me Seb? Just in case Bobby's trying to get hold of me."

I hand him the car keys and he disappears around the corner. Rosa gets out her phone and starts taking some selfies. "Rosa, you're too close to the edge."

She laughs. "It's perfectly safe. I've done it hundreds of times."

"Come away. Hand me your phone and I'll take some of you."

She hands me her phone and steps back to the cliff edge. I retreat several yards, put the phone to my face and say, "Wow, fantastic picture, just face the camera a bit more so I can get the horizon better." She steps back perilously and faces me smiling.

"Great." I pretend to take a photo. "Where's Seb got to? I'll just go and see. Here. Catch." I lob her phone towards her and dart off without looking back, pulling my hat down hard over my ears.

Seb has his bottom stuck out of the passenger door and emerges red faced. "Got it. It was jammed under the seat. You must have kicked it."

"Rosa's taking some photos. Shall we have a quick coffee?" I quickly grab the flask and start pouring. He hesitates and looks back towards the corner but gives in. "Just a quick one. I'm thirsty. Save some for Rosa if there's enough."

We settle in the car and I produce two chocolate bars as well, although I only pretend to eat mine. A car pulls up alongside us and a middle-aged couple get out, dressed in walking gear. We wave at each other, and they set off round the corner to the cliff top. "That will suit Rosa", remarks Seb. "She'll have a chat with them."

"Good. Let's enjoy a few minutes on our own. Top up?" I grab the flask and settle back in my seat.

Not the End

About the Author

Clare lives with her husband and family on the family farm in rural North Devon. She has been writing short stories and poems from the age of ten and, inspired by her husband's love of the South West Coast Path has written her first novel.